What people are
The Hung

A terrific novel and truly gripping! Ma

A captivating page turner. *The Hunger Crime* travels from the war torn streets of Somali to the cobblestones of Rome unraveling the world of NGOs, world famine, money and power, and the chaos it leaves in its wake. I loved this book.

Growing up amidst of a bloody civil war, I learned the ramifications of food insecurity and the need to be self-reliant. *The Hunger Crime* poignantly calls everyone to act in our shared interest. Food security is directly co-related to all other societal challenges and nowhere is this clearer than in the food desert of Chicago. I urge everyone to read this book and make an impact towards solving the Hunger Crime, because together we would be unstoppable. In the end, the lives we sustain will be ours, and the sooner we realize it the better our collective prosperity!

A good book is one that you get immersed in to the point that you are living in the story. Your book does that . . .

John and Trudy have written a truly compelling and powerful book that captures the plight of humanitarian aid workers, who seek to stop the use of food as a weapon in the world. It is a rare, brilliant book that calls forth your social consciousness. I started reading and couldn't stop until I finished! A must read!

Misti Mazurik,
Your Purpose Driven Practice, Director of Operations

From the opening lines, as dawn breaks over Mogadishu, Somalia, *The Hunger Crime* keeps the pulse racing.

Evocative descriptions and brisk dialogue draw the reader into a tale of international intrigue set against a wider landscape of civil war and famine.

Moreover, this book, based on true events, provides an inside look at the world of humanitarian operations alongside veteran aid worker, Ben.

A vivid character drawn with great sincerity, the book moves between Ben's earlier years and troubled personal life, and his present quest to bring food aid to a country devastated by war and famine, wherein he discovers a major criminal operation.

The story is framed by scenes of negotiations to create a humanitarian corridor, on the ground emergency operations and the strategic direction from headquarters, and nuanced commentary on food as integral to the fight against terrorism and the path towards peace.

It is also telling of the tireless work and personal sacrifices of humanitarian aid workers.

The story is dark at times, revealing truths from the frontline of disaster and conflict, and reflecting the burden of post-traumatic stress disorder in Ben's internal struggle.

At a time when world hunger is surging, *The Hunger Crime* is a gripping thriller set against a backdrop of the highest stakes.

Dr. Margaret O'Neill,
University of Galway, Ireland

Terrorism, hunger and the crimes committed globally has always struck a nerve with me. This story addresses all of this and more. It contains drama and intrigue on a high level with compassion that tugs at your heart strings and truth that is often taken lightly, but this story sheds light on a global problem that we as human beings should be ashamed of. This story is enlightening and most of all it's POWERFUL. All of the characters portrayed in this makes you feel as if you know them, or it could have been you. Bravo on the writing and editors. This without a doubt should become a movie.

Van Taylor
CEO Van Taylor Production Inc.
Music on the FrontLines

You succeeded in conveying the importance of humanitarian work, the impact on the lives of people affected by conflict and natural disasters and the prices paid by humanitarian workers on their own personal lives, including PTSD and family/work balance.

All the while you kept this reader's interest in what could happen next in the future for Ben and Food For Livelihood.

I was impressed with the Bitcoin angle which added a modern aspect to the story and to the descriptions of logistics and organization of relief efforts.

How well you were able to make the reader feel what it was like to be working in places like Haiti and Somalia and how dire the circumstances were for the people living there. You certainly made a case for the relevance of humanitarian work and the scale and urgency of needs in times of disaster.

It's not only the crime of stealing the money and fraud but also the crimes against humanity.

Bravo!

Angela Van Rynbach
Retired humanitarian aid worker

The
HUNGER
crime

John B. Crisci and **Trudy E. Bower**

The Hunger Crime
John B. Crisci and Trudy E. Bower
Published by Food4Livelihood

Project Management and Book Design: Davis Creative, LLC / CreativePublishingPartners.com
Copyeditor: Karen L. Tucker, CommaQueenEditing.com

Publisher's Cataloging-in-Publication
(Provided by Cassidy Cataloguing Services, Inc.).

Names: Crisci, John B., author. | Bower, Trudy E., author.

Title: The hunger crime / John B. Crisci and Trudy E. Bower.

Description: [St. Petersburg, Florida] : Food4Livelihood, [2023]

Identifiers: ISBN: 979-8-9870592-0-3 (hardback) | 979-8-9870592-1-0 (paperback) | 979-8-9870592-2-7 (ebook) | LCCN: 2022921910

Subjects: LCSH: Humanitarian aid workers--Fiction. | Food relief--Africa--Fiction. | Guerrillas--Africa--Fiction. | Conspiracies--Fiction. | Man-woman relationships--Fiction. | Secrecy--Fiction. | Blockchains (Databases)--Fiction. | LCGFT: Thrillers (Fiction) | Action & adventure fiction. | Romance fiction. | BISAC: FICTION / Romance / Action & Adventure. | FICTION / World Literature / Africa / General. | FICTION / Thrillers / Espionage.

Classification: LCC: PS3603.R566 H86 2023 | DDC: 813/.6--dc23

Inspired by true humanitarian events

This book is dedicated to the
humanitarians who risk their lives
on the frontlines of the war
against hunger, delivering food today,
and building a brighter tomorrow.

Note to Reader

The idea for *The Hunger Crime* was conceived in 2011 at a strategic planning event at our UN humanitarian agency. When John and I were asked what dreams we'd hoped to pursue beyond our careers, we both replied that we'd like to write a book. John proposed that we write a book together "to give something back." He became the draftsman; I, the painter.

Our motivation was to write a fictional crime thriller set against the backdrop of humanitarian events unfolding in real time. We sought to highlight "the hunger paradox": that hunger is on the rise in a world that produces enough to feed everyone, and the role of food assistance in saving lives and livelihoods. We especially wished to honor humanitarianism and our colleagues and friends who gave their lives in the service of fighting hunger.

Then, as now, the aid agencies are facing challenges to deliver emergency food assistance to victims of conflicts and cataclysmic natural disasters of increasing frequency and magnitude. The 2010 Haiti earthquake decimated Port-au-Prince; killed 220,000 people, of whom 102 were UN staff; destroyed government buildings and infrastructure; disrupted banking operations; and compromised the ongoing work of the humanitarian agencies. In 2011, the Horn of Africa suffered the failure of two sequential rainy seasons resulting in widespread famine, killing 260,000 citizens, half of them children. A decade has gone by, and sadly, these events are recurrent and topical.

In writing this book, we aspire to entertain you with a fast-moving plot while personalizing the stories of the humanitarians and the people affected by hunger.

Foreword

The Hunger Crime is situated in the arcane world of the humanitarian community. Although it's a fictional crime thriller with the requisite elements to keep us turning the pages—an international cast of heroes and villains, exotic venues, gripping plot twists that meld action, romance, betrayal, and intrigue—the subtext is a story of hunger and of hope. The story reveals how and where the lives of the humanitarians and the hungry intersect, what obstacles come between them, and the unique risks they face. Humanitarians are driven by a higher calling and yet run up against bad actors with opposite motives—to use food as a weapon of war. Many humanitarians have sacrificed their lives delivering food to the hungry.

The Hunger Crime was written in 2011 following two of the biggest humanitarian catastrophes of the decade--the famine in the Horn of Africa and the Haiti earthquake. With the recurrence of these events in the context of a global food crisis, this book is just as relevant today. In Somalia, 6.7 million people experience high levels of acute food insecurity and localized famine, driven by climate change--with a projected fifth consecutive season of lower-than-average rainfall--high food prices, and conflict. In Haiti, 4.7 million people, half of the population, need emergency food assistance following recurrent natural disasters, the earthquake of 2021, and armed gang activities (see IPCINFO.org).

But these are just statistics, and they do not adequately convey the gravity of hunger as experienced by communities living in the most remote and dangerous places. John and Trudy reveal their stories as a backdrop to the plot of *The Hunger Crime*, why they are the most vulnerable, how they cope with hunger, and the choices they make to migrate or die. Women are affected disproportionately as they eat last. There is a cost of hunger to society in terms of peace and stability.

It is not often that a work of fiction entertains, educates, and uplifts with such ease. My hope is that *The Hunger Crime* will engage readers on a thrilling adventure and raise their awareness along the way.

Catherine Bertini
2003 World Food Prize Laureate

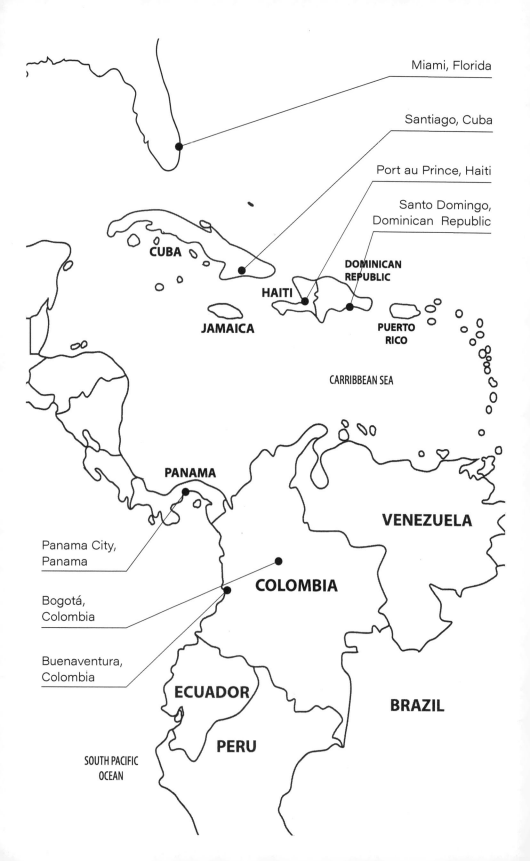

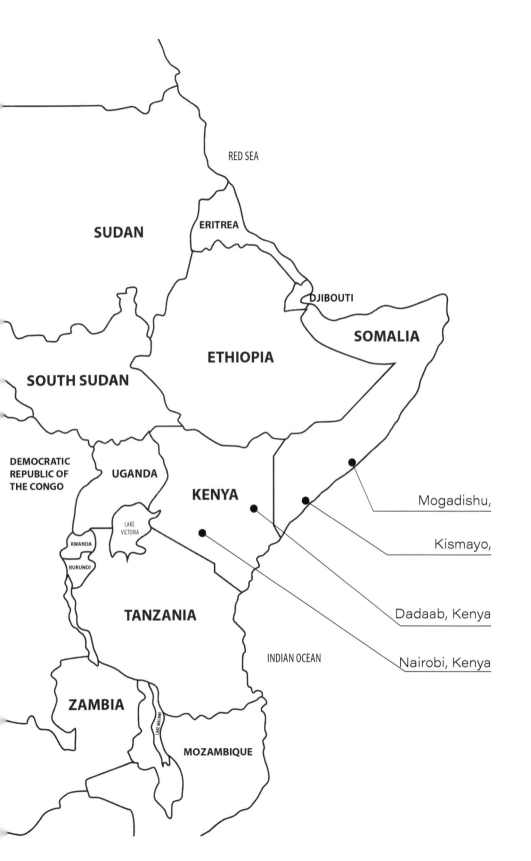

Prologue

The sound of hundreds of villagers running helter-skelter into their huts fills the air. Mothers race to scoop up their young ones. He runs toward the women, taking their bundles from them, running hard beside them. A woman with her baby slung over her shoulder frantically tries to gather the provisions she had been given with one hand while reaching for her small son with the other. He lifts the boy with his free arm and holds him tightly, continuing to run ahead. The woman running behind him calls, "*Waa caadi, Geedi.*" *It's okay, Geedi.*

Glancing over his shoulder, he recognizes the woman with the startling blue eyes. "*Waa caadi,* Geedi," he whispers. He lowers the boy to the ground and reaches into his pocket for a fruit-flavored candy. The boy looks at it in his open palm as though the toddler has never seen candy before. "*Nac nac?*" he asks, placing the candy in the boy's tiny hand. Geedi closes his fist tightly around his new prize possession just as his mother catches up. She grabs her son's free hand and keeps running, giving the slightest nod of her head in appreciation. Nodding back, he turns and rushes back to the Cruiser.

The pickups arrive at the village and circle at high speed, kicking up a thick cloud of sand and dust. Men's legs hang out over the sides, and the silhouette of weaponry poke above the cabins.

"Who are they?" he shouts over the noise. "Were they sent by the commander or Mogadishu?" A shrug is the only reply. A line of heads swathed in red-checkered scarves emerge above the dust cloud, carrying an arsenal of weaponry—anti-tank machine guns, RPGs, AK-47s—calmly and silently aimed at the FFL convoy.

Someone yells, "Red *keffiyehs* is YLF! YLF!"

What does it matter? An AK-47 pointed at your head doesn't need a name. "Oh, fuck!" he mutters. An eerie calm settles over him, as if he were in the eye of a storm. He lights another cigarette—a crutch to keep calm with guns pointed at him. He counts four gunmen standing at the back of each truck dressed in army fatigues and black boots. Some of them look like kids. Barely teenagers.

The driver, his hands clutching the steering wheel, turns and pleads with him through the open window, "Hurry! Get in! We can still escape. We've done it before. Our cars are faster than theirs."

Chapter 1

Mogadishu, Somalia, July 2010

Ben Tano climbed into the passenger seat of the Toyota Land Cruiser, his aviator sunglasses hanging from the neck of his white polo shirt. His security clearance was safely tucked into the breast pocket of his flak jacket. Dawn was breaking. It was the only thing he could count on in Mogadishu, which was so close to the equator that the sun rose and set about the same time all year long. Ben was an American, and at 35 years old, he had seniority within the nongovernmental organization (NGO) Food for Livelihood's (FFL) Emergency Response Unit, based in Rome, and was given the most challenging missions. He ran a hand through his thick dark hair, donned his FFL cap, and nodded to Jhamal, the uniformed driver whose ten-year service pin was affixed to his lapel. Jhamal pressed the gas pedal and began to drive through the gates of the FFL compound, proceeding slowly across the city toward the warehouse. The two men had taken this same journey, security permitting, several times over the past decade. Except for the mosques, little remained of Somalia's once grand capital on the Indian Ocean. The long civil war had decimated parts of the city and destroyed the country's infrastructure. The streets were war-pocked and congested with taxis and donkey carts. Herders crossed the city leading goats and cattle to pasture. Migrants from the country, eager for jobs in town, were tamping the largest holes with gravel produced by chipping away at the blocks of stone and cement from collapsed apartment buildings and luxury hotels.

The Cruiser passed an emaciated boy in torn trousers standing beside a pile of rubble, his hand outstretched. "Hey, stop a sec," Ben said, and rolled down his window to give the boy a few coins. The stench of raw sewage was overwhelming.

As they moved on, static poured from the radio on the dashboard.

"Whiskey Delta for Foxtrot Lima, what is your location, over?"

Ben lifted the microphone from its hook. "This is Foxtrot Lima. We are now in Sector Three, proceeding to Sector Eleven, over."

"Foxtrot Lima, avoid Sector Eleven; repeat, avoid Sector Eleven. Hostiles and exchange of gunfire in the vicinity. At the end of Sector Three, cross over to Sector Ten at the northern point and continue to final destination in Sector Fourteen. Do you copy, over?"

"Well copied, Whiskey Delta. Out."

Jhamal glanced at him and scoffed, "Sector Eleven...the YLF has been fighting the government for a patch of land there the size of my wife's vegetable garden."

Food for Livelihood was one of the few international NGOs remaining in Somalia after U.S. military intervention failed to establish a truce among the warring clans. The FFL had scaled down operations and staff, but they lived under constant threat of attack from the Youth Liberation Front (YLF), a shadowy group enforcing a strict interpretation of Islam who fought not only the weakened government but also the aid agencies who were trying to bring food to a famished population amid a shifting battleground.

One of the largest markets in East Africa, the Bakaara, was just ahead, a colorful sea of tables and stalls offering a bounty of merchandise for everyone from wealthy traders to those barely surviving on handouts from Western countries. On every corner, AK-47s, Uzi submachine guns, and pistols of all shapes and sizes were on sale. In a country where being well defended was more critical than being well fed, two-thirds of the population was armed.

The crowd scattered at the sound of gunfire. "The buyers are testing the merchandise," Ben said with a laugh.

Traders haggled over stacked boxes of medicine, tins of petrol and vegetable oil, and pilfered goods that had been donated by the U.S. Baskets of maize, sorghum, beans, and rice and colorful pyramids of chili pepper, curry, turmeric, and cumin were displayed next to cleaver-wielding butchers who reduced sides of goat and beef to edible portions of muscle and fat, while black flies gathered in the pooling blood.

Near the busiest intersections, at stalls fashioned from plastic sheeting, wooden poles, and scavenged concrete blocks, women wearing long colorful *baati* dresses with babies slung across their backs served *shaah hawash*— sweet, milky tea spiced with cloves, cardamom, and ginger. So long as they kept their heads covered, women were permitted to operate small businesses in Mogadishu, which was not governed by strict Sharia law.

When they reached the north end of the city, Jhamal pulled the Cruiser up to the FFL warehouse where eight IVECO trucks were being loaded. They were Italian dump trucks, donated years ago and converted into flatbeds, their sides painted with the FFL logo to signal that their cargo was humanitarian aid in the hope that the warring clans would allow them to pass safely. Day laborers trudged from the warehouse to the trucks, their bodies gleaming with sweat, their backs bent under the weight of fifty-kilo bags of cereal and beans, pallets of vegetable oil, and other commodities that comprised the nutritionally balanced rations.

Ben entered the warehouse where Salah, the portly manager, greeted him. Salah had begun as a day laborer and worked his way up through the ranks. Now he controlled every item that entered or left the warehouse.

"*Salaam Alaykum*, Ben. This will be your first visit to Kabuk, no?"

Ben nodded. Government troops had been fighting the YLF around Kabuk for months, making food deliveries impossible. The people in the village were reduced to eating roots and grasses. Mothers were too under-nourished to nurse their babies, and the starving children, if they survived, would be physically and mentally stunted.

"The South is infested with YLF," Salah said.

"UN security says the government has chased them out of Kabuk," Ben said. Salah handed Ben a waybill. "Khaled will accompany you," he said. "He is our best field officer. You can trust him…and he speaks good English." He summoned a slender young man in a khaki shirt and a colorful printed *macawis* tied around his waist.

Ben smiled, shaking the man's hand.

"Remember, the government forces strike back, but they do not hold territory," Salah warned.

Ben pulled a pack of cigarettes from his pants pocket and lit one, a nervous habit he hated as much as he needed it. "So, we get there before the YLF comes back again," he said.

"You are a brave man, Ben Tano. Promise to go easy on my old girls?"

"I promise. We'll have your trucks back in one piece before you lock up tonight."

"May Allah protect you on your journey."

Outside, a blond-haired, blue-eyed man with a sun-reddened face was examining the IVECO's tires and dented body panels. Ben slapped him on the shoulder. They had been through this many times since cutting their teeth as volunteers in Sudan. Leo was now in charge of logistics, based in the Kenya office. "Hey, Leo."

"I hope these relics can make it," he said. "This is one of our riskier missions."

"Getting cold feet, my friend?" Ben asked.

Leo laughed. "I'm not going to dignify that with an answer. How's it going, you workaholic bastard?"

"Same old shit. Serena is getting tired of being married to my voice mailbox. Can't say that I blame her."

They were both nervous and for good reason. Somalia had been at war for two decades. Now, the YLF was terrorizing the country. They saw themselves as nationalists, determined to rid Somalia of infidels and prove that they could feed their own people without foreign aid, no matter how absurd the claim. Boys were recruited from the age of fifteen, willingly or not. For many, joining the YLF was a means to escape hunger, poverty, and a bleak future without training or jobs. The YLF hated the relief agencies, especially the Americans.

Ben knew that every moment he spent in Somalia, his life was in danger. At least in Mogadishu, they had some protection. Traveling to a remote village was an enormous risk that required a military escort. He knew the odds, but he also knew that if they didn't make the trip, an entire village would wither away from starvation.

Two camouflaged Toyota pickup trucks with 50-caliber guns mounted in the rear pulled up to the front gate, honking their horns. Eight heavily armed soldiers were on board each truck. The commander leaned out a window and saluted.

Ben gave him a thumbs-up. "Okay, let's move out."

Ben, Khaled, and Jhamal jumped in one Land Cruiser, Leo and his driver, Hassan, in another. The two vehicles lined up behind the commander's pickup while the IVECOs got into position and the second military escort maneuvered behind the last truck to protect the rear of the convoy.

Chapter 2

The escort took a less traveled route over rugged terrain, doubling their travel time in an attempt to avoid YLF-controlled areas. Four hours later, Kabuk appeared, silhouetted like a mirage through heat waves rising from the scorched earth. As they approached the village, children with swollen bellies and emaciated limbs, who had been collecting branches and leaves, scurried away. Ben felt in his pocket for the bag of fruit-flavored candies he always carried as gifts.

The commander raised his right arm, directing the convoy to stop, then lowered it, a signal that they could proceed slowly through the packed dirt roads to the center of the village. Jagged rows of circular huts constructed from sticks and mud, covered by thatched roofs, were home to five hundred families. The roads were silent, empty, and as lifeless as the ground itself.

"They are hiding," Jhamal whispered. "They are afraid we're YLF."

Four village elders shuffled toward the convoy; behind them, a dark man, withered by age and hunger, emerged cautiously from his hut carrying a small child whose limbs dangled listlessly like branches of a dead tree. The child's eyes were hollow, and bright patches of frizzy orange hair barely covered his angular scalp—signs of kwashiorkor, a severe form of protein deficiency. As Ben, Leo, and Khaled stepped out of the Cruisers, other old men began to gather.

No women. The YLF flogged women who were caught with their heads uncovered or selling tea to men. Ben had seen this before. He would have to explain to the village that they gave food rations only to the women to be sure they reached the children. The men often bartered food for cigarettes and alcohol. But here, there seemed to be few able-bodied men. Drought and war had reduced the once thriving market town to a population of old men. The nomadic herders had undoubtedly migrated in search of water and grazing land.

He scanned the little crowd. No one seemed to be armed, so, in his friendliest tone, he began, "*Salaam alaykum*. My name is Ben Tano. I am the mission leader from Food for Livelihood, and this is my team," he motioned to the other men behind him. "We have brought emergency food for your village." Then, he turned to Khaled, who would act as interpreter and waited to discover which of the elders was the village leader.

A tall man of regal bearing stepped forward adjusting the folds of the *macawis* wrapped around his waist. "*Wa alaykum salaam, Mudane* Tano. I am Hakim, the village chief. You are welcome. I will offer you tea while my men carry the food from the trucks," he said. "Then, you can return to Mogadishu with Allah's protection."

Ben looked into his dark friendly eyes and grasped his hand. "Thank you, *yaabaa*." Hakim led them to a circle of plastic chairs where he, Leo, and Khaled sat down under a shadeless thorn tree. Ben spoke in a gentle tone, "I understand that you want to accept this food without further assistance from us. But it is important that everyone gets the right amount of food, especially the women and children. So, we must work together to organize the distribution process. If we bring back reports to our organization showing the number of people who received food, it will allow us to know how much to bring to you next time. Once the distribution is finished, we will return to Mogadishu."

He watched Hakim huddle with his elders. Ben understood that they were suspicious of the *gaal*, the white man, despite the presence of Khaled. But he was working under a tight and risky timeline. He needed their support, so he hoped they would understand his team's good intentions. Hakim broke out of the huddle and beckoned Khaled to translate. "We thank you for the offer to help, but we will decide how we will use your gift for our village."

Ben blinked, careful to keep his face neutral and not reveal his anxiety. He could see the men struggling to maintain their dignity, the illusion that they were still in control of the desolate village. It was hard to witness their powerlessness. When implementing development programs, FFL regularly monitored the villages, strengthening community partnership over time. But in countries without the privilege of good security and a fully functioning government, like Somalia, mere survival was the primary concern—and saving lives meant delivering the right food directly to the right people in the right quantities as fast as possible. He turned to Khaled, smiled, and moved on to his second line of defense. "Khaled, please explain that we must teach the mothers how to use this special food or their children will remain weak and small."

Khaled translated, but Hakim's eyes remained focused on Ben, searching for the intention behind his words. "*Mudane* Tano, we will consider this." He turned away, and the other elders followed him into one of the huts.

It was a negotiation Ben had often undertaken. He turned to Leo and said, "We're losing time here. The longer the delay, the higher our risk."

"I hear you," Leo said, passing him a cigarette.

Ten minutes later, Hakim returned and nodded his consent.

"*Yaabaa*, thank you," Ben said and nodded to Khaled.

"We will set up our distribution point over there by the school building," Khaled spoke to the elders. "We request everyone arrive grouped together as households—those who eat from the same pot."

Hakim and the elders began signaling to their people that it was safe to leave the huts. The women emerged, a rainbow against the drab earth, wrapped in long *guntiino* dresses and shawls, color upon color, pattern upon pattern, babies tied to their backs, baskets balanced on their heads, and toddlers clinging to their hands. Some of the men volunteered to help offload the food while others stood by to assist with the distribution. Khaled organized the registration process. Ben moved behind the table that was set up to help Leo, who was measuring out rations. One by one, warm, dark eyes lifted to meet his. He greeted each of them, "*Salaam alaykum.*"

"*Wa alaykum salaam, mahadsanid,*" they each responded in kind.

Time passed quickly, and the lines shortened. Ben and Leo, with their team of volunteers, were measuring and scooping out each food item in a smooth rhythm when they heard the commander of the military guard call out "Mr. Tano!" Ben broke away and hurried over to the Toyota pickup where the soldiers were milling about, watching the road in both directions.

Ben was a tall man, but the commander towered over him. "We are getting reports of fighting in the province, and the enemy strikes without warning." He glanced at his watch. "One o'clock. We will leave in one hour."

"We are on schedule," Ben said, "but I can't leave behind thousands of dollars' worth of food without knowing where it will end up, and I can't abandon these people who are waiting patiently in line to be served. I'll remind my team that we are on the clock, but I request some leeway here so we can do our job and you can do yours."

He had a mission and this man's job was to help him complete it. Ben chewed his lip as he watched the commander pick up his radio mic. If the military insisted that they leave earlier than planned, he'd have to comply; the safety of his team came first.

The commander replaced the mic on its dashboard hook. He was not a happy man. "Very well, Mr. Tano. But you need to work faster."

Ben nodded. "We will." The mission was still going as planned.

———————————

It was already two in the afternoon, but they were making good progress. The women were pounding the maize and singing, kneading dough for the flat *muufo* bread they'd bake over wood fires. Ben smiled as he watched them. This was why he loved his work, as dangerous as it was, as much as it distanced him from his marriage and family life; these hungry children would eat tonight, and the villagers would sleep without hearing their cries.

Suddenly, the commander was running toward him, and the soldiers were jumping onto the pickups. *He can't make us leave now,* he thought. *We're not finished.*

"Mr. Tano, I have a radio message from our central command. We are ordered to provide backup to one of our units nearby. We will return when you have completed your work. If we are delayed, another unit in the area will be dispatched to escort you safely back to Mogadishu."

Ben gripped the commander's arm. This couldn't be happening. *What kind of shit show are they running here?* Ben thought. "Commander, we were guaranteed military protection for the full duration of this mission. Our clearances were signed by the highest security and political officials. You are the only deterrent between us and the YLF. My staff is counting on me to bring them home safely."

The commander looked at Ben's grip on his arm.

"I have my orders."

Ben's mind raced in search of a solution. "Well, at the very least you can leave some of your men here to protect us!" he said, slowly releasing his grip.

"I'm sorry, Mr. Tano. I am ordered to report for duty immediately with our entire unit. Our government has its security priorities."

Shit, shit, shit! I'm screwed, he thought, a thread of fear rising in his chest. They were all screwed. These missions made him feel worthy. Fighting hunger was a cause far more rewarding than a powerful career in politics or business, following in the footsteps of his father. He had chased the approval of his father all the way into Harvard Business School and the corporate world, but his experience in Africa had continued to tug at his conscience. Making rich people more money made his father happy, but it ended up making Ben depressed, especially after witnessing the deprivation in Sudan. Humanitarian aid gave him the means to save the lives of people he truly cared about—and a career with a deeply meaningful purpose. He belonged here on the front lines where good people were starving through no fault of their own. He'd honed his effectiveness and high-risk tolerance over time, relying on good intelligence, gut instinct, and adrenalin. His purpose had always allowed him to push through any fear, but now he was stranded in no-man's-land without protection from the YLF—an unacceptable risk.

He asked himself the question that always lurked in the shadows. *Was this mission worth his life or the lives of his team?* He watched the commander sprint to his vehicle and speed off toward the horizon where the sky and desert melded in a trail of dust, the decision made for him.

Chapter 3

An hour passed, but the commander had not returned, and no unit had arrived in their place. The sun was bending toward the western sky, but the heat had not abated. The transporters had already departed for Mogadishu. The YLF wasn't interested in empty trucks. He and Leo were serving the last family in line. A tall woman with startling blue eyes gazed at him from across the table, her sunken brown face marked by starvation. Ben scanned her ration card. She was a widow with a small child and a baby. The woman's name was Suhila. She trudged on to receive her ration from Leo. Finished.

Ben hurried back to the Cruiser. He checked his watch and rechecked it. He had been sending urgent radio messages to Mogadishu requesting updates on the whereabouts of their military unit, but the security team had nothing to report. He was alone and responsible for the lives of everyone on this mission. Now, he would have to decide whether to drive back to Mogadishu unescorted or wait in Kabuk, hoping the military would reappear soon. Either way, they could be attacked. Ben and his team would be taken hostage or worse. He lit a cigarette to calm his nerves. He was in emergency mode, his mouth dry, trying to consider a logical way out. Finally, the radio crackled to life. The security team in Mogadishu was still unable to confirm the location of the military escort. They were scrambling to dispatch a backup.

Hakim and his three advisers approached the Cruiser with Khaled and Leo at their heels. "We are blessed," the old man said. "For weeks I have heard cries of hunger, but now my village rings with sweet music because our bellies are full. Allah is merciful."

He grasped Ben's hand in both of his and said, "The sun is low in the sky. It is dangerous for you to travel without protection. If you wish to stay, it will be my honor to welcome you as a guest in my home."

"What do you think?" Ben asked, scanning the faces of Leo and Khaled. "Jhamal knows the way, but we'll be without military intelligence on YLF movements. Should we risk it?" Khaled looked away unsure of the answer. He reached into his pocket to pull out a small plastic vile.

Leo shrugged and said, "It's a crap shoot." Ben was leaning toward making a run for it. A horn blared. Jhamal was standing on the running board of the Cruiser, pointing toward the horizon.

"Look! Look out there! They're coming! They're coming!"

Ben squinted his eyes. Two small dust clouds were moving in the distance. He yelled to the team, "Get ready to roll out! Our escort will be here in a few minutes." The muscles in his face loosened a little. It looked like they were going to make it out safely. There would be no blood on his hands today.

Khaled squinted at the trucks in the distance. Absentmindedly, he shoved the little bottle back into his pants and started walking to the Cruisers.

But Hakim didn't move. He stared out at the desert, silent as death.

Leo shaded his eyes with his hand, and when he saw the vehicles' escort approaching, he turned to Ben and gave him the high sign. Khaled got into the back seat of Ben's Cruiser behind Jhamal, who started up the engine. Hassan followed behind in the second Cruiser with Leo sitting beside him in the front seat, near the radio.

Ben stood beside his vehicle watching the dust clouds grow larger. Two Toyota pickups were now in view, engines roaring. Then, the screaming started—the sound of hundreds of villagers running helter-skelter into their huts, mothers racing to scoop up their young ones. Ben ran toward the women, taking their bundles from them, running beside them. A woman with her baby slung over her shoulder was frantic, trying to gather the provisions she had been given with one hand and reaching for her small son with the other. Ben lifted the boy with his free arm and held him tightly, continuing to run ahead. The woman ran behind him, calling, "*Waa caadi, Geedi.*" *It's okay, Geedi.*

Ben glanced over his shoulder and recognized the woman with the startling blue eyes. "*Waa caadi,* Geedi," he whispered. He lowered the boy to the ground and reached into his pocket for a fruit-flavored candy. The boy looked at it in his open palm, and Ben realized that the toddler had never seen candy before. "*Nac nac*?" he asked, placing the candy in the boy's tiny hand. Geedi closed his fist tightly around his new prize possession just as Suhila caught up. She grabbed her son's free hand and kept running, giving Ben the slightest nod of her head in appreciation. Ben turned and rushed back to the Cruiser.

The pickups arrived at the village and circled at high speed, kicking up a thick cloud of sand and dust. Ben could make out men's legs, hanging out over the sides, and the silhouette of weaponry poking above the cabins.

"Who are they?" Ben shouted over the noise. "Were they sent by the commander or Mogadishu?" Khaled shrugged his shoulders. A line of heads swathed in red-checkered scarves emerged above the dust cloud, carrying an arsenal of weaponry—anti-tank machine guns, RPGs, AK-47s—calmly and silently aimed at the FFL convoy.

Jhamal yelled, "Red *keffiyehs* is YLF! YLF!"

What did it matter? An AK-47 pointed at your head doesn't need a name. "Oh, fuck!" he muttered, and he felt an eerie calm settle over him, as if he were in the eye of a storm. He lit another cigarette—a crutch to keep calm with guns pointed at him. He counted four gunmen standing at the back of each truck dressed in army fatigues and black boots. Some of them looked like kids. Barely teenagers.

Jhamal, his hands clutching the steering wheel, turned and pleaded with Ben through the open window, "Mr. Tano, hurry! Get in! We can still escape. We've done it before. Our cars are faster than theirs."

Ben closed his eyes for a moment, considering. "No, we stay put." He'd been in bad situations before. He could handle this. He had experience and training, and he was counting on it now. He said, "Look at the artillery they're carrying. If we try to run, they'll blow us apart. There's nothing out there but open desert. We'd have no place to hide. Stay calm, and don't do anything to provoke them. We'll get out of this." Khaled nodded.

"Foxtrot Lima, Foxtrot Lima." Leo's voice was muffled. "It's YLF! We're in deep shit, deep shit! Our escort better show up fast and get us out of this fucking mess, over."

Jhamal handed Ben the receiver through the open window of the vehicle. "Foxtrot India, I read you, over. Move to channel eight and keep your frequency clear."

"Okay, moving to eight. Standing by, Foxtrot Lima."

Then Ben pulled the satellite phone from the pocket of his shorts, activated the tracking signal, and sent a message to the security team in Mogadishu: "SOS – stopped by hostiles at location."

Seconds later, a message arrived: "Military deployed, ETA 30 minutes. Stall them."

"Easy for them to say," he muttered. He picked up the radio receiver again and called Leo.

"Foxtrot India, Foxtrot India, ETA escort thirty minutes. Instructions are to stall them. Let me handle it, over."

"Copy, Foxtrot Lima, over."

Chapter 4

Ben watched a tall broad-shouldered man, clearly their leader, stand up in the roofless cabin of one of the pickups and raise his arm with a clenched fist. Five militants with their weapons cocked jumped down and formed a perimeter around the two FFL Cruisers.

"They're coming closer," Jhamal whispered.

"Don't move. Don't give them any excuse to shoot," Ben reminded them.

The leader stepped down from his vehicle to speak to his tall, pencil-thin lieutenant who gestured toward the convoy. They were both equipped with sidearm pistols in their holster belts, clips of ammunition, and machetes with deadly tips that reached to their knees. As the leader strode toward the Cruisers, Jhamal jammed his finger onto the button that rolled up his window.

"Stay calm and let me do the talking," Ben said, wondering why he felt so strangely in control.

Jhamal bowed his head and whispered, "May Allah be merciful to us all."

The militants stepped back, allowing their leader to pass.

Khaled's beads shook in his hands as he prayed softly.

The militants took aim at Ben's head, but he knew he couldn't flinch. He stood firm beside the Cruiser as the YLF leader came within a yard of him. Ben arranged his face in an expression of casual curiosity, as though he was both surprised and pleased to see him. He caught the reflection of his face in the dark-tinted lenses of the leader's Ray-Ban sunglasses and wondered if the man was reading fear in his eyes. Ben steeled himself. He kept his voice steady and answered the question no one had asked, "We are humanitarian aid workers with the NGO Food for Livelihood. We've brought food to the starving people of this village. Khaled, please translate."

The man reached up to adjust the bullet strap over his shoulder, and Ben saw that he was missing two fingers on his right hand. "There is no need," he said in flawless English. "I was educated in your country. I am familiar with your language."

Good, Ben thought. He couldn't read the man's face behind his *keffiyeh*, but he thought he detected a tone of amusement in his voice. He'd make this a cordial negotiation, ignore the AK-47s, pretend he could talk man-to-man with this guy, and stall by engaging him in conversation. "As you see," he said, "we are unarmed. We came here to save lives."

"Are you sure that is all you do?" the man asked, matching Ben's feigned congenial tone. "You think you're helping our people when, in reality, you're making them dependent on the West's handouts. The people of Somalia need to accept that sacrifice, suffering, and war will rebuild our great Islamic nation. You only corrupt them with your charity and politics."

At least they were talking. Africa had thrown off the yoke of colonialism and many Africans resented foreign influence in their internal affairs, but the country's transitional government was weak, and without foreign aid, the people would die of starvation. The UN and NGOs were giving the country a future by feeding its people today. Did this man really believe his people should starve until they could see things his way? Who was he to play God? Hungry people needed to eat in order to rebuild the nation.

Ben wanted to answer, but then he told himself to shut up. In a hostage situation, he knew better than to engage in political discussions. He would be baiting a man whose militants were pointing automatic weapons at him.

The leader bent his head to one side. "Where is the food you claim to have delivered?"

"Uh, there," Ben said, nodding his head toward the village, where wisps of smoke still rose from cooking fires.

Wrong answer. The leader shouted something to his men in Somali, and the gunmen dragged Jhamal, Khaled, Leo, and Hassan from the Cruisers.

A boy who couldn't have been more than fourteen years old kicked Ben squarely in the groin. He lay sprawling in the dirt, clutching his genitals, until another militant hauled him to his feet. The leader barked an order then retreated to his pickup truck while the young militants marched the FFL team in single file, their hands over their heads, toward the village school and lined them up, spread-eagled, so they could frisk them. They pulled various items, cigarettes, wallets, and passports from the men's pockets, including a small bottle of pills from Khaled. One young militant was elected to hand the items over to the skinny lieutenant who shoved most of the items into the pockets of his fatigues.

The lieutenant looked at Ben's and Leo's passports. "American, Norwegian. Allah is generous." These men were prizes they could hold for ransom. Then, he examined Ben's satellite phone. It was lit up and turned on. He began shouting in Somali and hurled it against the corrugated metal wall of the abandoned school, breaking it into bits. He grabbed Ben by the throat and pulled his face close. Ben saw death in those lifeless black eyes and struggled to breathe. "I would like to kill you," he spat at Ben. He knew this young guy was bluffing because Ben was too valuable as a hostage, but that was little comfort given the adrenalin he felt coursing through his body, priming him for fight or flight. The lieutenant shoved him back against the wall, and Ben caught a glimpse of his team to the right. Leo was muttering to himself. Hassan was sobbing softly. Khaled and Jhamal were motionless.

Ben heard the laughter of the militants who had taken the keys and were ransacking the Cruisers. He closed his eyes and whispered a prayer. Ben didn't believe that any god was watching over him personally, but if ever there was a moment for a god to intervene, it was now.

Just then, Ben heard the faint sound of engines approaching. *Please let it be the military,* he thought, a knot forming in his gut. *Maybe God did hear me.*

The leader heard it too and began screaming at his men, waving his fists for them to retreat. Ben watched as the militants ran to their pickups, hopping on as the vehicles started pulling away. He couldn't believe it. The YLF was fleeing. They were spared.

Khaled suddenly took off running after the departing pickup trucks, waving and calling out something in Somali.

No! No, no, no! What the hell is he doing? Ben thought.

"Khaled, come back, come back now!" Ben screamed.

Khaled turned and yelled over his shoulder, "They took my heart medicine."

Leo and Hassan rushed over to Ben's side. Helpless, they stood watching the scene like a movie in slow motion.

The skinny lieutenant, who was bringing up the rear, stopped and turned to face Khaled, holding up the plastic bottle of medicine, and said something indistinguishable in Somali.

Khaled held out his upturned hands in supplication. The lieutenant laughed, opened the small vile and, turning it upside down, splayed the pills onto the ground. He grunted and threw the empty bottle at Khaled.

Then Jhamal ran after Khaled. A stunned Ben tried to scream but no sound came out of his mouth. *This can't be happening,* he thought.

Khaled dropped to his hands and knees and began picking the little white pills out of the sand, returning them to the bottle one by one. A breathless Jhamal reached him and dropped down beside him to help. The two men locked eyes for a brief second, enough time for Jhamal to note Khaled's gratitude for his gesture.

But Ben had seen, up close, the cruelty in the lieutenant's eyes and knew this wasn't over. He felt the bile rise in his throat as he watched the scene unfold, powerless to stop it. The lieutenant pulled out his pistol and screamed at Khaled who looked up, pills in hand, just in time to see the lieutenant press the gun to his forehead. A single shot knocked Khaled backward, spraying brains, bone, and blood, bright red against the green of his fatigues. Next, the lieutenant turned his gun on Jhamal, still on his knees, who quickly bowed down to touch his forehead to the sand, desperate to initiate his prayer ritual. Ben could see a urine stain beginning to spread over the seat of Jhamal's pants as he rocked back onto his folded legs.

The lieutenant pulled back the hammer of his pistol and fired again. And just like that, his friend, Jhamal, toppled over onto his side, dead.

Then the lieutenant closed his eyes and brandished the gun to the sky, dancing and shouting in triumph, "*Allahu Akbar! Allahu Akbar!*"

"Run! Ruuuuuun!" yelled Ben. And the three of them hurtled along the side of the schoolhouse, trying to make it around the corner before the next shot.

It came swiftly. Gunfire, then a thud. Either Leo or Hassan had taken a hit. A second shot rang out, and Ben heard a body crash against the metal side of the building. He was next.

His heart pounded in his ears. His legs and chest were on fire. The corner of the school was just a few feet away. He had to reach it before the next shot was fired. Horns were blaring, engines were revving, and men were shouting. Then he felt a pain rip through his back, knocking him to the ground.

The world turned black; the noise stopped. He heard the voices of villagers who had come to check the bodies, turning them over one by one for signs of life.

"*Wuu dhintay. Naftiisu janno ha garto.* He is dead; let his soul go to paradise," Ben heard Hakim say through the fog enveloping his brain. Then Hakim knelt beside Ben's inert body, gently turned him over, and peeled away his flak jacket and shirt. He placed an ear against his chest.

"*Wuu nool yahay!* He lives!"

Chapter 5

Rome, Italy, eight months later

A soft breeze from the Mediterranean Sea wafted into the apartment window, bringing with it the scent of spring. The Eternal City was waking up from its long winter's sleep. Ben Tano slowly, painfully, lifted his head from the couch. The light pierced his bloodshot eyes. He closed them again and groaned. The empty scotch bottle on the table reminded him of the source of his misery. He swung his bare feet onto the floor and, after rising, lurched toward the bathroom and the promise of a hot shower.

Outside the building, dressed in jeans and a cotton sweater, he pulled down the top of his beat-up Alfa Romeo Cabrio, adjusted his new Carrera sunglasses, dropped into the worn leather driver's seat, and wove through traffic. It was a sunny Saturday afternoon, the streets were crowded, and the outdoor cafés were filled with Romans and tourists leisurely enjoying a glass of *prosecco* or a Campari soda.

Ben hadn't seen his wife for weeks, not since she had picked him up at the airport to begin work again after his long and difficult recovery and the therapy that followed. During one of his long absences on mission, Serena had opened a clothing boutique near FFL headquarters on a street lined with restaurants at the foot of the Aventine Hill. Now, five years later, business was booming.

She had just closed shop for the day. He slipped quietly through the still-opened door to find her sorting through piles of clothes clients had scattered haphazardly on the tables. "Serena," he said softly. She stopped, eyes widened, then ran to him, standing on her toes to plant a kiss on his cheek. They had been married for ten years, and he still felt immense joy whenever he saw her, as though he were connecting with this lovely, earthy woman for the first time.

After the YLF massacre, he'd woken up screaming in a Nairobi Hospital, his wife at his bedside. Serena stayed with him as he struggled with panic attacks and depression, but he was lost to her. He had retreated to the dark recesses of post-traumatic stress disorder, broken under the strain of bottled-up feelings of anger, guilt, and shame.

When he was transferred to Walter Reed Medical Center in Washington, they decided to take a break from their marriage. Serena returned to her boutique in Rome and moved in with her mother. When Ben was considered well enough to take up a desk job, he was sent to Food for Livelihood headquarters in Rome and stayed in the apartment they had once shared. He was off painkillers, but he was never really free of the night terrors.

While Serena finished tidying the shop, Ben sat down with his smartphone. Then they locked up together and strolled down the Viale Aventino to the Blue Jeans Café, a favorite of the Food for Livelihood crowd. Nico, the owner, lit up when he saw them. *"Bentornato! Come stai?"* He clutched Ben's right hand and shook it over and over again. Nico's ample belly, thick mane of dark hair, and chef's tunic gave him the look of a Roman senator on his way to the forum.

He ushered them to a corner table in the back of the room, giving them maximum privacy in a place where they risked running into FFL colleagues. They ordered plates of spaghetti bathed in spicy red *amatriciana* sauce, topped with grated *pecorino* cheese, and while they waited for their food, they sat peacefully, simply enjoying being in each other's presence.

"Tu sei troppo magro," Serena said. *You're still too thin.* "And you look tired. Have they found you a therapist in Rome?"

Ben unfolded his napkin and spread it on his lap, stalling. He was tired of answering this question. No one could understand what it had been like for him, and he had no words to explain it. "No, I'm done spilling my guts to total strangers. Reliving the memories just makes me feel worse."

"You went back to work too soon."

"The more I work, the less time I have to think."

She's even more beautiful than I remembered, he thought. Her long chestnut hair was tied back in a ponytail, and her warm brown eyes softened as she looked at him. He reached across the table to touch her hand. "The apartment is empty without you," he said softly.

"*Sono qui.* I am always here for you," she said, "and I pray for you, even if you don't pray for yourself. Maybe a little faith would help you right now."

"Maybe, but it's hard to know what to have faith in. You can't understand, you weren't there," he said. He could see the hurt in her eyes at his words and tried to soften his tone. "I'm sorry, it's hard to explain. And I know you worry. I'm not making light of it. I just have to do this my way."

"You can't keep working like this without help, *mio caro*," she said, reaching across the table to touch his hand. "Do you have any idea what you want to do?"

"What about you?" He avoided her by changing subject. "How's your mother? I'm sure she's happy to have you back home," he said, attempting to keep the conversation light.

"She's doing well after the surgery. She needs me now."

"I need you," he whispered. *Shit,* he hadn't meant to say it.

"Do you? Then why do you keep running away from me? Ben, I can't be with you now. Not if your work continues as it was. *Dio mio,* you almost died!" Serena pulled her hand away and sat back in her chair. She shook her head and with a wry smile said, "What am I to do with you, *mi amore*?"

He'd have to choose. The love of his life or his life's work. He had no idea what to say next.

The arrival of the spaghetti rescued him. *Thank God for pasta.* "*Buon appetito, amore,*" Ben said and dug hungrily into his food.

Dr. Samuel Adjei, known as Sammy to his colleagues, capped a fifteen-year career when he was selected to head the NGO Food for Livelihood.

When Ben met him, he had been youthful and vibrant, with clear, deep brown skin, tightly coiled black hair, and a clipped mustache. Now, two years into his presidency, his gravitas was bolstered by curly wisps of grey in his sideburns and a furrow permanently etched in his brow. He was looking sharp when he stepped up to the podium, his pin-striped suit offset by a tie the same green shade of the FFL flag hanging from the pole beside him.

Ghanaian by birth, Sammy spoke in the British accent that reflected his public school education and Oxford doctorate. With his usual flourish, he opened the meeting, "Dear colleagues, we must face the fact that FFL is facing unprecedented challenges to its legacy of excellence in delivering humanitarian food aid. At the recent board meeting, donors commended us for being able to keep boots on the ground in response to the increasing scope and intensity of conflicts and natural disasters. But they also expressed concerns that our agency is taking on too much risk."

Commodity losses had increased, and the reporting had become less reliable and timely. The board had suggested that FFL might have to curtail its operations in some of the most inaccessible and high-risk areas—notably in fragile states.

Samuel grasped the lectern and leaned forward. "Our organization has but one choice, to continue our mission, stronger and nimbler than before. We've progressed from mail pouches and telexes to email, e-banking, global communications, and corporate information systems. We have learned that the future of humanitarian aid must keep pace with technology in order to meet these new challenges. Now, another promising technology is on the horizon."

As murmurs broke out in the room, he paused to wait for quiet. "I strongly believe that blockchain technology will enable us to keep track of our funds and plug leakages in the supply chain, from the origin of food purchases to the mouths of hungry people. And this is only the beginning."

He cleared his throat. "Today, I am here to announce a new system-wide initiative to be known by the acronym FLITE: Food for Livelihood Innovative Technologies for Emergencies. Soon, areas in the deep field will be able to load up information onto a shared system and transmit it with only a solar panel, a computer, and a satellite phone. Everyone involved in the distribution of food will have the same financial and operational information delivered to them in seconds. FLITE will replace existing systems that do not talk to each other and multiple dashboards that require updating. We will use one system that delivers accurate, real-time reporting, one set of figures and data, a paperless trail, and full accountability. Better timing and synchronization will allow us to take advantage of market fluctuations. It will revolutionize the way in which FFL manages its billions of dollars in annual contributions."

He paused for a moment to take the pulse of the room. His face appeared on a big screen to his left, and two thousand members of the headquarters staff gave him their full attention.

"Someday in the near future, we will be able to give refugees and displaced persons without access to bank accounts a debit or credit card with digital money moved through the blockchain, which they can spend at the nearest grocery store or kiosk. Their identities will be verified with biometrics through their thumbprints. Our food distribution lines will be replaced by direct cash transfers, empowering individuals to get out of poverty and hunger by buying their food through local markets, a win-win for all. Humanitarian assistance is quickly adopting exciting new modalities for bringing food security to 900 million hungry people. The future is upon us now. Are we ready for this new challenge of harnessing technology in the service of humanity?"

The staff didn't limit themselves to loud applause. There was whistling from the finance and logistics departments and stomping feet throughout the auditorium. Samuel smiled and announced that an FFL project manager would be appointed shortly. Then he introduced a consultant from Albatross, the London-based company that would transition the organization into the blockchain environment, and the room clapped for Melissa Trask.

A tall striking woman with shoulder-length auburn hair wearing a black business suit and heels came to the podium. A close-up of her face flashed on the screen. Ben was used to working with women in the field. Some of his bravest, toughest colleagues had been women, and he'd thought of them as humanitarians first and foremost rather than women. But this woman was different—oddly compelling. Her strong jawline framed her full lips, and her eyes, a startling amber, were magnified on screen. She began clicking through a PowerPoint presentation, the first slide showing a map of the world dotted with the green FFL logo, representing all the locations the aid organization serviced.

"These will be consolidated and accessed by a single blockchain account," she said. She spoke with authority, her full contralto voice, with a slight accent Ben could not quite place, commanding yet warm.

"Albatross is not offering an answer to all of FFL's problems, but it can help restore trust and credibility. Let me explain how in simple terms: blockchain is a digital record of transactions. The name comes from its structure, in which records of individual transactions, called blocks, are linked together with other blocks to form a chain—a blockchain. Each record is time-stamped, and the writer is accountable for that record. For example, when a truck of food is off-loaded, the warehouse manager will write a transaction confirming exactly what has been received and when. The manager is responsible for that record or block. All the participants involved in this private blockchain, which constitutes your supply chain management system, will have access to the file and will be able to see that it is aligned with the other blocks. Recorded transactions are immutable, engraved in stone, and can't be changed by a single participant. In this way, the blockchain offers transparent accountability and a solid audit trail from the starting point of food procurement to the end user, the hungry people you serve. Any questions?"

Ben was interested in the concept, but he felt fidgety. He was a stickler for accountability, insisting they distribute the food according to protocol at Kabuk, even when it meant risking his life. But he had always worked in the field with the people FFL served. The intricacies of technology and data management had never been his thing, but Melissa Trask had kept his interest from the moment she was introduced until she walked off the stage. He liked her style and could tell from her demeanor that she had the best interest of FFL at heart.

Chapter 6

When Ben returned to his office suite, he was greeted by the senior technical advisor, Dalia, a petite Filipino American woman who had been assigned to work with him. Dalia knew the ins and outs of the FFL processes cold. Ben had been put in charge of the critical emergency preparedness and response service, where he'd spent his career as a member of the response team, but he wasn't used to desk work, so Dalia's guidance was much appreciated.

She immediately informed him that the country representative from Kenya had called with a request for an emergency budget revision to accommodate increasing numbers of refugees arriving at the Dadaab camp. "She said to let you know that roughly 25,000 additional people are in need of food assistance," she said.

Ben went to his inner office, plopped down at his desk, and flipped on his computer to review the request. The meeting had eaten up his morning, and his inbox was full of urgent documents to be cleared. The message from Sally in Kenya was labeled "RUSH." She reported that YLF attacks had been escalating, and the FFL early warning system predicted another drought. He got back up and returned to where Dalia was seated. "Okay, the request is fine. Go ahead and finish the paperwork," he said then headed for the door. "I'll be right back. I need a coffee and a quick smoke." He left Dalia to her work but she was soon at his heels.

He was removing a tiny paper cup of espresso from the vending machine in the stairwell when Dalia caught up with him. "Natasha in Samuel's office called with a message for you."

"Did she say what he wants?"

"He wants to meet you around eight at your usual place."

"Tell him I'll be there. Thanks."

Ben looked for Sammy's green Peugeot in the parking lot of the Sheraton, but it wasn't there. "Of course," he muttered. Sammy would be late as usual. The hotel had become their meeting place of choice because of the billiard tables in the bar where they spent hours playing eight-ball and talking business. Neither of them ever wanted to call it quits and would have stayed there all night if it weren't for their wives. Now that Ben was alone, he drove down there most evenings to avoid going home to an empty apartment.

The bartender knew him well. "Hey, Ben. Maker's Mark on the rocks?"

Ben lifted the glass of scotch and drained it. "Another one of these, please, and a Guinness for Sammy."

He had just taken his favorite cue stick from the rack when he saw Sammy stroll in pulling his rolling briefcase.

Sammy took off his tie and unbuttoned his collar with a tired, end-of-the-day sigh.

"Your beer is on the table," Ben said. "Grab a cue."

"Good man." Sammy took a sip.

"Prepare to observe the great art of eight-ball, my friend." Ben chalked up his cue and broke up the rack, scattering balls in all directions. One thumped into the far pocket, and the next shot was his. He circled the table, casually pocketing balls as he went until there were only a few left.

Sammy watched, grinning. "So, tell me, how was your day?"

"Busy. I was dealing with Kenya."

"Hmm…the Somali refugees."

"And you?"

"After the presentation, I met with the donors to convince them about FLITE," Sammy answered as Ben potted another ball. "It was exhausting, but they were open to the idea of allowing me to reshape the way FFL conducts business. FLITE will address their concerns and put us on the cutting edge of delivering humanitarian food aid."

"Oh yeah? How so?" Ben asked, lining up his next shot.

"If you leave a few balls on the table for me, I just might give you the highlights."

Ben laughed and sank another ball. "I know you're trying to distract me, but it won't work. I'm on a run."

Sammy took another long swig of his brew then balanced his glass on the edge of the table. "What did you think of this morning's meeting? I'm excited about this new technology. It's going to transform the way we operate Food for Livelihood."

Ben finished a seven-ball run and was lining up his shot to sink the eight ball in the pocket at the far-left corner.

Sammy continued, "The woman Albatross sent from London, Trask, is very capable; however, I need a team on our side, not only to manage a smooth transition, but also to ensure coherence and relevance to our field operations. We need the field staff on board so...I'd like you to head the project."

Ben's arm slipped and jacked up the cue. The white ball flew into the air, barely missing a beer mug in the hand of an elderly Japanese tourist standing nearby.

"Strike!" Sammy laughed.

"Did I hear you right? Repeat that, please."

"I am putting you in charge of the FLITE project."

"I need another drink," Ben sighed.

Sammy put down his cue and smiled. "Let's find a place where we can talk."

Ben had only been back at work for a couple of months, and he wanted to return to the field. The last thing on his mind was another big job at headquarters, anchored to a desk. But when Serena asked him what he wanted, he hadn't been able to answer. Maybe he should be glad. He could stay in Rome and repair his marriage.

"I don't know," Ben said, easing into a chair at a secluded table. "I'm not so sure how this whole thing will work. We're not a tech company, and I'm not an expert in data systems. I've always been in the field. Why me?"

Sammy leaned forward. "For that very reason! I need someone who really knows our field operations, who knows how to implement new systems. Take, for example, our emergency needs assessment and reporting tools. If I can win you over, others will follow. You know the organization, and you're familiar with our supply chain bottlenecks. Once it's set up, the system will do all the work. Listen, I'm handing you a dream job, a job most of your colleagues would die for. You can't run from an opportunity like this. I won't let you. There's too much riding on it."

Ben slumped back in his chair. "I'm not ready for more responsibility, Sammy. I have enough to do already. What I need is more time. As soon as I'm medically cleared, I want to return to the field."

Sammy shook his head and folded his arms. "I'm not convinced you've made peace with what happened in Somalia. Risk-taking constitutes your modus operandi. That's who you are. It's time to turn this trauma into a springboard for what motivates you—feeding hungry people—but this time doing it from the safety of headquarters. Remember, I was the one who recruited you from the private sector. I needed your skill sets, and you needed a calling—a win-win for both of us."

Ben knew he was right. Since Somalia, he'd developed a fear of taking risks. This job wouldn't be life-threatening, but he'd risk failing, and he didn't think he could handle it. This was unfamiliar territory. He needed to be on the ground, with the people they served. He needed the validation of seeing the results of his work on people's lives—not from data on a computer screen.

Sammy unzipped his briefcase, pulled out an oversized file marked "FLITE," and placed it on the table in front of Ben. "Take a look at this."

Ben opened the folder and found a few pamphlets from Albatross, schematics, and a lengthy proposal.

"Our collaboration with Albatross will streamline everything," Sammy said. "You know very well our food pipelines have been hemorrhaging in Sudan, Congo, Yemen, and Afghanistan, taking a toll on our credibility and finances. These militant groups steal food meant for starving families. The bastards use hunger as a weapon of war. With blockchain, we can track the movement of food deliveries in real time and hold all links in the chain accountable, closing the biggest gap we must deal with—trust."

Ben was used to watching his friend deal with high-stress situations and solve life-or-death problems, but he'd never seen him as enthusiastic about anything as he was now.

"The great advantage for us," he continued, "is that the platform is decentralized to monitor all our operations around the globe."

"Big Brother is watching?" Ben laughed and took another sip of his drink, trying to take it all in. This was not the vocabulary he was accustomed to using in the field, but it was intriguing. He could see the potential. Field operations would be streamlined. Working relationships with partners would be stronger. And they had to be very strong to feed a hundred million hungry people every day.

"So, what do you think, Ben? Are you with me? Food for Livelihood will be the first NGO to implement blockchain technology. No risk, no reward, remember?"

Ben's skepticism shifted to admiration for the brilliance of Sammy's vision and conviction, but he needed to mull it over. He was still traumatized by the massacre in Somalia, and he wasn't sure if he'd ever really be well again. He couldn't trust himself to make decisions anymore. Sammy's eyes were boring into him. He always seemed to know Ben better than Ben knew himself. Maybe Sammy was right—maybe the job would be good for him. It would give him a chance to prove he wasn't one of those damaged

PTSD guys they had to place somewhere out of the way. Sammy wouldn't have offered him the job if he didn't think he could do it. Maybe he wasn't so screwed up after all. The doctor had told him to take baby steps. This would be a giant step, but compared to confronting YLF, it was a walk in the park. After all, he didn't know if he'd ever be fit enough to go back to the field.

"Ben," Sammy said gently as if reading his mind, "you're not ready for the field yet. It's going to take time to heal from the trauma you experienced. What I'm offering you is another path to consider, and I need you by my side now." He swallowed the last of his drink. "Do you trust me?"

"Yes." Ben wasn't sure he trusted anything, but he knew Sammy was testing his loyalty and his willingness to reengage with the work that inspired him.

"So, are you in?"

Was he in? In what? He couldn't stop reliving the sights and sounds of his colleagues gunned down one by one. He had been running for his life ever since, trapped in a no-man's-land between past and present, where survival depended on numbing his emotions. He noticed that the hand clutching his glass was shaking. "I'm in. Together we sink or swim. When do I start?"

"As of this moment, you are under my direct supervision. I'll back you one hundred percent. Natasha booked you on a flight to London tomorrow morning. The managers at Albatross will bring you up to speed. Feel them out and let me know what you think of their operation. Then get back here and set up your team. You have carte blanche. Recruit anyone you like."

Ben nodded. Did he really have a choice? The wheels had been turning long before Sammy asked him to take the job.

As they left the hotel, Sammy squeezed Ben's hand. "Congratulations. You are now directly responsible for billions of dollars. Don't let the money out of your sight."

Chapter 7

A farmhouse near Taranto, Puglia, Italy, the next day

In the early hours of the morning, a stout, middle-aged woman wearing a faded red cotton dress and rubber boots was bent over her vegetable patch, her once-fair complexion lined and hardened from long hours spent under the sun. She muttered to herself while she vigorously plucked weeds from the hard ground and heaped them in a pile. She supported her lower back with her hand as she slowly straightened to survey the remaining clumps of crabgrass.

"*Prokleti korov!*" she snarled in Serbian. "Damned weeds! No more smothering my tomatoes and carrots."

Inside the house, a tall man in his late sixties crossed the room to answer the one landline phone they used to communicate with the world outside their farm. He was handsome, with high cheek bones, small dark eyes, and a thick, well-trimmed beard. His silver hair was cropped close around his head, leaving a thick crown on top. On his forehead, just below the hairline, a mottled purple birthmark was partially hidden under an unruly lock. He combed it back with his fingers as he bent to lift the receiver.

The phone rarely rang, and when it did, it was usually someone selling insurance or satellite TV. "*Pronto?*"

"Tata? It's Mihailo."

He had two children, a son and a daughter, both smuggled out of Serbia, both grown now, each a successful professional.

"Miha? Where are you? Are you coming?"

"I'm sorry, Tata. Still in London. Work is extremely busy. That's why I'm calling. I won't be able to fly out this afternoon."

"But your mother is expecting you. She made *sarma* and *burek* with cheese…"

"I know, but it's a big project."

The man's attention was distracted by the sound of tires crunching on gravel. *Who is this?* he thought. Not even the postman came to his house very often. He opened the heavy drapes a crack, but his view was blocked by the myrtle bushes that lined the driveway. The black hood of an Audi SUV appeared from behind the bend.

"Tata? Tata? Are you still there?"

"Sorry, Miha, I can't talk now. Someone is here."

"Who is there? Tata? Tata!"

He ended the call and stood motionless as he watched and waited. The windows of the vehicle were slightly tinted, so he could only see the profiles of two figures sitting in the front. They circled the long driveway that concealed the house from the road and came to a full stop in front of the door. Two men in shiny black leather boots emerged from the vehicle. A trim, middle-aged man wearing a dark linen suit and dark glasses removed his jacket and swung it over his shoulder with two fingers. He reached into his trouser pocket and pulled out a red handkerchief to wipe the perspiration from his bald head as the younger, stockier driver came into view carrying a briefcase. Both men seemed out of place. The old man hoped they were only real estate agents from Rome, nosing around for opportunities to buy and refurbish vacation homes.

The driver pointed to the white cord attached to a brass bell, looked to his companion for approval, then jerked it twice. He didn't wait for an answer but reached for the handle. At the same moment, the old man opened his door from the inside, causing the driver to lose his footing. When he regained his balance, he found himself looking into the amber eyes of the silver-haired gentleman.

"*Buon giorno.* What can I do for you?"

"*Buon giorno.* My name is Bruno Neri," said the bald one, "and this is my colleague, Ugo Bosco. We think you may be able to help us. We're looking for a man by the name of Trasjic—Rasko Trasjic." He repeated the name slowly while removing his sunglasses to get a better look.

The elderly gentleman stiffened and answered too quickly. "I'm sorry, who? I know no one by the name of Tra… Tra… What was the name, please?"

"Trasjic, Rasko Trasjic."

"No, I don't know anyone by that name. I'm sorry. I can't help you."

He started to close the door, but Neri jammed it with his right foot. "So, we finally meet you, *Signor* Trasjic, or would you prefer General Trasjic?"

The old man instinctively ran his fingers through his hair, letting the stray lock cover his birthmark. "Who are you and what do you want from me?" he said with a measured tone.

"Allow us to introduce ourselves. I am Agent Neri, and this is my colleague, Agent Bosco. We are here on behalf of the International Criminal Tribunal for the former Yugoslavia with the authority to hunt and bring to justice individuals accused of committing war crimes during the Balkan conflict when, of course, you were chief of staff of the Yugoslavian army." They both reached into their pockets and pulled out identification cards.

"If you are implying that I am guilty of some crime, I have been thoroughly investigated, and no charges were ever brought. Why am I of interest to you now?"

"Your role as the master planner behind these crimes didn't come to light until 2004. We have been trying to track you down for the past seven years. Who could imagine that a former Serbian general would assume the lifestyle of a Pugliese farmer?"

The general had been through far more brutal interrogations. He calmly smiled and gestured toward the sitting room, stepping aside to allow the agents to enter. "May I suggest we continue this discussion where we can be more comfortable?"

"No thank you, General," Neri said. "We'd rather stand."

"Suit yourself." The general went to the dining table and sat on one of the wooden chairs.

"Let me get to the point," Neri said. "What can you tell us about the Srebrenica massacre and General Mladic's role in it? According to our intelligence, he served under your command. Is that correct?"

The general paused, adjusting the lock of hair. "I'm afraid I have nothing to say about the Srebrenica massacre. The orders were issued by General Karadzic. Mladic was commissioned to capture the city, ostensibly to save Serbian lives..."

"Yes, he saved Serbian lives...fearing they would take up arms against you. He slaughtered eight thousand Bosnian men and boys who had taken refuge in the UN safe area. That was genocide, General."

The general shrugged his shoulders, saying, "I thought I might be held accountable for his actions one day."

"Do you know where Mladic is now?"

"I have no idea. I left the country immediately afterward. I had nothing to do with the killing of those people. I did not order any acts of genocide. I was a bureaucrat, a military strategist."

Neri nodded to Bosco who reached into the briefcase, pulled out a stack of pictures, and spread them on the table. The general froze at the images of mass graves, remembering the women who hanged themselves from trees after being raped by Serbian soldiers, men and boys with their throats slit, left to bleed to death. Neri picked up one of the photos and handed it to him. "General, look at this one very closely. The man in uniform to the left of General Mladic. Does he look familiar to you?"

The general knew he was trapped. "It was war... I had to serve my country," he said softly.

"General, General," Neri hissed, "you did so much more than that. You stood by while your soldiers killed innocent civilians who were the wrong race, the wrong religion. And you justified it by pretending that this slaughter was in the service of a greater Serbia."

The general shook his head, saying, "I never wanted this to happen."

"General, we have everything we need to bring your case to trial…"

The back door was kicked open, and the stout woman charged into the room like a bull, head down, aiming a double-barreled shotgun at Bosco's chest.

"You are not welcome here!" she screamed. "Get out of my house before I blow your heads off!"

Neri held up one hand and discreetly groped for his pistol with the other. "Easy. Don't hurt yourself with that thing," he said smoothly.

"Keep your hands where I can see them. Believe me when I say I will shoot you. Do you think I will let you take my husband without a fight?"

"*Tranquilla…tranquilla…*calm down, *signora*," Bosco said.

The general jumped to his feet, and the two men reached for their pistols.

"*Signora, per piacere*, put the gun down," Neri said.

"Lidija, please do what they say," the general told her.

But she only readjusted her aim and shifted her weight from one boot to the other. "You're not taking him."

"*Signora*, I promise you that we have not come here to take your husband away. We've come to discuss an offer that will mean his freedom. You don't need the gun. Please, put it down."

She lowered the gun and rested the barrel against her boot.

"Why should I believe that you are here to discuss my freedom?" the general asked.

"As I said, we have an extensive dossier concerning your activities." Neri lifted his chin toward Bosco who was still trembling from the shock of the shotgun being pointed at him. Bosco fumbled with the briefcase on the floor and handed the general a thick file.

Neri said, "As you will see, we've collected a great deal of evidence. If I alert Interpol, you will be arrested, and in all likelihood, you will be tried in the Hague with your friend, Karadzic, and sentenced to life in prison—the last ones to face justice. Mladic is in our sights now. I'd just have to make one phone call. Please, take a look at the file."

"No, that won't be necessary," the general replied. "I've seen enough."

"So, you know we are serious, but it is not our intention to have you arrested. We can come to an agreement if you're willing to do business with us. Are you interested?"

The general shook his head, laughing under his breath. "I know you're not agents from the International Tribunal. Your forged identification didn't fool me. Who are you and what do you want? Tell me now or leave my house."

Neri smirked. "You know what the thing is, General? It doesn't matter who I am or who I work for. All you need to know is that I have enough information to ruin your quiet retirement, and that if you cooperate with me, I can take care of you and your family."

The general sat down again and leaned back in his chair and crossed his arms over his chest. "How much do you want?"

"Twenty million dollars."

"Very funny!" the general barked a short, loud laugh.

His wife reached for the shotgun again, but he gave her a look and held up his hand. "Twenty million? Look around you, gentlemen. You've come to the wrong place," he said.

"Ah, but you see, General," Neri countered, "this will be very easy for you. If you simply follow our instructions, you will be a free man and a wealthy one. With your help, and the help of your children, we will obtain the twenty million we're seeking. You just need to encourage them to do the right thing when the time is right. Not only will you be a free man, you and your family will never have to worry about money again. I am sure you will come to see that our offer is very attractive."

Lidija lifted the shotgun again. "*Signora*, if you kill me, you will be unable to hide from the dozens of men who are my colleagues. Not one of them will find it difficult to shoot you wherever they find you and to make life very difficult for your son and daughter. Yes, you see, we know too much about you. Anything could happen. You might have an accident. Perhaps you will get lost coming home from the market."

"No more talking!" she screeched. "Get out of this house before I shoot you both!"

Neri didn't flinch, but Bosco was slowly backing toward the door, his eyes fixed on her shotgun.

Neri picked up the briefcase the panicked Bosco had left on the floor. "We'll leave you now, General, *Signora* Trasjic. Think carefully about complying with our demands. It will help you. And the alternative is…much less advantageous for you."

He turned and sauntered to the door then looked back and with a twisted smile said, "Before we go, I'll leave you with a thought. Your children hold the key to your freedom. We will be back soon when we are ready to move forward. The choice will be yours. I suggest you make the right one."

The general grimaced. His son and daughter worked with international companies. No wonder these two mobsters had decided to come after him. He didn't want them involved in his trouble.

Back in the SUV, Bosco relaxed into the leather driver's seat and laughed. "You almost got him, boss. Agents for the International Tribunal. *Fantastico!* A couple of Barese guys. *Si, si,* Agente Neri."

Neri smacked the dashboard. "*Chiudi la bocca, cretino!* You stupid kid! You almost pissed in your pants when the old *puttana* aimed her shotgun at us. You thought she'd have the balls to pull the trigger. Idiot! You left the briefcase on the floor. What would have happened if I hadn't picked it up? *Sei inutile!* Useless! If I didn't owe your uncle, I would never put up with you. Be quiet. I need to call him and tell him we found the old man. Don't make an ass of yourself. Let me talk to him without you running your mouth." Neri pulled out his cell phone and punched in a series of numbers while Bosco sat grimacing.

"We found him… *Si*, it's him, I'm certain," he said, pausing. "I understand. We won't let either of them out of our sight." He flicked the phone closed and glared at his partner.

"We have to do this deal perfectly. I can't betray the trust that's been given to me. *Capisci?* Either we're both rich or we're both dead, just like the general! You're not going to screw this up for me. This is my ticket out. My cut of this money means I'm done with all this *merda*. I got my eye on a vineyard in Corsica. Now, keep your mouth shut till we get back to Bari or I'll strangle you myself. In the meantime, we're stuck here until we know what the next steps are."

"*Va bene, va bene…*" Bosco said, trying to sound confident.

Chapter 8

Leonardo da Vinci Airport, Rome, two days later

Ben awoke with a start, soaked in sweat and breathing heavily. The jolt when the plane landed felt like a gunshot to his head. He was disoriented and looked around frantically. *Right, plane,* he thought. *I'm on a plane.* A woman's voice came on the intercom, soft and comforting words in Italian. *"Benvenuto a Roma. Siamo atterrati all'aeroporto Leonardo da Vinci."* He was back in Rome. He let out the breath he didn't realize he was holding, released his death grip on the arms of his seat, and relaxed his tensed muscles. He flashed an embarrassed smile at the stranger sitting beside him in the window seat. It was a full flight from London, a quick commute. Mostly businesspeople and the odd university student.

After two days of briefings in London with Albatross, he was convinced that FLITE would be a great thing for Food for Livelihood and had mustered genuine enthusiasm for his new assignment. He had spent a lot of time speaking to Melissa back in the Rome FFL office. He was learning a lot from her, and he admired how much she had learned, apparently in a short period of time. Blockchain was a lot to wrap his head around, but he saw the value in it especially with her tutelage. They spoke about the project during the day, but on his last night in London, he called her from his hotel room. He had some ideas he wanted to explore, but after some discussion about FLITE, they continued to talk for nearly two hours and slid from business to personal with an unexpected ease. The conversation remained light, mostly touching on things they enjoyed about the job, Rome, what they enjoyed doing in their spare time. But when Ben hung up, he felt a loneliness creep in. *Hmm, that was nice. Maybe a little too nice,* he thought, and as he drifted off to sleep, he could hear the sound of her laughter in his head.

He was following the other passengers into the terminal when Sammy called, asking to meet him at the café in Terminal One.

Ben found him sitting at a table by the window with his familiar black trolley stowed beside him. "Short trip?" he asked, gesturing to the trolley.

"I'm off to Brussels," Sammy said as they shook hands. "I have a meeting with the European Commission, but I'll be back tonight."

"Doesn't leave much time for sightseeing."

"Just one of the perks of working for a nonprofit," Sammy quipped.

"Your whole life is a perk." Ben laughed. Sammy traveled at odd hours when flights were cheap, saving money for the organization.

Sammy chuckled and said, "Sit down and tell me about London. Are we right in bringing Albatross onboard?"

"I think so. They're relatively new and hungry to get our business... and they have the available staff to pay us the kind of attention we're going to need. We'll be one of their biggest clients, so they're offering very competitive rates. I think the donors will be happy when they see how far their money will go with fewer losses and greater efficiency. I'm feeling a lot better about taking this on knowing I'm feeding more people, even if it's from a desk."

Sammy didn't answer. He was looking past Ben, shifting to the right in his chair.

"Sammy? Everything okay?"

"The bald chap behind you to the left appears to be listening to our conversation. Do you know him?"

Ben tried to get a look at the man without catching his eye. "Never saw him before." He wondered if the stress of the presidency was making Sammy paranoid. *Why would anyone spy on an NGO?*

"We should move," Sammy said and stood up, pulling his trolley along. Ben followed him to a table on the far side of the café.

"I can see the potential impact on our field operations," Ben continued once they were seated. "Our field staff will love it! The setup process will be pretty straightforward with the expertise of Albatross and a dedicated FFL team."

"I suppose you've thought of who they might be," said Sammy.

"Dalia, of course. I'd make her our business requirements manager. Akito from IT will plan out and execute upgrades to the off-the-shelf system. And Paul will be the change manager charged with identifying the training needed and organizing the rollout schedule."

Sammy folded his hands in his lap and nodded. "Jolly good. What else can you tell me?"

Ben took a file from his backpack and placed it on the table. "I jotted down some of the extracts from the Albatross presentations to illustrate my implementation plan."

"Excellent. I'll review this on the flight. Incidentally, our key board members are in Rome this week, so I've scheduled a conference tomorrow at 11:30. I'll need you to put together some sort of presentation for me, and it would be good if you joined us."

Sammy's flight was announced, and he stood up. "Well, right you are then. Next time you'll trust me when I tell you what's good for you."

Ben laughed. "I trust you, Sammy. I wouldn't be here if I didn't trust you. I might be making a million a year, or I might be lying in a gutter somewhere, but I wouldn't be here."

When Ben got to the office, he passed Melissa Trask installed at a computer. He noticed that her thick auburn hair was tied up in a knot, revealing the intent expression on her face. She looked up from her screen and smiled quickly as he greeted her, saying he would catch up with her later in the day. They'd be working closely together on the project so it made sense to plan to spend some time with her. *It would be smart to get to know more about her, right?* he asked himself, justifying the idea. He thought he'd made a good start in London.

Dalia took off her headphones, saying, "Welcome back, Ben! How was London?"

"You're going to hear all about it after lunch. We need to schedule a meeting with Paul and Akito at three o'clock…and ask Melissa Trask to join us. She's been set up with a desk, I see. Sammy will be briefing the board members on blockchain tomorrow morning, so we'll have to rush through a presentation for him. I'll give you an outline we can send up to his office."

Ben knew he had a strong team. Paul Emanuel, a Nigerian, was an experienced talent manager, aligning and upgrading staff competencies with the evolving needs of the organization. Akito Sato was the office IT wizard. He'd developed FFL's international communications systems, and the whole staff leaned on him. Dalia Reyes was the most efficient person Ben had ever known. He could count on her to ensure compliance with FFL's financial regulations and business processes. She'd backstop him by double-checking all upgrades prior to the Go Live phase.

At three o'clock, they were seated in his office. Sitting behind the desk, running the show, Ben had the realization that he was an executive now. It felt weird. At least he wasn't forced to wear a suit and tie every day. Melissa Trask looked much more like senior management in her well-pressed navy blue silk jacket and narrow skirt. His eyes drifted to her neckline where her white satin blouse was opened just enough to offer a glimpse of a lace bra. *Snap out of it,* he told himself. It had been a while since he had been with his wife, and there were no other women on his radar, but Trask was a colleague and an important one. He was just feeling the pressure of the work. He couldn't disappoint Sammy who had more faith in him than he thought he deserved.

"Guys, if you haven't already met Melissa Trask," he said, "she's our project developer and liaison with Albatross. We'll be working closely with her as we set up FLITE, and I'll ask you to brief her individually regarding your areas of expertise, and she will work with you as we bring all the pieces together."

They all smiled that perfunctory look coworkers give each other when they're hoping for a decent relationship but don't really care who the temporary person actually is.

Ben explained the blockchain system and their roles and responsibilities in setting it up.

"We have a huge task in front of us with cutting over our legacy data to FLITE, which will be accessed by our staff all over the world. Dalia will take the lead on that."

"What's our time frame?" Paul asked. "I'll need to finalize the training plan and rollout schedule."

"We'll schedule a launch date for headquarters only in four to six months. By then, we should have trained all the staff, finished the simulations, and ironed out the kinks so we can Go Live. Rollout to the field should take another six months. Ms. Trask will give you more details, but the short version is that using blockchain technology will save us all time, money, and labor. It will be well worth the effort in the end. So, are we good?" He looked around at their inscrutable faces, sensing their apprehension. "Okay, Ms. Trask will take it from here. She'll give you all the assistance you need to get up to speed. That's all for now, thanks."

Chapter 9

By the end of the day, Ben was in Sammy's office, watching the PowerPoint presentation on his big computer screen. Sammy handed the printouts back to him.

"You did well. Just one or two things. I'll need the corrected slides at least half an hour before the meeting."

"We haven't screwed up yet, have we?"

"There's a first time for everything. Just make sure it's not this time."

The board members provided the bulk of the financing for the organization. Sammy needed to reassure them that he wasn't making a disastrous mistake with his FLITE initiative. The technology was still new with reputational risks, and these people were conservative. He was taking a big chance, and Ben was taking it with him. To fail, to cause financial harm to FFL when every penny was needed to feed desperate people, was unthinkable.

The next morning when Ben arrived at the office, Dalia called to say she'd be late because her daughter had the flu. She wouldn't be able to enter the revisions on the presentation in time for Sammy's meeting.

This was bad news. Sammy trusted him to deliver the presentation without glitches. He needed help, and neither Akito nor Paul would know what to do.

The obvious answer was Melissa Trask. She would be able to catch any mistakes in his presentation of FLITE, but he had no idea if she knew how to use the program or even if she would be willing to pitch in. She was an outside consultant, and this wasn't in her job description.

He called her and asked her to step into his office then put his sport coat back on, smoothed his hair, and sat behind his desk. When he looked up, she was already standing in his doorway holding a notebook. She seemed taller than he remembered. Maybe it was the heels. Her eyes were hidden behind dark-framed glasses, and she was slightly intimidating in a fitted three-piece business suit.

"Good morning, Ben." He realized that he was staring at her, cleared his throat, and tried to sound professional. "Good morning, Melissa, good to see you. I'm glad I finally have the chance to sit down face-to-face with you. Thanks for all your help in getting me up to speed. Sit, please," he said and motioned to the chair facing his desk.

She sat gingerly on the edge of the seat and leaned toward him.

"I know this isn't your problem, but I'm in a jam. Dalia is coming in late today, and she was supposed to make the final changes for a presentation Dr. Adjei is giving this morning on FLITE. He asked for just a few things… but I have no idea how to use this software program, and I'm hoping that you do and that you'll have a moment to make sure I haven't made any errors in describing how blockchain works. I'm seriously embarrassed to ask, but the thing is…the presentation is at 11:30, so we only have ninety minutes."

"Let me have a look." He pushed the printouts across the desk to her, and she began reviewing each image, setting aside each page where Sammy had marked changes. "This looks impressive," she said.

Ben grinned. That was his work she was complimenting. "So, you're willing to help me out?"

She held his eyes for a moment while he fidgeted waiting for an answer in the affirmative.

"Of course," she said. "Can I find the files uploaded on the share drive, or do you have a pen drive?"

"I have a pen drive right here," he responded. Their hands touched momentarily.

Melissa smiled. "Thanks, Ben," she said. Standing quickly, she turned on her heels and walked out of his office.

Ben spent the next hour on the phone. Refugees were fleeing the post-election violence in Togo. The Philippines had been pummeled by a cyclone. Sammy's office called. The meeting had been moved forward thirty minutes.

He grabbed his tie and rushed to Melissa's desk. "Have you finished?"

"Almost," she said calmly. "I'll bring everything to you in ten minutes."

Natasha was much more than Sammy's executive assistant. She was on top of every detail that made the organization work, and the staff knew it. When Ben arrived, she was sitting at her computer lining up the delegates for the conference. She pursed her lips. "What's wrong, Ben?"

Since the massacre, any sort of stress set him off. His whole body tensed up, his heart beat out of his chest, and he sweated heavily. He thought he hid it well, but apparently not well enough if Natasha had noticed.

He forced a smile and thrust his sweaty hands into the pockets of his trousers. "Oh, just another typical day at Food for Livelihood," he said. "The slides aren't ready just yet for Sammy's presentation. Melissa Trask is reviewing them. She'll bring them up as soon as she's finished."

He paced nervously back and forth in front of Natasha's desk, terrified Melissa would be late. Natasha's phone rang.

"It's Dr. A," she said.

"Don't pick it up. He'll be asking for me. We need to give Melissa more time. I can't go in there empty-handed."

Natasha flashed him a look as she lifted the receiver. "Good morning, Dr. Adjei."

Ben grasped his head as though he were trying to keep it in place. He mouthed, "No, no!" His chest and throat began to constrict, and his mind raced through a current of panicked thoughts. If he messed this up, FFL would lose credibility. And he had to prove to himself that he could still perform under pressure. What had happened to the man who dealt with hostile governments, violent militia, the man who handled natural disasters and civil wars? Here he was freaking out over a PowerPoint presentation.

Natasha was still looking at him. "Yes, he's here. I'll send him in right away." Ben grimaced, trying to hide his fear by screwing up his face at her.

"What do I say if he asks to see the presentation?" Ben asked.

Natasha responded evenly with her usual cool demeanor, "Tell him that I'm making copies of the printouts, and I'll go check on Melissa Trask."

As Ben approached Sammy's door, he recalled the advice of his therapist at Walter Reed Medical Center: "When a panic attack feels like it's coming on, focus on your breathing." He closed his eyes and took a few mindful breaths before he knocked on Sammy's door.

"Ben, you don't look well. Are you sure you're okay?" Sammy said with concern in his voice.

"Yes, yes. Fine," Ben replied a little too quickly.

"Let me have a look at the presentation then."

He was formulating an appropriate reply when Sammy's computer screen lit up with the first slide.

"Showtime! They are already in the building."

"Uh, Natasha is bringing…"

There was a knock at the door and Natasha came in. "These are hard copies of the presentation and the briefs. The slides have just been loaded onto your computer. Anything else?"

"No, I guess we're ready. Invite the board members to join us." Ben breathed a sharp sigh of relief but was unable to let go of the tension in his body with the meeting to come. He had been warned that this was a common symptom of trauma—the tension remains even after the perceived danger has passed.

A group of men and women in business suits and native dress filed into the room. Ben recognized the U.K., Germany, Brazil, Canada, the U.S., Ireland, India, China, Saudi Arabia, South Africa, Egypt, and Japan, among others.

Sammy stood by the door shaking hands. "Ladies and gentlemen, welcome to Food for Livelihood headquarters. I believe you know Ben Tano."

Two hours later, Ben had moved from tension to excitement, and Sammy was grinning from ear to ear. The presentation was enthusiastically received. Blockchain technology would become a reality at Food for Livelihood.

When he got back to his office, Melissa was waiting for him, sitting on the edge of his desk tapping her foot in the air.

"Don't look so nervous," he said with a laugh. "We were a big hit. They agreed to FLITE. No objections, no reservations. We're on!"

"Thank God," she said, clutching her hand to her chest. "I'm not used to your humanitarian pace; I had to really race through those slides."

"But you stayed calm and delivered. That's what this business is all about."

"Thank you, Ben."

"Are you kidding? I have you to thank." He didn't know what to say next. Her lips were parted, and her eyes were shining as she smiled at him.

"Are you…? Are you available to have a celebratory drink later?" He said the words before thinking it through.

She lit up. "I'd love to!"

He hoped he wasn't grinning like an idiot. "Awesome. I'll stop by your desk at the end of the day."

Chapter 10

The restaurant on the top floor of the Food for Livelihood building was always crowded at lunch, but only a few staffers used the bar in the evenings, and from the terrace, the view of Rome was stunning. Ben stood with his elbows on a high table, a foot resting on the bottom rung of a stool, as Melissa maneuvered herself onto the stool opposite him, discreetly hiking her straight skirt over her knees. He lifted his glass of scotch and tapped it against her gin and tonic. "To Albatross," he said.

"To Food for Livelihood," she said. And they both took long swigs from their glasses.

She looked different at night. He'd only seen her under the fluorescent glare of the office overheads. The terrace was subtly lit to allow the city below to glimmer in all its glory. Her skin looked soft, and he could see now that her startling amber eyes were flecked with green. She'd let her hair down, so it framed her face in soft waves. He hadn't realized how young she was—late twenties, he guessed.

He reminded himself that they were colleagues. The success of the FLITE project depended on their ability to work together. He was used to working with women, and she was more than capable. Still, he couldn't help wondering if she was married.

"It's beautiful up here," she said, squeezing the lime into her glass.

"There's an even better view from over here," Ben said, picking up his drink. He casually strolled toward the edge of the terrace looking over his shoulder to be sure she was following. They reached the spot on the rooftop that offered an even better vantage point.

"Have you spent much time in Rome?" he asked as she took her place beside him.

"Not at all. My parents have a place further south, but it's a bit of a drive, and my life is really in London. The apartment where I'm staying for now is…right there," she said, pointing when she located it.

Ben's eyes followed her outstretched finger. "Yes, that's next to the Circus Maximus where they had the chariot races. Is it nice?" he asked.

"I enjoy the view. It has everything I need. I'm probably going to be here for a while, so I was glad they put me in a comfortable place. What's the beautiful building that looks like the Coliseum? I walk past it all the time but never take the time to ask."

"Yeah, it does look like the Coliseum. It's called the Teatro di Marcello. The Coliseum isn't far from here, though. And that wide road to your right leads to the Baths of Caracalla. Good jogging path."

"You know a lot about Rome," she said, brushing her hair away from her face.

Ben pushed away a thought about what it would be like to run his hands through her thick, shiny hair.

"Well, I do have Italian blood, and it's now my home base," he said. "I have an apartment here, but for years I spent most of my time traveling in the deep field."

"You live here with your family?" she asked.

He looked away, addressing his words to the night air. "No family. I'm…my Italian wife and I are separated. You?" He held his breath.

"Not married. Married to my job, I guess." She chuckled. "What's your story?"

"I got hooked on humanitarian work when I was an undergrad at Princeton. I volunteered for an FFL internship that sent me to Sudan, and I knew I'd found my vocation, what I wanted to do with my life. You've worked your way up to an impressive position in Albatross. Where did you start? Your accent doesn't sound like British English."

She laughed. "Do I still have an accent? Since my teens, I've lived in London where I completed my secondary studies before pursuing a degree at the London School of Economics. I'm from Belgrade."

"Really? Have you been back since the war ended? I know the city has been reconstructed."

She looked into her glass. Nothing was left but melting ice cubes. "Building a new city may cover the blood, but nothing can bury the memories. You grow up quickly as a child in war. I still have nightmares. The noise of the shelling. The streets littered with bodies. Bosnian friends I never heard from again. As a Serb, I'm so ashamed of that episode in our history."

This was not the confident professional he'd seen in the office. He could see that she was hurting like he was, and it surprised him. "I know it must be hard to talk about. I mean…many of my colleagues were there in the former Yugoslavia giving humanitarian aid…at the time of Srebrenica. I can't even imagine what it must have felt like for you to live through it. But I do know that once you've experienced war and death, you never forget it. I carry the massacre of my colleagues in Somalia with me every day, like a yoke around my neck."

She nodded, lowering her eyes. "My father has been withdrawn ever since the war. He never talks about it and would never admit that he suffers from post-traumatic stress."

Ben lowered his eyes. "Unless you have the courage to face it, PTSD is like a ghost that haunts you for the rest of your life."

In that moment, he felt an undeniable connection between them. Flustered, he didn't know what to say next. "Where's the waiter? We need another round. Are you hungry at all?"

She nodded in the affirmative, and they headed for a table where they ordered a bottle of wine and some small plates to share. Two hours passed easily as did the conversation between them, like a couple of old friends catching up.

Later, they went down to the office to collect their things. On his way out, he stopped by Melissa's desk to find her loading her laptop into a leather tote. He considered offering to drive her home. Would she think he was trying to come on to her, maybe trying to get her into bed? *Maybe I am.* He had to admit that the thought was a pleasant one, but it would only make things complicated. He had to work with this woman, and then there was Serena. He thought of her every day. This would hurt her and his chances to fix his marriage.

In spite of his better judgement, he realized it was late, and in an effort to sound casual, he said, "My car is in the lot if you need a lift."

"Thanks." She hoisted the bag over her shoulder. "I usually enjoy the walk, but it's been a long day. You don't mind?"

"Not at all," Ben said a little too enthusiastically. *Calm down, boy. She'll get the wrong idea.*

In the elevator they stood side by side, looking straight ahead. When they reached his car, he opened the passenger door for her and gently took her elbow to get her settled in the seat. "All set?" he asked. She nodded yes.

Ben navigated the car through the narrow streets following Melissa's instructions until he arrived at a small apartment building at the base of the Palatine Hill. He started to get out to open her door but she placed a hand on his arm to stop him. "I'm good. Thanks for taking me home," she said, her eyes locking with his.

On impulse, he leaned to kiss her cheek, Italian style, but she turned her head in time for his lips to lightly brush hers.

"Oops!" She laughed, flipped open the passenger door, and said, "See you in the morning."

Ben sat a moment, watching as she fumbled with her keys. Once she was safely inside, he slowly drove away in the cool night air of Rome lost in his thoughts.

Chapter 11

Southern Somalia, April 2011, nine months after the attack

Food security experts from Food for Livelihood had been monitoring the prolonged drought in the Horn of Africa, the worst in twenty years, affecting Somalia, Kenya, Uganda, Ethiopia, Eritrea, and Djibouti. Teams analyzed rainfall patterns, food consumption, and the prices in local markets. After two planting seasons without rain—the *Deyr* in October and the *Gu* in April—the maize and sorghum crops had failed, and livestock had died. Signs of distress were everywhere—low prices for livestock, household items sold off by starving farmers. The UN declared a famine. Those affected had two choices: migrate or die.

As dawn broke in the village, pale colors rose above the horizon. The savanna was scorched brown. In these unforgiving temperatures, the only signs of life were a few skeletal goats scavenging for sustenance. With nothing to trade and nothing to eat, most of the inhabitants had taken their few belongings and migrated south to the Dadaab refugee camp in Kenya.

Suhila was negotiating the sale of her remaining animals with the village elder. She had already sold her cooking pots, clothes, and jewelry—anything of worth—to pay for her passage to Kenya.

Hakim emerged from his hut clutching Somali shillings and crumpled dollars, which he placed gently into her thin hands—all he could offer in exchange for the four scrawny cows and goats lying listlessly in the shade of the hut. She sifted through the bills and looked up at him, her blue eyes pleading.

"My daughter, this is what I can give you," he said.

"May Allah bless you for your kindness, Uncle."

"Allah will guide you on your journey. That is Allah's purpose," said Hakim.

He stepped into his hut again and emerged with a few handfuls of lentils. "I offer these to keep you well. May you and your children have a safe journey, Inshallah."

As she put the food into her sack, careful not to drop even one precious lentil, a voice called out, "Sister, hurry now. We are ready to go!"

"Go, my sweet child," Hakim whispered with tears in his eyes.

She bowed her head in respect, and with her daughter strapped to her back, grasped her son Geedi's small hand, and hurried away to board the truck.

The flatbed Mercedes had traveled so many miles in the heat that patches of rust melded with the brown exterior of the body. Nevertheless, Assad, a transporter from Mogadishu who now carried people fleeing famine in addition to food and merchandise, took pride in his vehicle, handed down to him by his father, the family name painted boldly on its doors. Suhila ran toward him. "We must go now if we are to sleep at the border," he said.

While Assad found space for Suhila and her children on the floor of the truck, the other passengers were tying small sacks of food and jugs of water onto the side racks. Two dozen people from nearby villages, their faces hollow from deprivation, their eyes shadowed by darkness, crowded onto the flatbed.

Assad shut the doors, hoisted himself into the cabin, and started up the truck in a puff of black smoke. He had decided to use a less traveled route, but the treacherous and bumpy conditions soon took their toll on his passengers. Many suffered from nausea, vomiting thin bile from empty stomachs. Assad would stop for no one. They had no choice but to remain aboard.

The truck passed groups of men, women, and children trudging slowly on foot, carrying their possessions in small bundles. Scattered along these roads of death were the bones of animal carcasses, bleached white by the sun, and small mounds of dirt marking shallow graves where the smallest children had been buried—children too heavy to be carried and too weak to walk the distance. A woman wailed as she knelt before the body of a child, his limbs splayed at odd angles like a baby bird fallen from a tree.

A couple of hours later in their journey, the left rear wheel got stuck in a deep rut of loose dirt, and the truck lurched to a stop, slamming the passengers against the back of the cabin. Assad got out and ordered twelve of the youngest men to help him hunt for rocks, branches, and anything else they could find to create enough traction to pry the wheel out. When they had finished packing the materials around it, Assad ordered them to assemble behind the truck. "Push hard if you wish to reach Kenya. Together now, one…two…three!" The wheels spun furiously, flinging dust into their faces and causing the rubber tires to emit a foul cloud. Still, the old Mercedes refused to budge. Assad jumped down from his seat, shaking his head in frustration and commanded, "We need more help! Bring the women!"

They waited for the strongest of the women to timidly approach and, once again, were ordered to push, "One…two…three!" The truck rocked back and forth, its tires straining as the wheel slowly inched its way onto firmer ground. Assad yelled over the cheering and clapping, "*Alhamdulillah!* Now, let's be on our way."

Barely twenty minutes later, a young woman, swollen from the last weeks of pregnancy, began to whimper in pain. Suhila and two of the other female passengers knelt around her, wiping the perspiration from her face and offering sips of water. In desperation, Suhila turned to the oldest among them. "Please, I beg of you, we must stop or she will die!"

Two of the men began pounding on the roof of the cabin while the others leaned over the side of the truck, waving their arms and shouting in the hope that Assad would see them from the side mirror. "Brother, stop the truck! Our sister is giving birth."

Assad slowed down and found a suitable place to stop beside a patch of withered bushes. The woman was carried from the flatbed and set gently on the parched ground.

Thirty minutes later, her screams subsided, and a small mewing was heard. The newborn was thin and underweight, with curly black hair, chestnut eyes, its little fists clenched as though ready to fight. The baby fretted and searched hungrily for her mother's shriveled breast. "The mother?" Assad asked Suhila as she emerged from behind the bushes.

"They are both weak," she said, shaking her head.

"Let us rest here," he announced. "We will begin again at daybreak."

A dozen men began grumbling among themselves.

"Assad, you said we must cross into Kenya by tomorrow morning," one of them reminded him.

"If we travel by night, it is cool and safe," chimed in another man.

"No," said Assad. "This is my decision. Some of my passengers are too weak to travel. I do not want their deaths on my conscience. Have we not seen enough death today?"

"But we all risk death if we stay," they protested. Assad reached into his toolbox under the seat and pulled out a gun to remind them of his authority.

Night had fallen but a full moon illuminated the clearing around the truck. The men sat around the fire while the women prepared what each had to give in the tradition of Somali generosity. After a meager offering of bread and tea, they found places to lay down for the night and were soon consumed by an exhausted sleep.

At the break of day, Assad beeped his horn to awaken his sore and tired passengers. They rubbed the sleep from their eyes and began their prayers. The truck was loaded and ready to go when Assad heard one of the children crying, "Stop! I cannot wake *Awoowe*."

He stopped revving the engine and followed the boy to the spot where his grandfather had been sleeping, gently pulled back the threadbare *macawis* that covered his head and saw that the man's emaciated body was all that remained of him. He had not survived the night. They'd have to perform the funeral rituals. The old man's limbs were straightened, and his eyes were closed. There was no water to bathe his body, but a grave was dug and covered with dry earth and scrawny branches of umbrella thorn. Assad corralled his weary passengers back into the truck. "Soon we will reach the border. *Inshallah.*"

By midmorning, they reached the crest of a hill overlooking the border with Kenya. From the truck's cabin, Assad saw tens of thousands of Somalis milling around, guarded by a line of heavily armed Kenyan soldiers. In the excitement, his passengers stood up to look toward their new home, but their hopes soon faded to despair.

As far as the eye could see, the parched land was carpeted with starving men, women, and children, many of them sitting listlessly or lying where they had fallen. "Sit down—everyone! We go on!" Assad yelled as he shifted gears and drove carefully down the final stretch to the outer fringe of the crowds.

Assad stopped the truck and picked his way through the throngs of people clinging to life. When they spotted him, many began to moan, their hands outstretched. He inhaled the stench of misery and death, fighting back tears, mumbling words of encouragement, "*Inshallah,* may you be at peace. May Allah have mercy on you, brother." When he could go no further, he tugged at the long white robe of one of the men and shouted above the din, "What is happening?"

"The Kenyans have closed the border, brother. No one can pass."

"For how long?"

"Only Allah knows."

Assad turned and slowly walked back to his truck, his shoulders slumped in defeat. His passengers were on their knees, praying toward Mecca.

Chapter 12

Rome, Colle Oppio

Ben stared at the bedroom ceiling, listening to the pendulum clock in the living room chiming one, two, three in the morning. He sat up in bed, slipped into his flip-flops, and shuffled to the kitchen to prepare a cup of herbal tea, then he took it to the swing on his terrace where he had spent so many hours with Serena, rocking, snuggling, and planning their life together.

The full moon descended toward the horizon, its soft light reflected on the white marble of the Coliseum, the Roman Forum, and Constantine's Arch. His hilltop apartment in Rome's Colle Oppio zone was a jewel with a panoramic view that spanned three millennia.

He lit a cigarette and took a deep puff, feeling his body begin to relax. He had just turned thirty-five, a tipping point. He should have become the man he was meant to be by now. It was time to put the past behind him—to be free of it—but memories of the massacre in Somalia buried him. He felt frozen in time like the ancient marble ruins below him.

Unable to accept the stability a family might have brought to his marriage, he had been a part-time husband, not a partner Serena could rely on. So, there had been no children. An emergency anywhere in the world meant he could be called away at a moment's notice to put his own life on the line to save others. Now they were stuck in limbo, separated, immobilized by a decision he was incapable of making. Since Somalia, even the smallest decision was a trial. He had trouble ordering lunch. Reordering his life felt impossible.

He was still committed to a job that demanded all his time, his energy, his passion. Food for Livelihood's programs were changing the lives of the people who had no other resources. It gave him moral purpose, the conviction that his life meant something, that he was, in some small way, making the world a better place. Serena knew this, but she also knew that she needed a husband who was fully present, and Ben had been little more than a sometime lover.

His thoughts turned to Melissa. Was there really something there? She was, of course, attractive, capable, and they'd made an obvious connection. She had seen and suffered the ravages of war. She seemed to understand the part of him Serena could barely imagine. But he was technically her supervisor and hesitant to wade into murky waters. Too much was at stake.

Ben put out his cigarette, drained the remaining tea from his mug, and curled up on the cushioned swing, rocking himself to sleep.

The morning sun teased his eyes open. Then he heard his phone ring.

Across Rome, in the Monteverde Vecchio zone atop the Janiculum Hill, Samuel Adjei had been sipping his third tea laced with milk. He was bent over his laptop at the kitchen table, while his Kenyan wife, Esther, her long black curls tied up in a kerchief, was at the stove, stirring *uji*, her favorite porridge. CNN hummed along from the TV on the shelf. She stopped with her spoon in midair and stared at the screen. "The harvest in the Horn of Africa has failed. Starvation of epic proportions seems unavoidable." The commentator predicted that upwards of one billion dollars in humanitarian aid was needed.

She glanced at her husband, whose computer was buzzing with a flood of email.

"Switch to the BBC, please," he said.

A "Breaking News" banner streamed across the screen as a blond woman with a chic haircut announced, "Kenyan authorities have closed the border with Somalia to halt an influx of refugees."

Sammy was on his feet. "What the bloody hell are they doing? They will all die!" After the attack on Ben's mission in Somalia, he'd had to pull Food for Livelihood out of the country. He couldn't in good conscience sacrifice more lives to YLF. Food for Livelihood had been one of the last agencies to retreat to the relative safety of the Dadaab Refugee Complex in Kenya, which had been accepting thousands of starving Somalis who poured across the border.

He took the remote from his wife's hand and raised the volume. "Our John McLeish is here for you with a live report from Dadaab. We should warn you that some images may be disturbing."

The young man in a reporter's vest looked grim. "Humanitarian agencies were taken by surprise at 0800 hours when Kenyan authorities announced the closure of the border with Somalia, which is preventing thousands of starving Somalis from entering the Dadaab refugee camp. The entire zone is being reinforced heavily by security patrols due to an increase in kidnappings, bombings, and attacks on aid convoys. Kenyan authorities are scouring the area for weapons and YLF terrorists whom they suspect are infiltrating the camp, which is home to more than 200,000 refugees from six neighboring countries. I spoke with the representative of the NGO Food for Livelihood, Sally Singer, who said that if a solution is not found immediately, hundreds of thousands of Somalis will perish as they did in 1992."

Sammy lowered the volume, his eyes still fixed on the screen, and grabbed his smartphone. "Natasha, sorry to bother you on a weekend, but can you meet me at the office? It's an emergency. And have Ben stand by. I may need him."

"You'd better go," Esther said as she closed his laptop and slipped it into his rolling case. "Can you do something for the Somalis? The famine is worse this time, but the world didn't listen to your pleas for aid. Now there's no hope for the Somalis trapped in YLF territory. That poor country has suffered too much."

Natasha was already at the office when Sammy arrived.

"Who should I call first?" she asked, putting a cup of tea on his desk. "The U.S. ambassador in Kenya?"

He nodded. "Right, and the ambassadors for Canada, Japan, the U.K., and the Netherlands. We'd better find someone to talk with in Brussels… probably Charles Baron—I saw him last week."

"And Ethiopia?"

"Right, Ethiopia as well. I don't care who I speak with first. Just put them through as soon as you reach them. Has Sally Singer phoned from Dadaab yet? Never mind. We'll wait for her call. Interrupt me as soon as she's on the line."

A moment later, Natasha put through Charles Baron of the European Commission.

"I presume you've been briefed on the closing of the Kenyan border with Somalia?" he asked Ambassador Baron.

"I have. How will Food for Livelihood respond?"

Sammy was prepared for the question. He'd had a contingency plan since the agency pulled out of Somalia. "It's too late to mount an effective response from the Kenya side. The only option now might be to conduct a series of air drops in the vicinity of the migration routes." He paused for a moment, anticipating Baron's objection. "It's true we cannot guarantee that our food would reach the right people, and we know that YLF is capable of shooting down humanitarian planes, but we have an excellent supply chain. Our logistics network of ships, planes, and trucks spans the globe. We are uniquely positioned to provide aid. Can we rely on support from the EC?"

Sammy was tense. He faced an almost unsolvable crisis. But he had unwavering faith in the dedication of his staff, and he'd always succeeded by applying his political acumen and strategic thinking over his long career with Food for Livelihood. He buzzed Natasha. "Get Ben up here," he told her. He needed Ben's opinion. There was no one he trusted more, and he couldn't take the chance of making even one wrong move.

As the calls continued to come in, he solicited support from the ambassadors and individually assured donors that Food for Livelihood intended to coordinate with the other NGOs and UN agencies on the ground. His last call was with the U.S. ambassador in Kenya.

"Dr. Adjei, I've already spoken with the President, who assures me that the United States will respond decisively to avert a humanitarian crisis that could destabilize the entire region," said the ambassador. "We plan to work through the international aid community and support you in any way we can."

"Thank you, Madame Ambassador. We're reviewing our contingency plans and security assessments as we consider all available options."

"Do those options include returning to southern Somalia?" asked the ambassador.

"We'd need firm security guarantees from all factions of YLF before we could consider that. The factions are splintered, taking different positions vis-à-vis relations with the international organizations," Sammy replied.

"What about using the African Union or United Nations Peacekeepers to deliver food in areas you can't access?"

"The African Union and the UN have even less leverage than we do. YLF considers them enemy combatants," answered Sammy.

Natasha stood at his doorway, gesturing frantically.

Sammy's attention shifted. "Please excuse me. I have an urgent incoming call. I will keep you updated as the situation evolves."

He looked up.

"I have Sally on line four."

"Sally? Hi, what's the latest?"

Her voice crackled under the static. "The situation in Dadaab is deteriorating fast."

"Do you have any idea how many people are stranded on the other side of the border?"

"We don't know for sure. We estimate it's in the tens of thousands…but the biggest problem is that two to three million people might be trapped in YLF-held territory. We need to find a way to reach them… Sammy…Sammy?"

"I'm here, Sally. We're working on it. Keep me posted."

He hunched over his desk, pinching the bridge of his nose with two fingers. It was a matter of access—a political problem, not an operational one. All the available options meant shooting blind. Everyone saw the political problem as intractable. He'd have to find a way to change the conversation, and he needed someone to guide him. Someone who knew Somalia and YLF up close—their beliefs, their mentalities, their modus operandi. He buzzed Natasha.

"I've just had an idea. Book me a ticket to Nairobi and get the Egyptian ambassador on the line. I need a guarantee of safe passage into Somalia. Call Sally back and ask her to charter a plane. And call Ben. I want a full briefing on what to expect from the moment I land in Mogadishu."

"You're really going to Somalia?" asked Natasha, wide-eyed.

"I need to talk face-to-face with the YLF. They have to be convinced to let us get food to their people trapped at the border. I can't do it over the phone, and I won't let thousands of people die of hunger on my watch."

Chapter 13

Ben was about to walk into the Food for Livelihood building when he saw Sammy make his way through the front doors rushing toward a waiting taxi. He heard Sammy call out to the driver, "Fiumicino, Terminal Three," and before he knew what was happening, Ben scooted into the cab beside him.

"What are you doing here?" Sammy asked. "I thought we agreed your debriefing would be your only involvement with this mission."

"You're right, we did. But last night instead of sleeping, I thought about it and realized that if you want to come out of there with an agreement and your life, you'll need me by your side. I've looked the YLF in the eye. I've seen how easy it is for them to kill. The day they murdered my friends, they murdered me too. I'm a dead man, Sammy; I've got nothing to fear."

"Go home, Ben. You're not ready for this."

"Maybe I'm not. I might never be ready, but FFL needs me. Besides, I already bought a ticket." Ben chuckled.

"You don't need to do this. It wasn't your fault. You don't have to atone for anything by putting yourself in harm's way again."

"Even if I don't, I'm coming with you. I can't stay behind on this one. Just accept it." More than anyone, Sammy understood the risks of saving lives in a dangerous world. Nearly a year had passed since YLF turned Ben's life upside down, his spirit buried under an avalanche of guilt and shame. But maybe for Ben to find his stride again, he would have to face what happened in Somalia to let it go.

Sammy sighed, partly relieved, partly by way of giving in. He tugged at his earlobe. "Very well, then. But if things get rough, I'll be counting on you."

"Always, brother."

———————————

They spent a day in Nairobi meeting with government officials, ambassadors, and humanitarian agencies then boarded a small, single-engine Beechcraft capable of landing on a makeshift runway. Ben knew Sammy was anxious, unsure of his impulsive decision to negotiate with the YLF in person. But he'd explored every avenue, called on the UN and other intermediaries to convince the Kenyan government to reopen the border, and received only vague promises while hundreds of thousands of innocent people were dying of hunger. On the positive side, he knew that the YLF had been weakened by the counterattacks from Kenya and by the famine itself. Most of the militants were southerners with family ties to those who were hardest hit by the drought. Their public image was suffering, which had undoubtedly spurred them to consider Sammy's overture.

Ben looked out the plane's window at the peacefulness of the clear blue sky. He was returning to Somalia, the place that had finally broken his marriage—and in most ways, had broken him. His time there was the reason Serena and he had become strangers. He was reminded of their starkly different lives. While he distributed ration cards to starving villagers, she sold expensive clothes to spoiled women. He'd been fulfilled saving lives. She'd been endlessly lonely. He was more of an agnostic. She was a devout Roman Catholic. Maybe their differences would be insurmountable; the thought made him deeply sad.

From the open cockpit, the pilot announced that they'd crossed into Somali territory. Ben clutched the armrests to stop his hands from trembling.

Sammy noticed. "How are we doing?"

Ben forced a smile. "We're doing fine." But his confidence was wavering.

The Beechcraft made a rough landing on a narrow dirt runway just outside Mogadishu, throwing them forward against their seat belts. Through the window, they could see a convoy of Jeeps waiting to escort them to the hangar. Despite the cabin's heat, Ben's hands were cold, and he clenched his teeth to keep them from chattering. He kept telling himself he could do this. "Welcome to the land of YLF!" he said, forcing a laugh.

The pilot had been instructed to turn the plane around and wait for them on the runway, ready for takeoff in case they needed to make a quick exit.

As they descended the folding staircase, two soldiers toting automatic weapons rushed forward to open the passenger doors of the first Jeep in the convoy, and two men emerged.

Ben forced himself to take long, deep breaths. A tall man with a thick dark beard extended his hand and greeted them in English, "Welcome. I'm Dr. Ibrahim Saladin, the minister of welfare. This is my colleague, Mr. Mohamed Zaligi, minister of agriculture. We represent the political arm of YLF."

Sammy shook the man's hand. "My name is Dr. Samuel Adjei, president of Food for Livelihood, and this is my adviser, Ben Tano. We thank you and your delegation for receiving us this morning."

Ben knew that beneath their polished demeanor and business suits, they were YLF gunmen who would kill them if they didn't get what they wanted. His life was in Sammy's hands, and he'd have to trust his diplomatic skills. But his colleagues had trusted him, and they'd been massacred. His heart began to pound.

"Gentlemen, before we proceed, I must ask you to turn over your phones and any weapons you are carrying." Dr. Saladin was polite, but this was not a good beginning. Ben and Sammy reluctantly surrendered their phones before following the men into the hangar under heavy guard.

Ben scanned the surroundings for danger. The hangar had been ravaged by war and weather. The aluminum walls were perforated with bullet holes, and the roof had been partly ripped off, possibly by a cyclone or windstorm. His chest tightened as he entered the building behind Sammy, and he pressed his sweaty palms against his sides. They were escorted to a meeting room and seated at the head of a U-shaped configuration of tables and benches. Sammy was beside the two ministers, with Ben to his right.

A YLF militant, his face swathed in a red-checked *keffiyeh*, was stationed directly behind them. He could easily have been the man who had pulled the trigger on the day of the massacre. Ben closed his eyes and bent his head, fighting to stay in control.

Tribal elders and young masked militants filled the remaining seats. Ben forced himself to glance from one face to another, afraid he might recognize one of the men who had attacked them that day.

Dr. Saladin stood up to open the meeting. "Dr. Adjei, you have asked for this meeting to discuss the current crisis, but first, we would like to state our position clearly. We know Food for Livelihood and the work you have done in southern Somalia. We did not permit you to remain in the areas under our control because you travel with military escorts and collaborate with our enemies."

Ben lowered his head to hide his expression. The mentality of YLF would never change. They invariably began with accusations. "We support the closing of the border with Kenya. We alone are responsible for the people of Somalia. They belong here, on their own lands."

Then Minister Zaligi took the floor. "YLF does not accept dependency on international aid. We support the development of this country through our law, Sharia law, using our own labor and resources. We oppose the policies of the transitional government, which has no authority to speak for the people of Somalia because it is propped up by the aid agencies and their clients, the Western governments."

Samuel had been confident that he could negotiate access issues with them, but Ben began to think otherwise. Perhaps they had been wrong to come to Somalia.

Zaligi had effectively blocked all avenues for negotiation. Dr. Saladin interjected quickly, "My colleague wishes to explain that we are a strong, proud, and resilient people, and we ask you to respect this. Now, you have traveled a long way, Dr. Adjei, will you tell the council your plans?"

Ever the diplomat, Sammy stood up, his face impassive. "I thank you, my brothers, for receiving us here today," he began. "The purpose of our trip is to find a solution to this crisis that will benefit the people of Somalia. The drought is the worst in living memory. The rains have not come, and your people are dying. We acknowledge, by our presence here today, that the response to the drought is the responsibility of all those who claim to represent the people of Somalia."

He looked around the room to gauge the audience. The council members were nodding their turbaned heads in agreement. "Ministers and honorable members of the council, I believe that before the problem can be resolved, the migration of your people into Kenya must be managed, as it aggravates the political tensions between your two countries. This can be accomplished by stabilizing the populations within their own regions with a package of assistance. I am ready to immediately divert our vessels, now on their way to West Africa, back to Dar es Salaam and Mombasa. Ben, would you kindly elaborate?"

They had rehearsed their lines in Nairobi. Ben rose from his chair, careful to avoid looking at anyone in particular. "Honorable Ministers, we propose that food items will be trucked into Somalia through Kenya and Tanzania, our biggest overland corridors. We have received special clearances from those heads of state to pass through their borders. At the same time, we would like to commence emergency airdrops of grains, beans, and nutrient-enriched products for the children. This will keep people alive until we can deliver enough commodities to provide them with a stable diet."

The men seated around the table leaned forward in their seats.

"We estimate that the situation can be stabilized within a matter of a few weeks," Sammy added. "Mr. Tano will remain in Nairobi to support the start-up phase of the operation and ensure that everything that has been agreed to at this meeting will be implemented."

The room erupted in murmurs, and the two ministers consulted the YLF adviser standing behind them. Then, Dr. Saladin rapped on the table and began to speak, "We do not recognize aid from Western governments or their proxies. This has been said. What would be our reasons to change this policy now?"

"My brothers," Sammy replied, searching their faces as he looked around the room, "we know your own families are suffering. We know you have accepted aid from the governments of Egypt, Syria, and Saudi Arabia when it served your purpose. We are not here on a political mission to debate policy. We are here on a humanitarian mission to save lives so your country will have a future. That future is in your hands now. What will your answer be?"

The ministers huddled at the head of the table while the council members continued to debate in loud voices. Ben and Sammy kept their faces expressionless, but their palms were sweating. Finally, Dr. Saladin rose slowly from his chair.

"We ask you to put these plans into immediate effect, subject to two conditions: First, there must be no markings on the food, trucks, or planes. The people must never know they are receiving aid from our enemies. And second, you must keep your people out of Somalia. We do not always control the actions of our combatants."

Ben leaned toward Sammy and whispered, "This will never fly. No one will be willing to give millions in aid without accountability or visibility."

"Not so fast," he whispered back then turned to Dr. Saladin. "I fully understand your position and acknowledge your concern for the well-being of my staff. However, I regret that I cannot accept your conditions. I respectfully remind the council that our organization is not driven by politics, religion, or private interests. My staff must be present to ensure that the food reaches the people for whom it is intended. The mothers need to be taught how to feed these products to their children."

Ben detected a shift in the room. The men seemed agitated, alert to the change of dynamics, and began talking loudly among themselves. "Forgive me, Dr. Adjei," Mr. Zaligi replied coldly, "but is not the food you are about to deliver a gift to the people of Somalia? Your aid is a poor gift if you insist on invading the country to deliver it."

The men pounded the tables, clapped, and stomped their feet in agreement.

Sammy smiled and held out his hands, inviting them to listen. "Yes, of course it is a gift to the people of Somalia, but we are accountable to our governing body. Food for Livelihood must monitor the food. It must be labeled with the Food for Livelihood logo as humanitarian food aid from the point of departure to the mouths of the beneficiaries. In order to do this, we will need your guarantees for the security of our staff."

Ben elbowed Sammy and whispered into his ear, "Go slowly. You need to give them time to process, and please, don't be so confrontational."

But he pressed his advantage. "Regrettably, without your agreement to these two conditions, my colleague and I will be obliged to end this meeting and return to Nairobi. And I must caution you that if I leave here today empty-handed, the international community may take matters into its own hands, authorizing Kenyan troops to cross your borders in order to open up humanitarian corridors."

Ben was horrified. Sammy had threatened YLF. The young militants erupted, shouting and vehemently shaking their heads. He heard the terrifying clicks of soldiers releasing the safety catches on their weapons.

The YLF adviser held up his hand to calm them as he leaned over to whisper to the minister of agriculture, who stood up and said, "Dr. Adjei, the threats of infidels do not sway our resolve. We fear no one. We place our faith in Allah… Allah will bring us victory."

The elders were on their feet, stomping the floor and shaking their fists. Ben found himself trapped in yet another nightmare, surrounded by enraged YLF militants. "Sammy," he whispered, "you went too far! You can't talk to them like that."

Ben concentrated on his breathing to slow it down so he could focus on saving the negotiations—and getting out of there alive. He stood up. "Ministers and honorable members of the council…" He had to shout to be heard. "I believe you misunderstood Dr. Adjei's intent." He looked to the ministers who raised their hands to quiet the room.

"We are here as nonpolitical actors. We believe our proposition is the right one and that our goals are the same as yours. We have a unique opportunity to work together, without outside interference, to alleviate the suffering of your people. The only obstacles separating us from achieving this goal are these simple conditions. Our trucks and our food will carry the Food for Livelihood logo, but YLF soldiers will be with us. The people will see that YLF is helping to bring them food, that YLF is saving their lives. Your soldiers will maintain our security and protect our staff. For the sake of your dying women and children, I implore you to accept these conditions. In return, we promise that our planes will be loaded, fueled, and ready to deliver lifesaving food within hours."

Again, the ministers consulted with the YLF adviser and the room was filled with chatter. After a few moments, the minister of welfare rose from his seat and waved his hand to bring the meeting back to order.

"Dr. Adjei, Mr. Tano, we will consult privately with our membership. The guard will escort you to my office."

Chapter 14

Locked in the minister's office alone with Sammy, Ben lost it. "What the hell are you doing? They shot my field officer in the head when he begged them to return his heart medication."

Sammy shrugged his shoulders. "It's a game of brinkmanship. Maybe our good cop, bad cop routine will succeed. You were brilliant in there. That's the Ben Tano I remember. I promised the capitals of the world I'd come back with a deal, and if we succeed, we'll not only be saving lives but we'll also be demonstrating how food can be an instrument of peace. That's our job and worth putting all our chips on the table."

Ben laughed bitterly at his logic. It had once been his own mantra. All or nothing. Put your life on the line. His colleagues had followed him to their deaths. Now he was following Sammy. It was only fitting. "Yes, it's our job, but you weren't listening to me. 'All or nothing' doesn't mean coming home in a body bag. That's not a healthy career objective."

Sammy sat behind the minister's desk, swiveling in the chair. "You always thought saving people's lives was a mission worth dying for."

"Fine, but with your methods, we'll both wind up dead, and our mission will fail anyway. That's the difference," Ben huffed.

Minutes later, they were back at the table, still sore from their blowup.

"Dr. Adjei and Mr. Tano, we have reached our decision. We, alone, are responsible for the lives of the Somali people, and it is our duty to put this consideration first. Your conditions are granted. All of us present today will guarantee safe passage to Food for Livelihood staff and vehicles, and we are ready to participate in all phases of the operation. We trust you will adhere to your promises and protect our common interests."

Sammy stood to address the room. "Brothers, you have my word. I will uphold Food for Livelihood's end of the agreement."

"Then, please proceed. As you say in the West, 'you have the green light.'"

Sammy shook the ministers' hands then worked his way around the table. At first, Ben was too relieved to grasp what had happened, but after a moment, he stood up and followed him, shaking hands until he came face-to-face with the YLF adviser. When he reached for his hand, Ben realized that the man was missing two fingers. This was the leader whose young militants had botched a kidnapping attempt, slaughtered Ben's colleagues, shot him in the back, and left him for dead.

He tightened his three-fingered grip on Ben's sweaty hand, leaned in, and said in a low voice, "If your men died, it was Allah's will. Their blood is not on my hands...or yours. Allah has spared your life for a higher purpose. Go in peace, Ben Tano."

Ben's mouth was dry, his lips glued to his teeth, but he found his voice. "I haven't known peace in nearly a year. But it is still my purpose to bring food to your people."

An hour later, a jubilant Sammy and Ben were escorted back to their chartered plane for the return flight to Nairobi.

Ben boarded the plane and settled into his seat. He could not get the face of the YLF leader out of his head, the man whose lieutenant had taken the lives of his colleagues and nearly killed him. He still felt the man's three-fingered grasp. He would have done anything to avoid this man who haunted his nightmares, but having confronted him, he felt lighter. They had crossed paths in a war zone, where hunger was politicized as a weapon of war and those who delivered food became collateral damage. The leader had spared him, but his lieutenant had not. And yet he had not died. He had lived, and he could continue feeding the hungry. But he had a choice now. He could try to make peace with a new image of the YLF leader in his mind. He would never forget, but maybe he could forgive himself. Maybe now he'd be able to renew his sense of purpose without carrying guilt or shame.

Within days, the international press had the story. Samuel Adjei and Food for Livelihood were recognized for spearheading a mission that would save millions of Africans from starvation, and contributions poured in to support that effort.

Ben stayed in Nairobi for a week to organize the operation then took an overnight Kenya Airways flight back to Rome. As he left the arrivals terminal to find a taxi, he heard a familiar voice shouting his name and saw Serena rushing to his side.

"Hey!" he said. "What are you doing here? How did you know I was on that flight? You've been calling Dalia, haven't you?"

"Oh, Ben." She wrapped her arms around him. "I've been worried, and I had to see you. How could you go back there?"

He was amazed at how glad he was to see her too, at the way all the stress left his body when she held him. "Let's go someplace where we can talk," he said.

She had parked her Fiat 500 at one of the meters near the terminal. "Where to?" she asked.

"How about home?" he said, without really knowing what "home" meant for them.

When they got to the apartment, he dropped his bag and threw open the terrace doors. He didn't know what to do next. He felt awkward, trying to act like a host in the home they'd shared for years. "Would you like a coffee?"

"No, thanks."

"So…let's sit."

The terrace swing was so heavy with memories it barely moved when they sat down.

"Serena…" He wasn't sure what he wanted to tell her, but he had to say something. "We've been through a lot together. You were there for me when I couldn't even get out of bed. You've been a wonderful wife, and I've been a lousy husband. Don't you think you deserve more happiness than I've been able to give you?" *What was he saying? Was he sending her away? Ending the marriage?* He had no idea if that's what he wanted, but it seemed fair. If he loved her, he couldn't burden her with his problems, his absences. He couldn't keep her in limbo, waiting for him to show up.

For a while, neither of them spoke. He felt as though his limbs were breaking apart, but he was doing the right thing. He bent his head to see her face. She was crying silently and trying to hide it. He tried to say something that would make it better.

"When we separated, I think we both knew in our hearts that our marriage was over. Somalia broke me, and it broke us." He was devastated by the failure of a marriage that had begun with such love and commitment, not realizing that his humanitarian career, the source of his fulfillment, was pulling him away from the woman he loved. He believed that setting her free was the best thing he could do. "Going back there helped me see how stuck we were, how far apart. I love you so much, Serena. You're beautiful, kind, and generous. But I'm also married to a cause. I can't leave Food for Livelihood…I can't. It's who I am. I need it now more than ever."

She was sobbing now. "I know. I know."

He put his arms around her and held her until she calmed. He had unburdened the guilt and shame of surviving the massacre, only to replace it with the guilt of hurting this woman who had given him so much.

She looked up at him. "I love you so much, Ben, but there is no space for me in your life. I suffered every time you went away, never knowing if you would come back. When I saw you in that Nairobi hospital, unconscious and covered in bandages…so close to death, it was…"

"I'm so sorry that I caused you so much suffering," he whispered, kissing her hair. "That's not what I wanted for us." No matter how much they loved each other, they had come to realize that they couldn't be together if they were each to honor what was best for themselves.

They held each other, rocking slowly. Now that he'd finally found the courage to let her go, he felt more connected to her than he had in years.

"I'll come by later," she said and stood up, wiping the last of her tears from her face. "I left a few things in the closets."

"Take your time, *cara*. There's no hurry."

Ben didn't move. He continued to rock back and forth, the sound of the door closing behind her like the last note in a concert that had gone on too long.

Chapter 15

Puglia, Italy

The farm near Taranto had begun to decline. Since the unwelcome visit of Neri and Bosco, the general and his wife had lost all interest in tilling their arid fields, and the garden was wild with undergrowth. The general didn't dare leave the property, but Lidija couldn't bear sitting indoors another day and needed to go into the village. "We agreed to stay out of sight," he scolded her. "We don't know who is watching us."

"Rasko, please, look at us. We're nothing but starving skeletons. Since those bastards showed up, we've become prisoners. In the village, they will think we have died."

She wrapped a well-worn silk scarf around her neck and stomped out the door to the barn to fetch her rusted old scooter. She puttered down the wet driveway to the main road, avoiding potholes along the way. When she began to accelerate around a curve, she saw a black Audi SUV coming toward her from the opposite direction, veering into her lane. She frantically pressed on her horn, but the SUV forced her onto the gravel shoulder, and she skidded left and right until she tumbled into a thicket of bramble bushes that covered a drainage canal.

"Tut...the *signora* should know better." Neri laughed as he lowered the window. "These country roads can be very dangerous. Don't you think so, Bosco?"

"*Si, molto.* Very dangerous." They quickly drove on toward the farmhouse.

"Why didn't you run her over? It would be one less headache for us." Bosco, in the driver's seat, watched in the rearview mirror as Lidija struggled to push the scooter back up the embankment, her dress torn and spattered with mud.

"You lunatics!" she shouted, waving her fist at them.

"*Guarda*, Neri," Bosco laughed, adjusting the rearview mirror, "that will keep her busy for a while."

The general was outside repairing the shutters when he heard the familiar sound of a vehicle pulling into the driveway. He hadn't been expecting Neri and Bosco to return so soon, but he was ready for them. He dropped his tools, checked the pistol in his holster, and took cover behind a corner of the house. He watched the SUV round the bend and circle the driveway to park.

Neri stepped out. "General, we need to talk," he called out. He waited a moment and furrowed his eyebrows. "General…we know you're here."

The general stepped out from behind the house and walked slowly toward them, his hand covering the handle of his pistol.

"Cover me," Neri whispered to Bosco. "He's armed."

Neri cautiously approached the general with Bosco close behind him until they stood face-to-face in the middle of the driveway.

"What do you want?" the general asked.

"The first phase of the operation is on track, General. We're ready to start the second phase, which will be considerably more complex."

"The second phase?" The general's eyes narrowed.

"Yes, but first let me congratulate you… Your children are very resourceful," Neri said with a smirk.

"*Si, molto intraprendente.*" Bosco waved his hand under his chin and laughed. "Your daughter is spearing our 'phish'…and soon our 'phish' will be spearing your daughter."

The arteries running down the side of the general's neck began to throb as he whipped out his pistol and pointed it at Bosco. "I'll kill you if you don't shut your mouth right now."

Neri held up his hand. "Now, now, my good general, ignore him and put your gun away," Neri said. He kept his eyes on the pistol as he shouted at Bosco, "*Tu cretino!* Keep your mouth shut."

The general lowered his gun, but his finger stayed on the trigger. He hadn't survived the war by being a slow shot.

"Now, let's get down to business. We can talk over there." Neri switched to a genial tone of voice and gestured toward the SUV.

Bosco followed, carrying the briefcase. He placed it on the hood of the vehicle and popped it open.

"How much longer before this is over?" the general asked.

"In two months…maybe less…depending on when we get the money."

"Continue." The general unconsciously flicked his head so his hair covered his birthmark.

Neri reached into the briefcase and extracted an envelope labeled with a file number and the name "Trasjic" then opened it and selected four large black-and-white photos, which he placed face up on the hood of the SUV. "Do you know these men?" he asked.

The general carefully examined each one. "I know two of them. We worked together during the war. I thought they were dead."

"These are the suppliers we want to do business with."

"What business?" the general snapped.

"As I was saying," Neri continued, "your two friends will be waiting for you in Belgrade. You will assist us to deliver a few large packages, shall we say. Consider it a family reunion."

"Belgrade? Why Belgrade? If I go back there, I'll be arrested!"

"*Un po' di fiducia*, General, have a little faith. Everything will be explained once you get there. We've taken every precaution to ensure your safe passage."

The general tightened his grip on his pistol, and Bosco reached for his gun. "All you have told me so far is that you need my help to get twenty million dollars. You never mentioned going to Belgrade."

"*Senti,* General, if you value your freedom, you will go to Belgrade. We need you to do this. Put your hands on the hood where I can see them. I want to show you something."

Neri opened the file again and took out a British passport and three thousand British pounds. The general opened the passport to find his picture with a new identity: Mr. Reginald Richards, born in Sussex, United Kingdom, 5 December 1944.

"British?"

"We couldn't find a Bosnian passport." Bosco laughed. "Or would you prefer a Serbian one?"

"Go to hell!" The general's hand slid back to his pistol.

"*Basta!*" Neri glared at Bosco. "I told you to shut up."

"When do I leave, and what are the travel arrangements?" asked the general.

"Wait for our instructions. We will be in touch with your son and then you."

Bosco packed up the file before getting back into the car.

"And where do we deliver these 'packages'?"

"Somewhere warm, so pack your suntan lotion," Neri said with a smirk.

"Where is warm?"

"All in good time, General." Neri waved as he climbed into the passenger seat. "No false moves. We wouldn't want anything to happen to your beautiful daughter."

Chapter 16

Dadaab refugee camp, Kenya-Somalia border, May 2011

An old General Motors truck branded with the "Christian Grace" logo on both sides raced across the maze of crisscrossing paths the convoys had left in the dirt.

"There it is." Sister Chiara pointed. An Italian, recently ordained by the Missionaries of Charity, she was the oldest of the three and an experienced veteran in service to refugees. Her two American volunteers had difficulty distinguishing the small schoolhouse amid thousands of tents housing displaced Somalis, punctuated by the brightly colored flags of a multitude of UN agencies and international NGOs.

The young man behind the wheel was an all-star college football player with a rugged, handsome face and curly brown hair. "Jeez, look at the size of this place," Bradley said. "It's freakin' enormous."

Sister Chiara never failed to be moved by the magnitude of the refugee camp. "Yes," she said. "The fact that so many people made it here is a miracle."

He pulled the truck to a stop in front of a cement brick building in a small, open compound where the cheerful voices of children filled the air. He blew the horn in greeting, and the children abandoned the maize meal and beans lunch they'd been eating to get a closer look at the visitors. They were fascinated by people with white skin and the long flowing white tunic with blue stripes covering Sister Chiara from head to toe.

A petite young woman wearing the traditional *guntiino* wrapped around her shoulders and head came out to greet them.

"Welcome to our school," she said in accented English as she shook their hands. "I'm the school's headmistress. My name is Noor, which means 'light.' What are your names?"

"My name is Sister Chiara. This is Jill, and he's Bradley. We brought you supplies."

"*Mahadsanid.* Thank you. What did you bring us today?"

"We have maize meal, pigeon peas, cooking oil, salt, and high-energy biscuits, and we managed to get chalkboards and colored chalk for the classroom."

The children crowded around Jill, staring at her blue eyes, pale skin, and long blond hair.

Noor clapped her hands. "The children will be so happy…"

"How many children are in school here?" Bradley asked.

"We have nearly fifty students today. The numbers change as people move in and out, but no matter how many turn up, they are always welcome here. Please follow me."

Inside the school, four wooden crates topped with boards served as a teacher's desk. The floors consisted of packed dirt and the walls were plastered with mud.

Noor said, "I suppose it doesn't look like much compared to your American schools. We have only what you see in front of you." A teacher, who had been sitting on a plastic chair, rose to greet them. "This is our head teacher, Asab. *Saaxiibadeena Mareykanka ayaa sahay noo keenay.* Our American friends have brought supplies for us."

The teacher smiled and bowed her head.

"We are teaching basic reading, writing, arithmetic, and study of the Koran," Noor said, nodding toward the wall that was being used as a black-board. We have had to explain to the parents the importance of sending girls to school, and we are proud to have as many girls as we have boys. Many are illiterate, but they learn that girls bring better health and wealth to their homes. The children are given a hot meal every day, which is an incentive for parents to keep them here. We have no desks or writing materials, so the students copy their lessons in the dirt using a small stick or their fingers. Your gift of slates and chalk will mean so much."

"Where would you like us to put them?" Sister Chiara asked.

"We will move them to the storeroom behind this building to keep them safe," Noor said. "Now, Kahalia will show you where we cook and offer you some tea." She pointed to one of the older girls.

As they turned to follow Kahalia to the kitchen, Jill stopped and held up a hand. "Do you hear that?"

"Hear what?" Bradley asked.

"It sounds like…horses."

"There aren't many horses out here."

"Brad, I'm from Oklahoma. I learned to ride before I could walk."

Kahalia turned and ran, frantically waving her arms and shouting, "YLF! YLF!"

From the nearby tents, they heard hundreds of displaced Somalis shouting in terror, racing to gather their children and belongings.

Noor trained her eyes to the spot where Kahalia was pointing. A cloud formed by dozens of hoofs kicking up the dry ground was moving in their direction.

"Asab," Noor ordered, "*caruurta gudaha ku hay.* Keep the children inside. Make sure they stay quiet."

"What's going on? Why is everyone leaving?" Bradley asked.

"It's the YLF," Noor said. "They cross the border on horseback to avoid the checkpoints. I need to hide you…follow me quickly! Give me the keys to your truck. I will find someone to move it."

As the galloping grew louder, Noor shepherded the three aid workers into the cement block enclosure that served as a storeroom and motioned them to hide behind the stacks of maize meal. They sat on the ground, huddled together as Noor covered them with a plastic tarp. "Stay here and don't make a sound until I come and get you," she whispered. She locked the door and returned the key to Kahalia.

"Kahalia, make sure they do not go into the storeroom. They must not find the foreigners, or they will be killed...*ma fahantay*?"

The girl nodded gravely.

Behind the school, a man was staring in the direction of the dust cloud, leaning on the rake he'd been using to clear the playground. Noor threw him the keys. "*Qari gaariga xamuulka ah!* Hide the truck! Quickly!"

When the attackers arrived, she was standing alone in front of the school, bent in a submissive posture. Seven horsemen, their heads wrapped in red-and-white *keffiyehs*, carried guns, swords, and automatic rifles. The leader rode forward. "*Allahu Akbar.* Where are the foreigners? We know they are here. Bring them to us now, and we will spare your lives."

Noor kept her head down. "*Halkan ma joogaan,*" she said. "They ran away when they heard the horses approaching. They fear you."

"And the truck...where is it?"

"It is gone."

He dismounted and stormed toward the schoolhouse. Noor rushed past him and blocked the entrance, pleading with him. He lost his temper, hit her sharply on the head with the butt of his rifle, then swung the barrel to the side to knock her down.

Asab was cowering in a corner with the children, the youngest ones cradled in her arms. When she saw the man step over Noor's crumpled body, she began to wail.

"I want the foreigners," he shouted. "Take me to them now or we will burn the school!"

"*Fadlan,*" Noor whispered, struggling to push herself up on her elbows. "Please believe me. They escaped."

"You tell too many lies," he said and then ordered his men to dismount and search for the foreigners.

"Please don't hurt the children. Please, I beg of you," Noor cried. She struggled to sit up, but a black boot came to rest in front of her face.

"*Halkan ayaad joogtaa!* You stay here!" The children were screaming in terror. "*Aamus!* Silence!" he shouted, waving his gun around the room.

He stood guard and shouted to two of his men who were looking around, finding nothing. "You! Go behind the school. There are other buildings."

Kahalia was standing with her back against the wall of the storage shed, nervously twisting the tip of her headscarf.

"What's in here?"

"Food and s-su-upplies," she whispered.

"If you are lying, we will kill you. Open it."

"Noor keeps the key."

They kicked the door furiously and smashed the butts of their rifles against the hinges until it fell to the ground. Inside the dark room, one of the men flicked on a lighter and trod quietly, swatting cobwebs from his face, then fired at the stacks of maize meal bags, engulfing the room in dust.

A muffled sneeze.

One of them trained his rifle at the tarp, while the other ripped it away, uncovering the three terrified aid workers, their hands held over their heads in surrender.

"Don't shoot," Bradley said, his voice shaking. "*As-salamu alaykum.* We come in peace."

One hauled him to his feet while the other took charge of the two women. Jill was clinging to Sister Chiara in fear. The militant laughed and grunted as he stroked Jill's blond hair then grabbed the sobbing girl by the arm and marched her out of the storeroom, followed by Sister Chiara and Bradley with a gun pointed at the middle of his back. Outside, they looked for Kahalia. She should be executed for having lied to them, but she wasn't worth pursuing.

They brought their hostages to the front of the schoolhouse and checked their pockets and bags, removing phones, ID cards, passports, wallets, and notebooks.

"In the name of God, be merciful. We are here on a mission of service," Sister Chiara pleaded as the men pushed them to the ground.

"Sister, Sister, are you alright?" Bradley shouted, but he was silenced by a fierce kick to his ribs.

Noor stretched out her arms from the doorway of the school where she lay and pleaded, *"Fadlan, ha yeelin iyaga. Waa caruur." Please, don't hurt them.*

The leader cocked his rifle and pointed it at Bradley's head. "Silence, woman, or I will kill them all!

"Give me their documents." When he saw the two blue passports and an Italian ID card, his eyes lit up. "This time we will get what we want. Load them on the horses."

Noor continued to beg for their lives until he walked over and dealt her another blow with the butt of his pistol. "You tell too many lies," he repeated.

The hostages averted their eyes from Noor's inert body as they were dragged to the horses where they were blindfolded, trussed up, and slung unceremoniously across the withers.

The YLF quickly mounted and rode off with their booty, disappearing into the void.

Chapter 17

State Department, Washington. D.C., early morning

Secretary of State Edwin Howard sat behind his curved wooden desk gazing over the heads of the four advisers seated opposite him and out at the rolling green lawns that surrounded his office. He was being briefed on his upcoming trip to the Middle East, but he preferred contemplating the lush scenery to discussing the complex problems he was facing.

His chief of staff entered from one of the service doors. "Jim, we're still in a meeting…"

Jim leaned over and whispered, "I'm sorry to interrupt, but we have a situation."

"Excuse me a moment," Howard said and followed Jim to the far end of the room.

"What is it?"

"Two young Americans and an Italian nun were taken hostage six hours ago."

"Where?"

"Kenya, at the refugee camp on the Somali border."

"Do we know by whom?"

"YLF."

"Son of a bitch."

Howard turned to his advisers. "I'm sorry, but we have to interrupt our session. Jim will be in touch with you to reschedule."

Once they were alone, he asked, "What else do we know?"

"The Italian Sister and the Americans are volunteers working for the Catholic NGO, Christian Grace, last seen at a school in Dadaab. The CIA and the AISE, the Italian external intelligence and security agency, are in communication and confirm they were kidnapped by the YLF in Kenya and most likely were taken across the border to Somalia. They have an idea where they are being held, but they haven't been able to pinpoint the exact location yet."

"Have there been any demands?"

"We all received a video a few minutes ago. It's loaded in the system."

"Do we know if they are still alive?"

"Alive and well, sir, for now."

"Show me the video."

Jim pointed the remote control at a screen mounted on the wall. The three volunteers appeared seated cross-legged on the ground, their hands pressed behind their heads, which were covered in black hoods. Standing behind them, three YLF militants, their faces hidden by *keffiyehs*, pointed Kalashnikovs at their heads. The black hoods were removed to reveal the terrified faces of the young Americans, a woman and a man. The Italian nun stared out at the camera with no expression at all.

The man was handed a piece of paper. "I have been asked to read this statement," he began, his hands shaking. "We, the Youth Liberation Front, are holding two Americans and one Italian citizen. In exchange for their freedom, we demand three million U.S. dollars to be delivered before sunrise tomorrow. If this demand is not met, the hostages will be executed."

The camera zoomed in on Jill, whose face was smudged with dirt and sweat. One of the fighters nudged her in the back with his rifle, prompting her to speak, "Please...they're going to kill..." The screen went blank.

"Jim, roll that again. And can we slow it down this time? Okay. Stop at the shot of the girl, to the left. Hold it!"

He stared at the frame. "Oh, no. It can't be."

"What is it, sir?"

Howard moved closer to the screen and pointed to the image. "That girl...with the long blond hair...isn't that Bill Winter's youngest daughter, Jill?"

Jim took out his smartphone and pulled up Bill Winter's file with photos of his family. He showed the images to Howard.

"How the hell did this happen? What were they thinking, letting his daughter go to Dadaab of all places? If the YLF finds out that they've got the daughter of a high-ranking State Department official, they'll have us by the balls. We sent out travel advisories warning Americans to stay out of there! How am I supposed to ensure the well-being of Americans when they're able to slip into the camps?"

Howard hated having to play God with American lives. He checked his watch: 9:30 a.m. "What's the time difference with Somalia?"

"It's about 4:30 p.m. there, sir."

"I'm guessing that gives us about thirteen hours. Not a word to anybody until we have a clear plan to bring these people home."

"Understood."

"Imagine if the press gets a whiff of this."

"What are you going to do, sir? We can't negotiate."

"That's always the problem. If we agreed to their demands, we'd set a precedent that would put every American abroad at risk. Every desperate son of a bitch out there would snatch our citizens in exchange for supplies from aisle four at the local Walmart."

Howard sat down at his desk and closed his eyes for a moment. When he opened them again, he was calm. "Okay, get my African team in here right away. Also, CIA and Homeland Security...Defense, in case we need the Seals. And I want to speak immediately with our ambassador in Kenya."

Jim was furiously taking notes.

"Jim, on second thought, put down your agenda," he said. "They don't likely know who Jill is yet. We need to do an end run around this thing before they figure it out and raise the stakes." He silently stared at the images of the three volunteers frozen on the screen as he rocked back and forth in the high-backed chair.

"Get Italy on the line."

Chapter 18

Food for Livelihood headquarters, Rome, late afternoon

Samuel paced the floor reviewing his speech for the unveiling of a memorial plaque in honor of the fallen Food for Livelihood heroes. He was tense. After the ceremony, he was scheduled to meet with the Italian foreign minister. Manenti's office had called with an urgent request, and they'd been vague about the purpose of the visit.

He took the elevator down to the auditorium where the audience was already seated. Natasha was waiting for him in the wings. "We're ready for you," she said. It was a solemn occasion. No applause greeted him as he strode across the stage to the podium. He looked out over the staff and dignitaries, pulled the microphone closer, and waited for the chatter to subside.

"Ladies and gentlemen, today we gather to honor our colleagues who have given their lives in the service of humanity. In a world of abundance, the crime of hunger is a travesty of social justice. Every six seconds, a child dies of hunger. This is the equivalent of a large passenger jetliner crashing every twenty minutes, seven days a week, three hundred and sixty-five days a year. And yet, this news does not make headlines.

"Our mandate takes us to the frontlines of the war against hunger: to Iraq…Somalia…Afghanistan…Congo…Sudan…and Rwanda, where the humanitarians we honor today worked tirelessly to stop the senseless killing of innocents. I will read their names, then we will observe a moment of silence in memory of their sacrifice."

As the "Introitus" from Mozart's *Requiem* played softly in the background, he stepped away from the podium to uncover the plaque on the wall behind him, then as the faces of the fallen appeared on a screen, he returned to the microphone to intone the names: "Hassan Abdurahman, Somalia; Leo Larson, Norway; Jhamal Omer, Somalia; Khaled Sharif, Somalia."

Seated in the front row, Ben stared at the faces of his fallen comrades for the first time since the day they were murdered: Jhamal, who had been by his side for years; Leo, whom he'd met as an FFL volunteer when he was still at Princeton; Hassan and Khaled, who had been pulled into joining the team. He heard the shots again, the thud of bodies hitting the ground, and for the first time, he surrendered to grief, sobbing without realizing it until someone handed him a tissue.

After a long pause, Sammy raised his head, folded his speech, and left the stage.

———————————

The last plaintive notes of the *Requiem* were drowned out by the wail of sirens and the whirring of blades as a blue-and-white Carabinieri helicopter streaked past the window and hovered over the roof of the Food for Livelihood building, while below, security guards rushed to take their final positions. The Italian foreign minister had arrived.

A dark blue sedan, escorted by four motorcycles and two squad cars, was ushered through the gates. The minister, along with his chief of staff, stepped out and shook hands with Samuel.

When they arrived at Samuel's office, the chief of staff waited discretely in the anteroom as the two men settled comfortably in armchairs. Natasha placed a tray of coffee on a low table then left, closing the door behind her.

"I have only a few minutes," Manenti said.

Samuel cleared his throat. "I would like to extend my thanks to your government and to the Italian people for your generous contributions to Food for Livelihood. I am sure you are aware of the important work we are doing."

"We are proud to host Food for Livelihood in Italy; however, today I have come on an urgent matter, and since time is critical, I will get straight to the point. He lowered his voice, "What I'm about to tell you is classified, of course."

"Please, *Ministro*, continue."

"About an hour ago, I received a video from our embassy in Nairobi. The YLF has taken three hostages—two American volunteers and an Italian Sister—while they were delivering supplies to a school at the Dadaab refugee camp on the Kenyan border with Somalia. The U.S. Secretary of State called me to share their latest intelligence, but their only option, of course, is to go in. One of the hostages happens to be the daughter of a high-ranking official in the State Department, so this option remains on the table…but my government has constraints too; the Vatican has taken a special interest in the release of Sister Chiara and the others without the use of deadly force. Do you understand the predicament?"

"Why have you come to me?"

"We want to negotiate their release with the utmost discretion, but we simply do not have the means nor the contacts to meet their deadline tomorrow at daybreak. First, we need your help in identifying an intermediary, trusted by both sides, to successfully make the exchange."

"I see," Samuel replied.

"Given the time constraints and the complexities on the ground, Secretary Howard and I agree that yours is the only organization with the experience and contacts in the region to facilitate such a delicate operation. Your success in negotiating the humanitarian corridors is a case in point."

"Ah. Exactly what do you want us to do?"

"Your intermediary would be tasked to coordinate the delivery of the ransom money and secure the release of the three hostages."

Sammy whistled softly. "That's a tall order."

The minister pulled out his smartphone and tapped the screen a few times. "Look at this," he said and passed the phone to Sammy, who slipped on his reading glasses.

"Pay close attention to the screen. These images were recently sent to us at 16:00 East Africa Time."

Sammy studied the images then pulled off his glasses and shook his head. "*Ministro*, Food for Livelihood would like to help, of course, but we're not in the business of rescuing hostages…other than our own, of course. What do they want?"

Manenti said, "They are demanding three million U.S. dollars, delivered to an airstrip near the border checkpoint before sunrise. It is a very short time frame. We have the money, but we cannot get it there in time, so I am asking you to find a way to bundle the cash locally. The sun will rise in Somalia in about ten hours. When your intermediary confirms that the hostages are alive, the exchange will be made. You are a leader in managing the logistics of food and cash transfers to Africa, are you not?"

"We are," Sammy said, "but since the YLF forced us to withdraw our permanent presence from South Somalia, we go in, distribute food, and get out. Our networks are curtailed." He stroked his chin nervously. He was in a delicate position. He had just succeeded in a tense negotiation with YLF leadership to deliver food to areas under their control. He couldn't do anything that might jeopardize that. "What you are asking presents more than the usual risks for everyone concerned, particularly if things go wrong. There are many factions of YLF beyond the control of their leadership."

Manenti pressed him. "Your organization is in the business of saving lives, and we are in urgent need of your expertise and contacts. These volunteers are part of the NGO consortium that delivers assistance to the refugee camp. I have no doubt that you will find a way to make this negotiation work beneath the radar and, should things go wrong, your agency and your intermediary will not be held accountable. I will take responsibility."

Sammy stood up and strolled to the window to clear his head. He gazed at the green and white Food for Livelihood flag waving in the breeze and was reminded of what it stood for. A lot was at stake. This was the best option. If the U.S. was forced into a military solution, it would become more dangerous for all those involved, including the hostages. Despite all the risks, he knew he couldn't refuse. "Do we know where they are?"

"Not exactly, but the Americans have located a small airstrip near the Somali border, within range of Kismayo, where the exchange could take place. They have confirmed it is operable," Manenti said. "My concern is whether YLF will release the hostages after they receive the ransom."

Sammy turned from the window so he could study Manenti's expression. The minister must have known that he was asking him to take a huge risk. "It will be very difficult," he said. "Everything is difficult in Somalia, but we must try."

Manenti sat forward in his chair. "*Va bene*, and there's the other matter of airspace…the Kenyans won't allow anyone to violate their airspace to get the hostages out of Somalia. Could you intercede on our behalf?"

"Food for Livelihood saved millions of Kenyan lives during their worst drought. The president knows that keeping his people alive keeps him in power. Consider it done."

Manenti stood up and crossed the room to join Sammy at the window. "Do you have an idea who could be our intermediary?"

"We have a supplier in Somalia who might be willing if the price is right. He does business regularly with YLF. He could handle the transport and the exchange."

"*Ottimo!*" Manenti clapped his hands together. "While I do not wish to minimize the risks or dangers, I am fully confident we will succeed."

"And why is that?"

"Because we will have God's ear."

"Ah," Sammy said, "but I'm sure they are saying the same thing."

Manenti took a pen drive from the inside pocket of his jacket. "All the information we have is here." He handed Sammy a business card. "And this is a secure number for your intermediary to reach the YLF."

Sammy studied the card for a moment. The number had been added in pencil. "*Ministro*, rest assured you can count on our full cooperation and discretion."

"We are grateful to you, Dr. Adjei, and will be praying for the safe return of the hostages."

Sammy returned to his desk, the minister's words echoing in his ears. The names on the humanitarian plaque were grim reminders of his duty to protect them. Saving three humanitarian lives was the right thing to do. He picked up the phone and punched in an internal extension. "Ben, I need to see you in my office right away!"

Chapter 19

"What's it about, Sammy?" Ben was still panting from having run up the stairs.

Sammy leaned over, pushed a button on his desk phone, and spoke into the microphone, "Natasha, hold my calls, thank you." He looked up, his expression grave. "What I am about to divulge is strictly confidential. You understand? This conversation never took place."

Ben nodded.

"The Italian foreign minister has unofficially requested us to help them to negotiate the release of three volunteers—one Italian nun and two young Americans with the NGO Christian Grace—who have been kidnapped by the YLF at the Dadaab camp."

"Run that by me again?"

"Food for Livelihood has been requested to identify one of our reliable contacts to serve as an intermediary to negotiate the hostage exchange. The deadline for the ransom payment of three million dollars is sunrise tomorrow morning."

"What? That doesn't leave much time! The sun rises in Mogadishu around five." He glanced at the clock on Sammy's desk. "We're on *ora legale* here in Europe, daylight savings time, so they're two hours ahead of us. That means we have less than ten hours to arrange the clandestine transfer of millions of U.S. dollars. No problem! Sammy, are you serious? I'm assuming they've tried to negotiate an extension?"

"This is YLF, Ben. You know they don't negotiate. One of the hostages is the daughter of Bill Winter. He's high up in the U.S. State Department."

"Oh, Jesus," Ben moaned.

"They will all be dead in ten hours if we don't figure out a way to orchestrate this ransom exchange. We're their last resort."

"Okay," Ben said. "Let me get this straight. Two Americans and one Italian were kidnapped in Kenya—one of whom happens to be the daughter of a top government foreign policy adviser. YLF is demanding three million U.S. dollars in cash, but U.S. policy forbids paying ransom, so the Italians are taking the lead. They passed this hot potato onto us because they think we're expert hostage negotiators, and we must pretend none of this is happening."

Sammy leaned back in his big leather desk chair and cleared his throat. "That is an accurate summary of the situation, Ben, but we don't have time to debate it."

Ben was dumbfounded. The exchange, was risky on so many levels. "You've got to be kidding me. The stakes are too high. We don't just risk money, we risk lives."

"I've given the minister of foreign affairs my word. Now we have to put our heads together and find an intermediary and a way to bundle and deliver that money by plane to Kismayo in less than ten hours."

Ben stood up and began pacing the room. "Why Kismayo? And how are we going to get the money together?"

"Reach out to our money traders in Mogadishu to help bundle up the cash. The exchange has to take place on an undisclosed airstrip near Kismayo. We'll need a small plane that can land on a makeshift airstrip, and it can only seat the crew and the hostages and no one else. The only aviation company in the area with that kind of plane…"

"…is owned by Jawa," Ben finished. "He knows how to deal with the YLF and his equipment is good, but the plane needs to get to Kismayo. Flying time to Kismayo is thirty minutes from Mogadishu. We need to deliver the money before that plane takes off."

He fell into a chair opposite Sammy's desk and began working his smartphone. Twenty minutes later, he stood up.

"They all need seventy-two hours to bundle up that much cash. They're as bad as the banks. I tried putting it together by going wider and asking them for smaller amounts, but I couldn't get more than a million. That will cover Jawa but not the ransom."

"There must be another option," Sammy said. "We run billions of dollars through the banks. Our credit is good. Someone should be able to deliver three million in cash to the plane."

Ben shook his head. "I tried everyone." He looked at the clock. Nine hours and ten minutes left. "I don't know how big your appetite for risk is, but…what about cryptocurrency, specifically bitcoin… digital money traded on the internet? I've been learning about it from the guys I deal with in London. It gets moved from one account to another using blockchain without involving a middleman like a bank. It's called P2P, person to person, because it's a direct payment without a verifier, based entirely on trust. If the YLF accepts cryptocurrency, we can transfer the money to their account in seconds."

Sammy raised his eyebrows and took a deep breath. "That sounds like the so-called Darknet. Isn't that how unlawful solicitation is transacted? Hiring of hit men…arms trafficking…drug dealing?"

Ben started pacing again, waving his smartphone. "No, that's a misconception the banks are perpetrating because they're afraid blockchain will take away their business. But some very reputable banks are handling bitcoin now."

Sammy pressed his lips together and shook his head. "It's too risky. We can't have FFL associated with it. As a nonprofit organization advocating for the right to food, we have to remain beyond reproach. Trust and transparency are key."

"I know, I know, but look at this," Ben said, handing Sammy his smartphone. "This article explains how bitcoin is becoming legitimate. It already has a value of more than 100 million dollars, and it's growing rapidly. You're the one who said that FFL needs to take advantage of the new technology. Well, here's our test case."

"Yes, of course, but we're in the business of feeding hungry people. I'm just not ready to go that far out on a limb, Ben."

"Really? People's lives are at stake? But if they come home in coffins… do you really want that on your conscience? This is an extraordinary request, and we have the means to help with no quid pro quo."

"I get it. I'm not sold on the idea, but we don't have time to worry about it. I'm going to call Jawa now." He unlocked a drawer in his desk, pulled out a secure smartphone, punched in a number, and spoke slowly, laying out the proposed operation. Taking the minister's card from his breast pocket, he read the contact number and hung up. "Now we wait," he said. "He says they never answer, but they always call back."

Within minutes, the phone buzzed. Sammy said, "It's Jawa." He pressed the speaker button. "They accept bitcoin, and so does he. His fee is $500,000. The account details for them will be provided at the time of the exchange, and Jawa is sending his account info now."

Ben whistled loudly. "Wow! Hostage rescue doesn't come cheap, but at least we're in the game. Now all we have to do is find three and a half million dollars and a kiosk where I can exchange it for bitcoin."

A rueful smile began to form on Sammy's lips. "Except that the banks are closed at this hour, remember?"

"In Italy, my friend," Ben countered, "but not in Panama. I'll get Melissa Trask to help. She knows all about this stuff."

"Be careful what you say to her, Ben."

"It's fine. I'll tell her that we have to Go Live with FLITE now, earlier than planned, due to operational expediency. It will be a good test of the system, after all the simulations. Cryptocurrency is blockchain-based and the perfect instrument to get them the money fast and under the radar."

He walked slowly down the stairs to his office, holding on to the banister, fighting to stay calm.

When he passed Dalia's desk, he asked her to call Melissa to his office. He'd have to depend on her to help set up the bitcoin transfer. No one in the building understood FLITE better than she did.

Melissa wandered in, dressed more casually than usual in a soft blue blouse and tailored slacks, and for a moment, he forgot what he was going to say. He stood leaning against his desk, his hands in his pockets. Recovering, he said, "Given that the FLITE simulation phase is successfully on track, Sammy has decided to Go Live. New developments in the field make it imperative we get the system up and running sooner rather than later."

"How quickly?"

"Now…tonight…but there's more." He tried to sound confident, but he doubted that what he was asking was reasonable or even possible.

"What is this about?" she asked.

"Sammy has stressed the absolute confidentiality of this plan. Nothing I say leaves this room. Nothing. All I can tell you is that lives are at stake." He paused to choose his next words carefully. "We need your expertise to create a bitcoin account for three and a half million dollars in cryptocurrency. One transfer will be made to a Somalia-based company called Jawa Logistics that's registered in our system, the other to an account number to be provided later. For our purposes, let's call it logistics services. We have eight hours to complete the transactions, so there's no room for error, no time for second chances. Can it be done?"

He couldn't read the expression on her face as he waited for her answer.

"I'll have to think this through, but yes, it should be possible. In order to create an account in bitcoin, I'll first need a photo of the account holder with a passport I.D. to verify him or her as the user. I assume that will be you."

Ben sprinted behind his desk and began rummaging through the drawers until he emerged waving a blue American passport. He turned to the page bearing his photo and held it open next to his face.

"Okay," she said, holding up her phone to take multiple shots. "That's done."

She turned and hurried out of the room. She'd looked uneasy...*and very beautiful*, he thought. *Keep it together, Ben. She's just a colleague, like any other. I need to stay at arm's length.* Feelings aside, it was all up to her now. He hoped he'd made the right decision getting her involved.

Chapter 20

Ben looked at the clock on his desk for the tenth time. They had five hours to transfer the funds. He decided to check on Melissa to see what was taking her so long. She was one of the most professional people he'd ever met, which made him fear the worst. As he approached her desk, he could hear her speaking very softly into the telephone. He caught the words, "Yes, I know. I need three and a half million U.S. dollars in bitcoin…not tomorrow… now…now." And he froze in place. "It's going to make everything easier for us. I know the bank closed hours ago, but this is an emergency… Figure it out… I'm not the crypto guru, that's your job… No, no profit margin… Because it's for a humanitarian cause… Of course… The transfer must be recognized immediately… The name on the account should be Benjamin Tano… Yes, T-A-N-O… I don't know who…it's all very secretive… Must run. Love you, Miha."

When she swiveled around in her chair, she saw Ben, who looked horrified. "Who was that?"

"My brother, Michael. He works in cryptocurrency at Mitchell Bank specializing in international corporate transactions. He can help us to get the bitcoin."

"That's fine, but you do understand that everything about this mission is highly confidential. If you said anything…"

"Yes, of course. I fully understand the need for confidentiality… but we need his help to execute the transaction this fast. I'm sorry I didn't run it by you first."

He noticed that she was twisting her hands in her lap, and his anger vanished. This was a lot to ask her, and he had to be patient with her.

"Forget about it. Where are we?"

"Michael is creating your bitcoin account. FLITE is going through its last Go Live simulation. I'm finishing the paperwork, so we should be ready in about two hours." She was still tense, biting her lip.

He held her eyes for a moment, sorry he'd upset her. Then he did the math. They had four and half hours before the hostage exchange. If he didn't have five hundred thousand dollars for Jawa in three hours, the plane wouldn't leave the tarmac. The timing was incredibly close.

"No more than two hours, Melissa. Swear we'll be ready to go then. Lives are at stake. I'm counting on you. Bring the paperwork to the operations center the minute you have it. I'll be waiting for you there with Sammy," he said. Realizing the strain he was placing on her, he added, "And then go home, okay?" He paused for a moment. He'd been so panicked he'd forgotten she was doing him a huge favor. This wasn't her job. "And Melissa…thank you so much for doing this. You have no idea how much this means to us."

At two in the morning, the glass and steel FFL building was in complete darkness except for the lit stairwells and a top floor office. The cleaning staff had left hours ago. Only the security guards were still on duty. The sun would rise in Somalia in a little more than an hour; no leeway there.

At the conference table, Sammy locked eyes with Ben as they heard the click of Melissa's heels. She opened the door looking exhausted, her usually impeccable chignon in disarray, her lips pale. She carried a large file folder, which she dropped on the table as she sat across from the two anxious men.

Ben gave her a pallid smile. "What do you have for us?"

"I'm still working on it. The coins should be ready for purchase in just a moment."

Sammy sighed. "Thank the Lord."

"My brother works in cryptocurrency exchange at Mitchell Bank, which deals in bitcoin on its trading platform. Luckily, he's been able to help.

Otherwise, I don't know how we would have been able to buy three and a half million in bitcoin so quickly. He had to call his boss in the middle of the night and persuade him to sell off part of the bank's bitcoin portfolio at market value with no gains. I told him to play the humanitarian card." Her smartphone beeped. "Excuse me, this could be it—fingers crossed." She read the text message. "It's my brother. The transaction will be a P2P straight trade between Mitchell and FFL no bid—no buying off the platform for fear someone might scoop up the coins before we did. This is safe and secure."

Sammy was jubilant. "Well done!"

Melissa began organizing the contents of the file folder, which was filled with paperwork. "Thank you. Now, I need to explain the extraordinary actions required and the risks involved. Due to the extreme time constraints, I've taken the liberty of speaking with the directors of IT and finance to find the best avenue. They have jointly come up with a profile that will keep the inspector general off our backs. Keep in mind that I have gotten incredible cooperation from your colleagues, whom I have called at their homes in the middle of the night. After looking at all options, they have concluded that what I am about to present is the only workable alternative.

"In order to execute the payment within the prescribed time frame, we'll need to create a temporary finance profile specifically for Ben, which has no financial or oversight controls and gives him, and only him, a single-line access to the FFL treasury module."

Sammy glanced at Ben. He hadn't expected this. She was asking him for a major breach in protocol. "With no oversight?"

Melissa nodded. "Yes. Basically, you're giving him the key to the vault, under exceptional circumstances."

"That access has never been granted to anyone," Sammy said. "This is a humanitarian organization entirely funded by contributions. We can't operate without the complete trust of our donors, which is why what you are asking is not possible."

Ben and Melissa exchanged looks. He was no more comfortable with the idea than Sammy. She said, "It's only valid for forty-eight hours, after which Ben's access will be denied."

"We have less than sixty minutes to make this happen," Ben said. "Believe me, Sammy, I am totally uncomfortable with the idea of having that kind of access. But if we have no other options…time is running out."

Sammy let his head fall back and closed his eyes. "I'm thinking," he said.

Ben put his head down on the table and clenched his fists. This was a nightmare. Now he was being asked to take responsibility for FFL's entire treasury—with no safeguards and a whole lot of risk.

Sammy opened his eyes and with a deep sigh of resignation responded, "There's no choice. We've come this far. Let's do it."

Melissa smiled. "Good." She handed the documents she'd prepared to Sammy and Ben.

"This is a decision memo approving exceptional authorization for Benjamin Tano to access the FFL treasury module. Please read it carefully and review the step-by-step controls that are being circumvented to conduct this financial transaction. These include vendor management and due diligence, tendering and contract awarding, service quality check, payment oversight, and compliance with FFL rules and regulations."

The memo was brief enough, but Sammy took time to examine it carefully before signing.

Ben blew out a long breath then picked up a pen. "My neck is on the line here too. This means I'm accountable for any wrongdoing that takes place in the next forty-eight hours."

Melissa's head was down as she replaced the paperwork in the file folder. A tense silence filled the room. Then she looked up and, in her most professional tone, said, "Ben, if you'll allow me to have a look at your computer, I'll upload everything you need to set up your account from these pen drives, and then I'll show you exactly what you need to do to release the coins. We'll send the money to Jawa now, and when it's time to transfer the coins to the other account, your screen will be ready to execute the order."

Ben slid his laptop across the table, and she inserted a pen drive in one of the USB slots. He noticed that her hands were shaking. *She's exhausted,* he thought. *We've put her through a lot. This isn't what she signed up for.* When she lifted her head, she seemed to be looking at something in the distance.

She cleared her throat and swallowed hard. "What I'm uploading is the online banking app for Mitchell Bank. Once you transfer the three million, they will send the bitcoin to your cryptocurrency account." She glanced down at Ben's laptop screen, removed the pen drive, and inserted a second one.

"Now I'm uploading your bitcoin account, which allows you to trade, buy, sell, or pay with cryptocurrency. Once it's uploaded, your account will be open. You will then insert your password, specify the amount and the recipient's account number, then press enter. A checkbox will confirm the transfer was successful."

She slid the computer back across the table to Ben, pushed back her chair, and stood. "That's everything, gentlemen. Goodnight then," she said and, without looking at either of them, exited the conference room.

Ben called after her. "Wait... I mean...thank you!" But she was gone.

Chapter 21

The time was 03:00 in Rome, 21:00 in Washington, and 05:00 in Somalia, where a Cessna 206 was flying through dark skies in search of a landing strip. At the U.S. State Department in Washington, the Ministry of Foreign Affairs in Rome, and FFL headquarters, anxious ears were listening to the voice of a middle-aged Australian bush pilot who had lost all patience. There was no airport, nothing, no lights on the ground. In the copilot's seat, Jawa, FFL's private sector transporter, checked his smartphone for further instructions. Nothing. Then the phone rang, and he held it up to the pilot. "YLF."

"Tell your pilot to maintain his current course, reduce engine speed, and commence descent to 1,000 feet, then hold until he sees the runway… flyover of the runway is not allowed…if he misses the approach, abort and go back to Kismayo."

"Listen, mate," the pilot said, "this is mad. I've flown over these parts for fifteen years, and I've never seen a dirt strip. I'll commence descent, but if I don't see anything when we hit 1,000 feet, I'm going right back up to cruising altitude and turning around."

Jawa turned his narrow shoulders to stare out the window as the pilot reduced the engine speed. There was nothing out there, not even the dark shadow of a cloud. Then he thought he saw pinpoints of light. Maybe he was imagining it.

In the FFL operation center, Ben and Sammy glanced at each other, barely breathing. Their video screen was still black. Jawa's voice came through the speaker. "I see it! A corridor of lights on the ground. Hang on!"

The plane pitched as the pilot commenced the final descent. Parallel lines of Toyota pickup trucks, using their headlight beams, were creating a makeshift runway. A few moments later, Jawa could see YLF militants manning fifty-caliber guns mounted to the cabs of the trucks.

Ben gripped the top of the table as the speakers blasted a loud thud. "Jawa?" Sammy leaned into the microphone. "What's happening?" Then the video screen lit up.

"We've landed, Dr. A. YLF is on the ground in force. Body cam operational… I don't know if you can see the line of trucks. They've just turned their lights off."

"The bastards don't want to be spotted from the sky," Ben mumbled.

On the video screen in Rome, grainy images began to come through. Lights flashed as a truck approached the plane and led it to a stop. Militants surrounded the aircraft, scouring the storage bins and examining the fuselage.

The pilot lowered the stairs, and Jawa appeared at the top, a slender man dressed in jeans and a white cotton tunic. The YLF militant in charge was waiting for him on the ground, flanked by other militants, rifles drawn. He motioned Jawa to come down. The pilot didn't even unbuckle his harness. They couldn't pay him enough to get out of the plane.

As he descended the stairs, Jawa's bodycam picked up the three hostages, kneeling on the ground, their heads hooded, automatic weapons pointed at them from all sides. The militant nodded at him, holding a satellite phone to his ear.

In Rome, Ben began to tremble. He crossed his legs under the table to keep his knees from shaking and tightly clasped his hands, trying to steady himself. The sight of these armed men, their faces hidden behind red-and-white *keffiyehs*, ready, even eager, to kill, was unbearable. All the terror he had fought so hard to resolve overcame him. He was back in the Somali village, heart pounding, hearing the gun shots, the thud of bodies hitting the ground, gasping for breath, running for his life.

The militants removed the hoods from the hostages, and Jawa approached them. On the screen, Jill's face came into focus. Then, one of the militants pushed her head to the ground, and the others lowered their guns, preparing to shoot her. She was hysterical, begging Jesus to save her. Jawa moved from Jill to Bradley to Sister Chiara.

Sammy leaned into the microphone again. "Washington? Confirm hostage identification?"

"Confirmed."

"Rome? Confirm hostage identification?"

"Confirmed."

"Jawa, ready for account details." Sammy wrote down the numbers and handed the paper to Ben. "Okay. Let's do this."

Ben entered all the information and paused, his hands hovering over his laptop keyboard. Now all he had to do was press "enter." But he couldn't do it. He couldn't bring himself to give YLF three million dollars to buy more guns, more ammunition, more pickup trucks. He couldn't pay them to murder more people.

The YLF militant was still holding the satellite phone to his ear. He was waiting, and then he was not waiting any longer. He was screaming.

Sammy turned to face Ben. "What's happening?"

Ben was frozen. He couldn't speak, couldn't move.

From the speakers, he heard heavy boots hitting the ground, angry shouts. On the video screen, the militants were surrounding the plane with heavy artillery. One of them dragged the pilot from the cockpit.

"Ben!" Sammy was frantic now. "What the bloody hell? Complete the transfer! Press the bloody key or these people die!"

Ben's hand was suspended over the keyboard. He blinked, and his whole body quivered.

"Ben, press it now! Now!"

Ben watched his finger in slow motion pressing down on the key marked "enter." The payment authorization icon popped up.

Sammy shouted at the screen, "Jawa, the money is in their account now. Tell them!"

The militant's phone rang. Fingers were hooked to the triggers of a dozen AK-47s aimed at the three hostages, at Jawa, at the pilot, ready to shoot. The militant listened to his phone, nodded. He gave the thumbs-up, and the barrels of a dozen rifles were lowered.

Sammy dropped back in his armchair. Ben began to sob uncontrollably as he watched Jawa run to the hostages, hurrying them onto the Cessna. He had choked and nearly cost these people their lives. He was no longer fit for anything.

The pilot revved the engine.

Ben's head was in his hands. "Sammy, I'm sorry, I…for a minute… I don't know what happened to me."

"It's alright. It's over. They're safe."

Sammy's phone rang. He pressed "speaker" and picked up. "*Complementi,* Dr. Adjei," said the minister, "for your aid in facilitating the release of our three hostages. Despite these ongoing threats, we know that our important work in the service of refugees will continue. I have also been instructed to read this message on behalf of His Holiness, the Pontiff."

Sammy nodded to Ben who sat up straight in his chair.

"Blessed are the peacemakers for they shall inherit the earth. May God bless you and keep you safe."

Chapter 22

It was still dark when Ben began the drive toward his apartment. The streets were deserted, and the city was shrouded in silence. Sammy had asked him to stay for a celebratory drink, but he didn't feel much like celebrating. The one person he wanted to thank hadn't been present. FLITE had been launched. Mission accomplished. But that also meant Melissa would be returning to London. The thought of her leaving suddenly made him feel empty, adrift. He was upset about the way he'd pressured her, and he hadn't had the chance to properly thank her. She'd done the impossible for him, and he'd given her nothing in return. She would never know what had been at stake nor be recognized for the lives she'd saved. She'd leave without knowing what it meant to him, what she meant to him.

It was four in the morning when he parked in front of her building. He hadn't thought to text or call first. He hadn't thought at all. He stood outside, wondering if she was sound asleep or as hyped up from adrenaline as he was. Should he wake her up? Would she let him in? What would he say? He strolled up to her door, squinting at the names on the buzzer, not knowing which one was hers. He pulled out his smartphone.

"Ben? What happened? Did the payment go through?" asked Melissa.

"Yes, we did it. Hey, I'm in front of your building."

"You are?"

"I need to see you. Can I come up?"

"Of course."

He paced for several moments before the door buzzed, letting him in. The old wrought iron elevator squeaked as it carried him to the third floor.

She was standing at the door outside her apartment, leaning on the doorframe in an oversized T-shirt and grey leggings, no shoes, no makeup, thick auburn hair flowing over her shoulders.

"Are you okay?" she asked.

"I want to be," he answered.

"So do I." She sighed softly, looking down for a moment. "Let's go inside." She took his hand, but he didn't move.

"Do you want some coffee or tea or…"

"No, I…" He realized in that moment that all he wanted was her. He pulled her close and kissed her without stopping to wonder if he should. But she was kissing him back, and her hands were caressing his head. She slowly pulled him into the apartment, hesitating for just a moment, then led him to the bedroom.

She pulled the T-shirt over her head. Her breasts were beautiful, her nipples pale pink and hard against his lips. She moved her hands slowly over his chest. The smartphone in his shirt pocket was buzzing with incoming messages. He took it out and threw it on the chair while she unzipped his jeans.

He awoke a few hours later with the morning light pouring in through the window. He reached for Melissa, but she wasn't there. He sat up and looked around, suddenly remembering where he was. A wooden crucifix was mounted over the bed. *Oh Christ, a witness,* he thought and searched for his boxer shorts. He stood up and began gathering his scattered clothes from the floor. Melissa had decorated the wall of her temporary home with family photos. He moved closer to examine an image, shot in a living room somewhere, of who must be her parents and brother. Her father was dressed in a military uniform displaying a chest full of medals. His hair was slicked back, and Ben noticed a shadow on his forehead from hairline to eyebrow, perhaps a scar or a birthmark.

Melissa came in behind him and put her arms around his waist. "Did I wake you when I got up? I'm sorry. I haven't been sleeping well lately. Too much on my mind."

He turned to face her and laced the fingers of his right hand in her thick hair. "It can't be work. Go Live was successful!" He mused, "I hope it isn't me?"

"No, it's family stuff—my parents, you know. I'm leaving for Puglia tomorrow to sort some things out."

"Really? How long will you be gone?"

"Just overnight. Let's not talk about it now. Come back to bed," she said. "I'm sure Dr. Adjei won't be expecting us today."

He tossed his clothes back onto the floor and complied happily. They made love again and again. Later, they lay in each other's arms, contented. Ben realized that as much as he was happy being there with this amazing woman, in reality, he knew very little about her. He wanted to know every detail about her life, what food she loved, her favorite color, what she wanted in life. He wanted more time to explore every inch of body, but now, all of a sudden, she was leaving. He felt a familiar kind of urgency he wasn't used to other than when he was on assignment. But this time, the only person who was hungry was him.

"Tell me things about you, Melissa. I want to know you, not just do… this," he said, kissing her lightly on the mouth.

"But I like this," she said, playfully kissing him back with more intensity.

"I'm serious," he said. "I know you've been through a lot. I have too. I want to hear about your family, what you were like as a kid." He pointed to the picture of the man in uniform. "Is that your father?"

"Yes," she said, resting her chin on his shoulder. "What about your family? You never mention them."

"My mother died when I was in college, and my father and I are worlds apart," Ben shared. He had not talked about them with anyone in a very long time. He pivoted back to her. "Your father was in the army?"

"He was a bureaucrat."

"It looks like he was a high-ranking officer."

"He was chief of staff."

"You sound proud of him."

"He's been a good father." She edged away from him a little and propped her head up on one elbow.

"Okay, but tell me more about him. What is he like?"

"I will…sometime."

She was avoiding the subject. She'd told him about growing up in Belgrade, about her mother and brother. She never said much about her father. Ben had assumed he'd been some sort of executive and had been surprised to see him in uniform. He'd wondered why they'd chosen to immigrate to Italy. He was a Serbian general. Maybe there was more to it, but he wouldn't press her to answer. There were a million other things about her he wanted to know. *Maybe there will be time to learn them,* he hoped.

"Let's go back to sleep," she whispered. Then she pulled him close and wrapped her leg around him as he drifted off in her arms.

When Ben woke up at noon, he was alone again. He instantly felt an unexpected loneliness. This time, he found a message from Melissa saying she was out doing errands. He gathered up his things and went home to shower and change clothes. When he unlocked the door, his apartment was dark and empty. He'd left dishes in the sink and a half-eaten pizza on the kitchen counter. After the adrenaline rush of Go Live and the hostage exchange, he should have felt relieved, but all he could think about was Melissa. He didn't want her to go. Since the shooting in Somalia, he hadn't been able to let Serena in, and he thought he'd never be able to open up to anyone again. But Melissa was a survivor too. She understood him, his reticence, his fears. And she allowed him to be able to reveal himself to her without pressing him with questions. He felt a deep connection with her and thought—or at least hoped—that she felt the same way about him. *But she's leaving for Puglia.* He wanted to tell her how he felt before she left. This wasn't just about sex. He wanted more from her…way more. He decided to invite her to his place for a quiet dinner, hoping there would be a moment that seemed right to talk things through. *Everything has to be perfect.* He felt that old twinge of anxiety, and for the remainder of the day, he busied himself with shopping, cooking, and cleaning his long-neglected apartment.

In the early evening, he was putting the final touches on the table setting, feeling happy and hopeful. For the first time in a long time, everything felt possible again. When Melissa arrived with a bottle of chilled *prosecco*, he immediately pulled her into his arms. She noticed the candles and flowers on the table.

"You've gone all out," she said.

"Of course. You know what they say—the way to a woman's heart is through her stomach…and a knack for table setting," he said smiling.

"I thought that idea only applied to men," she teased him. "But I like this domestic side of you."

"Just showing off how well trained I am."

He was proud of his efforts but nervous. He didn't want to come off as desperate or perhaps a little silly. "Honestly, I wanted to show you how much I appreciate everything you did for us, and trust me, what you did meant everything to a lot of people."

"No thanks needed," she said, looking away from him. She quickly changed the subject. "Smells good. What's on the menu? I'm starving." She was speaking a little faster than usual. *She sounds as nervous as I feel,* Ben thought. *I hope it's for the same reason.*

He laughed, encouraged. "I know how to cook two meals. Scrambled eggs with bacon and pot roast with potatoes and carrots. Tonight, we're eating pot roast, and this," he said, pointing to a platter of antipasto with sliced *prosciutto*, olives, and an array of cheeses. "Let's have it with the *prosecco*," he said, heading toward the living room.

"Wait," she called after him. "You have a terrace? It's such a lovely evening."

"All right then," he said. "When in Rome, you might as well be looking at Rome. I think you'll like the view."

He opened the door, and they stepped outside, breathing in the scents of jasmine, garlic frying in olive oil, and freshly baked pizza. A crescent moon was beginning her ascent above the horizon, and stars were faintly twinkling beyond their reach.

Melissa gasped slightly. "How beautiful!" she said, taking in the view.

"I know. It's the main reason I never gave this place up even after…" He trailed off, but she caught his meaning. His separation from his wife was still a fresh wound.

Ben set everything out on the small wrought iron table, popped the cork, and filled their glasses, waiting for the bubbles to come to rest. Melissa leaned on the railing for a moment, taking it all in. The lights of the city were always magical to see, highlighting the contours of the ancient monuments. It was cool but pleasant, yet she shivered slightly. He guided her to the cushioned swing and put an arm around her to warm her. For a moment, memories of sitting here with his wife made him hold in his breath.

"Everything okay?" she asked, sensing his sudden tension.

"Perfect," he said, exhaling slowly. He took his free hand and buried his fingers in her silky hair, pulling her in for a long, deep kiss. "I'm glad you're here," he said softly when the kiss ended.

"Me too. This is very romantic," she said, looking out over the splendor of Rome.

"Yes, it is," he replied, but he was looking only at her.

She returned his gaze. Nervously, Ben pulled back slightly. "I...uh, want you to know how much I've enjoyed our time together. Thank you again and...*salute*," he smiled, and they clinked glasses.

She looked down. "Please don't keep thanking me, Ben."

"I know this is very new, but I didn't want you to leave without knowing that I feel a special connection to you. When you come back from Puglia, I hope we can continue and see where this goes. I guess what I'm getting at is...I hope you feel the same way I do, that this is something special."

She leaned over and kissed him, locking eyes for a moment. He saw the tiniest of tears forming there, but she quickly looked away.

He reached into his pocket and pulled out a small red box tied with thin gold ribbons.

"What's this?" she asked, looking at the box in his hand nervously. "You don't seem like the kind of guy who proposes on the second date."

"Oh! Hell no!! I'm not that kind of crazy. But I thought pot roast and cheese weren't enough to show my appreciation."

He placed the box in the palm of her hand. "Open it!"

She carefully untied the ribbons. A smaller velvet box was nestled inside. When she flipped open the lid, she found a necklace with a small emerald pendant set in swirls of gold Florentine.

"Oh, Ben...it's so beautiful. I don't know what to say." She lifted the necklace from its cushion and held it up to the light, the green flecks in her eyes sparkling with the intensity of the stone.

Ben lifted her hair to fasten the clasp then leaned in to kiss the back of her neck. "Emeralds are the symbol of rebirth. I haven't allowed myself to feel anything since that day in Somalia, but I feel closer to you than I have to anyone for a very long time...like we've always known each other."

She held the pendant in her hand for a long time without saying anything. He watched her, waiting for her reply. Then she said, so quietly he had to lean forward to hear her, "I feel connected to you too, Ben, drawn to you. Working with you these past months, I've been very happy, but…I fear the past will always be with us."

"You know," he replied, "I've been so immersed in my work, my purpose, my FFL family. That's who I was. There was no time in my life for anyone else. I was a terrible husband, but I'm a different person now. Somalia changed me. I want you in my life, Melissa. That's what matters to me now. I think we could be happy together."

She leaned back, and a sad expression crossed her face. He began to think he'd made a terrible mistake. Then she turned to him and held him tightly. "I think so too," she whispered.

He nuzzled her neck and said softly, "Dinner can wait."

Early the next morning, with the scent of her perfume in his hair, he drove her to the airport for the short flight to Brindisi, where her brother would meet her for the drive to the family farmhouse.

"I don't get to see my family often," she said. "But now, I can't wait for the visit to be over." She smiled up at him.

"I'll be waiting for you when you get back," he said and kissed her one last time.

Chapter 23

Mihailo unlocked the farmhouse door and called out, "Tata...Mama... we're here!"

Melissa dropped her suitcase and stood waiting at the threshold, grateful for a moment to be lost in her thoughts of Ben—his eyes, his smile, the way he looked at her. He really did care about her. She put a hand to her throat and felt the emerald pendant hidden under her turtleneck sweater. Ben was a good man, an honest man who trusted her with his deepest feelings. He'd risked his life to save others, and now she was about to frame him, a man with whom she might have had a real life, for embezzlement from the humanitarian agency he loved so much, making it look like he had betrayed his mission and his best friend. She would gain her father's freedom, but at which price? This would surely destroy Ben, damage the reputation of Food for Livelihood, and compromise their mission to save lives. On the other hand, her father's freedom and possibly her parents' lives hung in the balance. She and her brother were in an untenable position.

She felt sick to her stomach. *How will he feel about me when he finds out who I really am and what I've done? Once he knows the truth, he will hate me.* No matter what choice she made, she would destroy someone she loved. She had made this impossible promise to go through with the fraud to save her father, but now she stood frozen in the doorway of her parents' home. *I don't know if I can do this,* she thought, her mind racing. The events of the last few weeks and her unexpected romance played like a movie with no good ending.

Lidija came running from the kitchen and hugged Miliitsa, breaking the spell. She lingered in her mother's arms a moment longer than usual, fighting back tears. The general emerged warily, but his face lit up when he saw them. He shook hands with his son and pulled his daughter close, saying, "Welcome home."

"Thank you, Tata." Her father loved her so much that he had risked his life to protect her and the family. It was her duty now to save him, wasn't it? But why did the price have to be so high?

"Come, sit," Lidija said, taking Mihailo by the arm.

She put a steaming plate of *sarma* on the table. "My favorite," Miliitsa said, trying to sound enthusiastic as her mother filled her plate with the warm stuffed cabbage rolls. Comfort food, but it brought her little comfort.

They ate quietly, stopping to squeeze a hand or share a smile. Miliitsa and Mihailo spoke of their work, promised that they weren't working too hard or eating too little, refusing second helpings, then agreeing to just one more bite. They examined their parents' faces, looking for signs of illness, of exhaustion, of worry. They exchanged sideways glances, pressed their lips together, tense. Miliitsa would never hurt her mother by not eating her food, but she was so full of guilt, fear, and regret, she felt she might explode.

When Miliitsa and her mother had cleared away the dishes and served the *torta praska* of apricot jam, walnuts, and sour cream, Mihailo pushed his chair back from the table and lit a cigarette.

"Tata, soon you'll be a free man," he said, exhaling smoke. "Miliitsa has done her part...which wasn't difficult, under the circumstances." His voice dripped with sarcasm.

Their father shifted uncomfortably. "Not now, Mihailo."

They were all silent. She had to say something. She owed it to her father to be truthful. "It's all right," she said. "Miha thinks that I've seduced Ben Tano only to win his trust. But what he doesn't know is that I do care about Ben Tano. My feelings for him are real, and I know he feels the same way about me. Or at least he did. If I do this..."

Her mother's eyes widened, and her father glanced at Mihailo, who appeared stunned by the news. "I see...well..." Lidija looked from her husband to her son, waiting for one of them to say something.

Mihailo exploded. "*If* you do this? You stupid girl! You were supposed to seduce him, not fall in love with him! How could you be so selfish? Neri was right. He said there would be complications."

Miliitsa's eyes flashed. "Selfish? Selfish?! Everything I've done has been for this family. And Neri can go to hell. He's the enemy here. Since when are you on his side, Miha? How can you say that my happiness, my life, my future are complications?"

"Stop now, both of you," their father ordered.

"I will not stop, Tata," Mihailo said. "The plan is in place. Your freedom is nearly secured. Her craziness is putting everything in jeopardy and… What does this mean, Miliitsa? Are you so insane about your new lover that you can't see what's at stake? They'll send Tata to rot in prison. You're putting us all in danger too. There's no way out of this."

"Enough!" the general commanded.

"I can access Ben's computer now," Miliitsa said quietly, staring at her hands. "I installed Spear Phishing and a Trojan on his hard drive so I can log into his account. And the FFL firewall will be down for the next forty-eight hours. But I don't want to do it. I can't let this man I so deeply respect and care about suffer for a crime he did not commit! He'll be the one to rot in prison! His life will be over! And so will mine. There must be another way."

Their father took a deep breath and spoke softly, "It's too late to call it off without repercussions. I would have to disappear again, and I am ready to do so if it's the only solution. You and Miha shouldn't have to take risks for me. I've lived my life. You still have yours ahead of you."

"Tata, don't talk like that," Miliitsa said. "You were not a war criminal. You were just a bureaucrat. You didn't kill anybody. If you go to the Hague, you can clear your name. You'll be declared innocent."

Mihailo folded his arms and glared at her across the table. "You are a fool, Miliitsa. Why do you think we fled to this remote village? Tata was a high-ranking officer under Milošević. The tribunal will want to make him pay for all the unsolved war crimes. It's too late…these mobsters are ruthless.

No matter where we go, they'll come after us—all of us…including you. You're too involved to back out now. You can't choose your new boyfriend over your family."

"And destroy an innocent man's life? Bring scandal to Food for Livelihood? Allow more children to die?" she asked.

"Don't worry about your Ben Tano. He'll despise you the second he figures this all out, and all he will get is a slap on the wrist for his stupidity."

She couldn't listen anymore. She got up and left the table.

Mihailo turned to his parents and continued in a low voice, "If Miliitsa talks, we're all dead." The general looked down at his plate, sadly shaking his head. Mihailo excused himself from the table, went outside, and made a phone call.

Mihailo listened intently, then answered, "I know, but we have a problem here that could put everything at risk. My sister is backing out. She thinks she loves Ben Tano."

He shifted from one foot to the other with the cell phone pressed to his ear and replied, "Yes! She's here with us in Puglia… Hello? Hello?" He looked at the phone in his hand for a moment, shook his head, and went back inside. *Maybe I can still talk some sense into her.*

Miliitsa took her leather tote and the satchel with her laptop from the hall and retreated to her room. She quickly called Ben's number and let it ring until the voice mail picked up. "Ben, call me. I love you," she whispered. She pocketed the phone and raced past the kitchen toward the front door where she grabbed her coat and Mihailo's keys from the table.

"Wait, Miliitsa! Stay here…we need to talk," Mihailo called after her, but she threw open the door and sprinted to his car.

She went to the driver's side, grappled with the key remote, and flicked it, watching the four locks pop up, then opened the door and slid behind the wheel.

As she was turning the key in the ignition, Mihailo's face appeared at the window of the passenger side. She ignored him and fumbled for the lock button while he struggled with the door handle and pounded on the window. "Miliitsa, wait! Wait!"

Mihailo flung open the passenger door and managed to get one foot inside the car before she jammed the gearshift into drive and floored the accelerator. The tires screeched as the vehicle jumped forward, causing him to lose his balance and fall out of the car backward, hitting his head against the gravel.

Dazed, he looked up to see the taillights disappearing around the curve. He rolled over on his side and slowly got back to his feet, brushing the dirt and gravel from his clothes. He had no choice. He pulled out his phone and pressed redial.

"You need to defuse the situation now. She just drove off in my car... back to Rome, I guess... Yes, she has her computer... Yes, her cell phone should be on. Look, I don't want Neri or that nephew of yours to hurt her... Do you hear me? Answer me!"

He punched the off button, put the phone back in his pocket, and walked resolutely to the house where his parents sat anxiously waiting.

———————

It was beginning to get dark, but Melissa took the coastal road to avoid the main highway. Her vision was blurred with tears as she groped for her phone and pressed "B."

"Come on, Ben, pick up. Pick up the phone, Ben. Where are you?"

A bright light flashed in the rearview mirror, temporarily blinding her, followed by a hard jolt that caused her to swerve dangerously into the other lane. She tightened her grip on the steering wheel and turned sharply to the right and then to the left to regain control as the car fishtailed. When she finally succeeded in steadying it, she checked the rearview mirror and floored the accelerator to escape whoever was behind her. The car took a second hit—much harder than the first one—and she screamed as her head snapped back and the airbag deployed, its impact loosening her grip on the steering wheel. She was terrified now, screaming, "No! No!" while the car veered off the road, crashed through the guardrail, and rolled over and over as it tumbled down the ravine.

A black SUV pulled up on the shoulder, and a man in an oversized dark coat got out and picked his way down the steep hill. He yanked open the passenger door, gun in hand, but there was no need to use it. He pulled out the satchel containing Melissa's laptop and tucked it under one arm and tossed her leather tote onto the ground a few feet from the car. He took one last look at the young girl jammed behind the steering wheel, immobile. *Probably dead anyway,* he thought as he walked toward the car's engine.

With his free hand, he pulled a bottle from his big coat pocket and poured out its liquid onto the ground from the front of the car and for several feet alongside it. Casually, he tossed a match at the ground and jogged swiftly up the hill, turning in time to watch as the small car exploded into flames.

An hour later, Mihailo's phone rang. "Yes?" he answered. He paused as he listened to the caller. Then, with a heavy sigh, he went to the door of his parents' house. On the ground outside lay the satchel containing his sister's laptop. A hastily scribbled note said only three words: "Finish the job."

Burning wreckage and flashing police cars lit up the dark sky. The heat from the flames and the dense smoke made it impossible for rescue workers to find any survivors.

A police officer scrambled up the ravine toward one of the police cars. Bent over and panting to catch her breath, she held up a woman's leather tote bag. "Firefighters retrieved this bag near the wreckage," she told the captain.

"Have you checked for ID?" She rummaged through the bag and pulled out a wallet and a British passport. "Serbian national, female…late twenties…name Miliitsa Trasjic on the Serbian ID and Melissa Trask on the British passport."

The captain lifted the mic from the dashboard radio. "This is Alfa forty-six for Base… over."

"This is Base…Alfa forty-six…over."

"Do we have any information on a Miliitsa Trasjic, T-R-A-S-J-I-C… over?"

Chapter 24

Puglia, later that night

Deep into the night, no one slept at the Trasjic farmhouse. The general and his wife had shut themselves in their bedroom. He was racked with guilt, and his wife had been inconsolable since they'd received the terrible call from the Carabinieri informing them of their daughter's death.

At the kitchen table, Mihailo had set up the two computers: his sister's laptop beside his Mitchell Bank laptop. Her laptop had been configured to mirror Ben's FFL network profile. His laptop gave him access to Mitchell Banks's network and validated his profile, so he'd have the authority to override security checks. Once he transferred twenty million dollars from the FFL treasury to Mitchell Bank, it would be converted into bitcoin and transferred to Ben's bitcoin account where it would be sent to the list of addresses Neri had given him. All the withdrawals, purchase requests, and transfers of bitcoin would appear to have been executed from Ben Tano's computer, and because FFL had an account with Mitchell Bank, the bank would recognize the money as soon as its system received the notification of transfer without the usual twenty-four- to forty-eight-hour delay. The FFL financial barrier would be back up within the hour. He had to get this right. His thoughts turned to his sister for a moment, and he was filled with a sudden rush of anger and grief. *How could she have let Ben Tano get into her head?* He ran his hands through his hair and looked toward his parents' closed bedroom door. *No time to think about that now,* he thought and went back to the job at hand.

Mihailo opened his sister's computer and inserted her password. Then he navigated to connect with Ben's network profile. Within seconds, the "Insert Password" screen popped up. The system would likely require a six-digit password including a letter, a number, and a symbol. He scanned Ben's files for a clue. Most people keep all their passwords somewhere. Melissa must have discovered Ben's, but she was no longer available to help. He tried notes, memos. Finally, he searched for "passwords" and a document popped up. He typed "#Tano1," and the FFL portal opened. He sat back in his chair and covered his mouth with one hand. He was in, but his excitement soon vanished.

"Welcome Mr. Tano" appeared on the screen. He clicked on the treasury module icon. Nothing. This couldn't be happening. He couldn't fail. He watched the seconds tick by on the computer's clock. A minute passed as panic began to set in. Then, an instruction window popped up. "A five-digit code has been sent to your email address." If Ben was on his laptop at that moment, he might intercept the email. Mihailo found the code, wrote it down, and erased the message. He could complete the fraud now. He had been a good son, tried to be a good brother. As a young teenager, he'd fled the war with his parents, crossed borders illegally. He'd known stress before, but nothing like this.

He entered the five-digit code. The payment page appeared. He typed $20,000,000 into the amount field and filled in FFL's account number at Mitchell Bank. In the justification box, he noted IT equipment and requested the full amount be converted to bitcoin and pressed the Transfer button. He was now officially a criminal. If anything went wrong, they might have the whole family executed. He himself would certainly face years in jail.

A check mark appeared on the screen. Transfer successful. He checked his Mitchell Bank email account for notification of the transfer received from FFL and overrode the request for a forty-eight-hour waiting period.

He logged onto an online cryptocurrency exchange trading platform. The Sell column displayed only $10,000,000 in coins available. He purchased all of it and transferred the coins into Ben's wallet. The time on the screen read 11:13—less than one hour remaining until the financial controls at FFL would be activated. To attract sellers, he rushed to place a buy order above the trading price and waited. Melissa's computer soon began emanating a series of pinging sounds, indicating that coins were being deposited into Ben's wallet. Her computer went silent after the desired amount had been reached.

He pulled up the list Neri had sent him of accounts and amounts to be transferred and entered the numbers. He checked it to be sure. Then he took a deep breath, stood up, and walked twice around the table to shake off his nerves before sitting down again to check the figures a third time. If even a single number was wrong, the money would be lost forever. He pushed the Transfer button and closed his eyes for a moment. "A five-digit code has been sent to your email address" appeared again. He found it, entered it. He had to prove he wasn't a robot by completing a virtual jigsaw puzzle. He put the missing piece in place, and the bitcoins vanished, instantly delivered to their specified destinations.

His phone rang. Unknown number. He pressed the respond button and listened without saying a word. Neri's voice said, "*Ben fatto, amico.* Package received. Get the general to the airport and wait for my call."

Back in Rome, an exhausted Ben ate a late lunch at a small restaurant in the neighborhood. After a big meal and a couple of glasses of chianti, all he had wanted to do was relax. Melissa was with her family, and Sammy was spending time at home with his wife after the last few grueling weeks. By the morning, everything would be back to normal.

Chapter 25

Rome, the next day

Ben arrived at the office whistling, still floating on a cloud of happiness from his time with Melissa and counting the minutes until she returned from Puglia that evening. He had taken the previous night to unplug and regroup. Exhausted, he had fallen into a deep sleep and missed two calls from Melissa, but one was a voice mail saying she loved him. This was going to be a very good day, or so he thought.

Dalia looked so serious that he stopped whistling when he passed her desk. "What's going on?"

"A Carabinieri officer is waiting in your office."

When he opened his office door, a tall man in the elegant uniform of the Italian military police was standing near his desk.

"*Signor* Tano? I am Colonel Passerini."

"Yes?" Ben wondered if this might be about the ransom payment.

"One of your colleagues was involved in an accident on the coastal road near Castellana Grotte." He handed him a photocopy of a British passport and Serbian ID that had been faxed over.

Ben sank into a chair and opened the passport. Melissa's face was smiling at him.

"Uh, where is she now? She's okay…isn't she?"

"*Mi dispiace molto, molto. La donna è deceduta.*"

"Dead?! No, that's impossible… She called me yesterday… There must be some mistake."

"No, *signor*, there is no mistake."

Truth was beginning to settle in. "When did this happen?" he asked.

"We found her bag. It seems she lost control of the car. It skidded into a ravine, turned over, and..." He reached into his jacket pocket and showed Ben a police photograph. The car was a smoldering skeleton of burned and twisted steel. No one could have survived that.

Ben couldn't bear to look at it. Melissa was dead. It made no sense. He glanced at the second document, the Serbian ID, also with Melissa's face but much younger, with a Serbian name printed underneath: Miliitsa Trasjic. Miliitsa Trasjic? She must have anglicized it when she applied for her citizenship. He leaned over and hugged his stomach. He couldn't breathe, couldn't see. His brain wasn't working properly. He wasn't sure he could formulate a sentence. "Where is she? I want to see her."

"Her remains were taken to the morgue of the *Ospedale Santissima Annunziata*. The next of kin have been notified. We're told her brother will come to claim her body. I was asked to inform her employer here in Rome. *Sono molto dispiaciuto.*" With that apology, he left.

The numbness and the shock were not new. They were familiar, like slipping back into an old, ugly robe. Ben had worn that robe a long time to protect himself from the pain of Somalia. Now here it was again. Maybe he would wake up bathed in sweat and realize this was just another nightmare. Maybe the officer was mistaken. He pulled out his smartphone and frantically punched in "M." Nothing. Not even a ring. He tried it again and again. Maybe she really was dead.

"No!" he screamed. His office door was open. Dalia peeked in then closed it and left him alone. He thought of the Somali women who had buried their children along the roads of death. He felt the weight of collective grief for all the children who had been annihilated by hunger and all those who would starve in the years ahead. For most of his adult life, he had been surrounded by death, and now he was being strangled by it.

He leaned back in the chair and covered his face with his hands. He felt as though he were about to explode, but his pain was too great for tears. He thought of the dreams he had dared to believe just moments before... the possibility of a life with Melissa, feeling alive again, a new start, finally.

But death had always been there, waiting to kill him or his dreams. And he began to wail.

When he stumbled out of his office, heads lifted at every desk, but he didn't care. He went to Melissa's desk, sat in her chair, and tried to tell himself that she would never sit there again. He went through her desk drawers, trying to find some part of her, some lingering scent. A snapshot of the FLITE team was taped to the partition above her computer. He took it down and slipped it into his shirt pocket. Then he stood and stumbled out of the building.

———————

Ben drove through the streets of Rome without thinking about a destination until he noticed that he was nearing Melissa's apartment. He pulled up to the curb, glanced up at her window, and bent over the steering wheel, sobbing. He saw the face of the Carabinieri officer, the messenger of death. He saw Khaled on his knees in the sand, a gun against his forehead. He saw Jhamal, praying for his life. He saw Hassan and Leo. "All gone!" he moaned. "Why? Why?"

When he looked up, it was dusk. How long had he been there? Where could he go? He could go to his place, but it would be empty, and he couldn't bear to spend the night alone. He pulled the car into an empty space and began wandering the streets. Offices were closing, bars were filling up. Couples held hands. And he was more alone than he'd ever been in his life.

He walked aimlessly along the Tiber River, then crossed the Ponte Regina Margherita into the Prati district. Serena's mother's apartment was just a few blocks away. He pressed the button and waited. He knew that her mother was in the hospital again and wondered if Serena might still be there. He checked his watch then pressed the button again. "Who is it?" She sounded a little annoyed, as though she hadn't been expecting anyone.

"It's me."

Chapter 26

As he stepped out of the sliding doors of the Belgrade Airport arrival area, a waft of cool, crisp night air hit him squarely in the face. It was just as the general remembered it. The lights, the sounds, the smells of the city were sharp reminders of his past life and, moreover, his past transgressions. His mind flooded with pictures of his children growing up, his home, but these were quickly replaced by the images of fallen bodies and the stench of gunfire and death.

He closed his eyes to try to shut it all out for a second, but the sound of a car horn blasting next to him shook him back to reality. The black car that slid to a stop in front of him held Bosco at the wheel, and he was gesticulating wildly at Trasjic to get in.

"Welcome to Belgrade, General Trasjic. I'm sure you're pleased to be home," Bosco grunted.

"Let's just get this over with," he replied.

Bosco navigated from the airport and through the city. They passed the Beogradska Tvrđava, and the sight of the imposing fortress where the Danube and the Sava Rivers meet made the general sink further in his seat. How often had he taken his children there to learn about their rich history or even just to play and explore.

Bosco kept quiet during the drive, for once adhering to Neri's threats. Neri had warned him of the consequences of screwing with the general at this critical juncture. They needed him to make this go smoothly. He was their insurance policy.

They arrived in an old part of the city where the buildings were run-down and the storefronts were less than inviting. They pulled into the alley behind a set of stores and eateries and parked the SUV. "Get out," Bosco said sharply. Trasjic followed Bosco to a steel door, and they entered the kitchen of a busy restaurant. Surprisingly, no one seemed to even notice them.

Bosco headed to a set of stairs leading to the basement with the general at his heels. They descended the rickety wooden steps and then tread through a corridor past a few doors to the last door on the right. "After you, General," Bosco said with feigned politeness, pushing the door open to a dimly lit room where two men sat, one with his feet up on the table in front of them, his leather boots worn and scuffed. They were clearly expecting company. When they saw Trasjic enter, they jumped to their feet. The general recognized the two men immediately. They had served under him during his administration but were not big players in the events of the war. *Looks like they've upped their game a bit,* Trasjic thought. *Arms dealers make a lot more than clerks, I bet.*

"General Trasjic, it's been a long time," said the man who had been sitting with his feet up. "You do remember us, yes?" He smiled, but it was an unpleasant smile, not the kind that puts a person at ease.

"Yes," he replied softly. "Milorad and…" He groped for the other man's name.

"Branko," the other man replied and reached out his hand to shake the general's, but the gesture was denied. His face tightened into a grimace as he looked at his empty hand. He shrugged and returned to his seat.

"What do you want from me?" Trasjic asked, looking from one man to the other. Just then, the door opened and Neri entered, shoving Bosco to the side.

"They want assurance that you are part of this operation," Neri said. "They trust you, the fugitive."

"Yes, General. We have been told that you will accompany our goods to the delivery point. If that's the case, the deal is on."

"I'm here, aren't I?" the general answered. "I will do what is expected of me. But I need to know the risks I'll be taking."

"All right, then," Milorad said, gesturing toward an empty chair. "Everything is ready to be loaded onto a cargo plane headed to Cuba. You will be on that plane." He leaned forward and locked eyes with Trasjic before he continued, "Our people will meet you and unload the cargo in a designated warehouse where the contents will be stuffed into four shipping containers. You will be given papers saying you are an agent for Food for Livelihood, a humanitarian organization, with a manifest to clear the containers for export by ship from Santiago de Cuba to the final destination, Buenaventura, Colombia. The manifest will read that the containers hold IT equipment to be used as humanitarian aid. We will then fly you to Panama City, where Food for Livelihood has its headquarters, so it will appear plausible that you work for them, but you must keep a low profile until you board the ship. Are we clear?"

"Yes," the general said, his lips tightening. He was not a fool. He knew the stakes.

"Once you clear airport customs, you will be met by our agents who will arrange the paperwork to transit the canal and assist you to board the ship. They will be informed that you are an agent for Food for Livelihood accompanying the shipment as an IT expert to assist in setting up the equipment in Buenaventura. Mr. Neri and Mr. Bosco will meet you in Colombia to handle clearances at that end."

Trasjic looked from Bosco to Neri. Neri's face was like a stone, but Bosco wore a silly grin. *This man is an imbecile,* Trasjic thought. *How did he get involved in something this complicated?*

Milorad continued, "Once the cargo is handed over to the buyer, your job is done. You can collect your share and disappear for good. But...it is critical that you be present for the loading and unloading operations as a neutral party so you can guarantee the contents to our buyer. Our transit points are routine now—the only risk might be in Panama—but we have excellent contacts on the inside. You will get all the details on a need-to-know basis for your own protection. Any questions?"

"Why do you need me?"

Milorad looked directly at Neri then back at the general. He locked eyes with him and said, "I know you, General. We are risking millions of dollars on our new clients. We trust you will protect our investment."

"I'm not a general anymore. I am just a man with a family…or what is left of it," he added bitterly.

"Exactly," Milo replied. "We remember your devotion to your family. We know you will do whatever it takes to protect them, and we know you will do whatever it takes to stay away from the Hague. Are we clear?"

"We're clear," Trasjic said with a sigh.

Chapter 27

Meanwhile, on an island in the Caribbean Sea

Port-au-Prince, Haiti, 4:53 p.m.

Jean-Bertrand and Lucien had completed their last delivery of food assistance to a shelter in the foothills of Pétion-Ville on the outskirts of the capital and were on their way back to the FFL country office when their pickup truck began tossing about.

"Qu'est-ce que c'est?"

"Tremblement de terre! Earthquake!"

Lucien gripped the door handle. The roadside shacks were disintegrating, and the tarmac was shredding into thick, black ribbons. Jean-Bertrand couldn't control the steering wheel. The truck veered off the road and collided with a pile of debris.

"Putain!"

Fifty-three seconds later, the earth stilled and an eerie silence settled over the city. A magnitude 7.0 earthquake—equivalent to 32 million tons of exploding TNT—had hit ten miles southwest of the capital.

The two men slumped in their seats, dazed from the impact, coughing up white dust.

Lucien stumbled out of the truck to brush away the debris that had accumulated on the windshield. *"Dieu, sauvez-nous!"* he murmured. *God save us!*

Port-au-Prince had been leveled, its skyline replaced by a thick cloud of dark smoke. The force of the quake had set off a chain reaction, causing buildings to crash to the ground, story upon story. Utility poles were scattered about, the severed ends of their high-voltage wires sparking like strings of life-threatening Christmas lights. Hundreds of fires raged amid the rubble.

Within minutes, the eerie silence was broken by sirens, and the cries of survivors rose in waves. Jean-Bertrand frantically turned the key in the ignition, but the engine refused to spark. Lucien began pushing the truck downhill until it picked up enough speed for Jean-Bertrand to pop the clutch, and they began to navigate the destroyed road.

They drove slowly through piles of debris, veering left and right to find traction. "Watch out for that woman!" Jean-Bertrand slammed on the brakes, missing her by inches. She banged on the hood with her bloodied hand, crying, "*Je vous en prie,* help me!"

They stopped, although every minute they delayed could mean the difference between life and death for their own families.

"*Merci, Dieu vous bénisse.*"

"Don't worry, we'll help you," Lucien said. "What's your name?"

"Marie-Louise."

"Marie-Louise, give me your apron. I'm going to wrap your leg to slow the bleeding until we find a hospital."

They gently lifted her into the back of the truck. When they reached the outskirts of the city, they were struck by the extent of the devastation. It looked as though Port-au-Prince had been swallowed up by the earth, leaving only piles of burning rubble behind. Survivors wailed as they dug under the debris with shovels, picks, and bare hands in the hope of finding a loved one still alive. Many of the wounded lay where they had fallen, while others wandered the streets in a daze, their clothes in tatters, their bodies covered in dirt and blood.

As Jean-Bertrand and Lucien drove on slowly, survivors began to crowd the truck, banging on the doors and holding their bleeding children up to the windows, begging for help. They stopped to assist as many as they could until the truck could hold no more.

At first, they didn't realize that only one wall of the Hôpital Sainte Marie was left standing. The hospital grounds had already been trans-formed into an open-air operating theater where medical teams worked frantically to help the scores of wounded, prioritizing those with life-threatening injuries. Those who had survived unscathed waited to donate blood until supplies could be flown in to meet the overwhelming demand. Jean-Bertrand stopped the truck to evacuate the wounded and hurried on.

All that remained of the Food for Livelihood office was the flag, which hung limply from its pole. Petra, the country representative, was speaking to headquarters in Rome on a satellite phone while shouting instructions pell-mell to staff desperately digging through the rubble.

Jean-Bertrand and Lucien called out, "Petra! What can we do?"

"We're still looking for Angeline and the others. Go check on your families first. Hurry!" Jean-Bertrand stepped on the gas.

The streets leading into the neighborhood were blocked by mountains of debris, so they were forced to abandon the truck and continue on foot.

Lucien found his youngest son, four-year-old Jacques, wandering naked through the rubble, bloodied by cuts and scrapes that covered his body, his face expressionless. Lucien waved and shouted, "Jacques, Jacques, *voici* Papa," and thrashed against the tide of debris to reach the little boy. Jacques froze in his tracks, tears streaming down his cheeks, until his father scooped him up and hugged him to his chest.

"Shhh…it's all right… Papa's here now." He kissed the boy's forehead and rocked him back and forth, cupped the tear-streaked face in his hands, and asked the dreaded questions: "Jacques, where is Maman? Where is your brother?"

"Papa…" he sobbed, "*perdus…*" Pointing his tiny finger to the ground, he added, "*Là-bas!*"

Chapter 28

It was nearly midnight in Rome, but Sammy had convened an emergency meeting in Food for Livelihood's operations room. Four flat-screen monitors flashed the latest newscasts and photos of the situation while the emergency team rushed to assemble the latest briefing materials—color printouts of the country showing the infrastructure of Haiti's ports, road networks, and airports as well as statistics on Food for Livelihood's global assets. Every moment of delay would cost lives.

Twenty of FFL's most experienced managers, coffee mugs in hand, crowded around the table. Natasha was organizing a conference call on the Spider, a five-pronged speaker phone. An automated female voice confirmed the participants as they connected to the group: "Panama has joined the conference." Then Washington, New York, and Brussels.

"What about Haiti?" Ben asked.

"We're still trying… I'm calling Dr. A. now that everyone else is present," responded Natasha.

While they waited for Port-au Prince, Sammy rushed in and seated himself at the head of the table near Natasha, who leaned over and whispered updates.

"Thank you for coming at such short notice," he began. "We have a lot of ground to cover, so we'll get started as soon as Haiti is on the line."

Everyone in the room was silent until they heard the crackle of static, followed by the computer voice, "Haiti has joined the conference."

"Hello, Petra, Sammy here speaking from Rome. Can you hear me?"

Petra was a middle-aged German, one of the toughest and most experienced Food for Livelihood country representatives. Her voice came through faintly. "Yes, Sammy, I hear you, but please move closer to the mic."

"Petra, we have Washington, New York, Brussels, and Panama on the line. In Rome, I am joined by logistics, IT, procurement, shipping, programs, personnel, finance, donor relations, and public information. Before getting into the operational details, I want to know about the staff. Are you all accounted for? How are you coping?"

"We were lucky to have one of the stronger buildings." She sounded exhausted. "It gave us time to get out before it collapsed…but not everyone from the upper floors made it. Three of our staff are dead, and five are missing. I lost my secretary, Angeline…" Her voice cracked. "She was expecting her first child." Ben stared at the speaker phone. "Emergency Services hasn't arrived yet. We're trying to dig them out with our hands and whatever we can find."

"Bloody hell!" Sammy ran his hand through his hair. "What about their families?"

"We don't know yet. Many of the staff have stayed here to help start up our relief efforts. Those who went home haven't reported back yet, but from what I'm seeing, I'm afraid the numbers will be high."

"Keep me updated on the casualties. I'll need a complete list of staff and their family members. Food for Livelihood must come together to provide extraordinary assistance to our families in need."

"I'll take care of it."

"What about you, Petra? Your home…Dan?" Sammy asked.

There was a small pause. "My home is gone and I haven't been able to find Dan," she said, her voice strained.

"Damn! Well, your better half is a tough character. I'm sure he'll turn up," Sammy said.

"I hope you're right. I'll let you know as soon as I hear," Petra replied.

"All right, well then," Sammy continued, "can you give us a preliminary assessment of the situation and tell us how FFL should respond?" Sammy knew Petra was torn between saving her staff and finding Dan.

She and Dan had been partners for over ten years. He was her support system, her rock. But she was a rock herself. He knew she would carry on with the job no matter what. He was counting on it.

"Sammy, this disaster is unlike anything I've ever seen. Preliminary estimates are more than two hundred thousand dead and two to three million affected. The quake obliterated the infrastructure, the communications, and the entire economy of the country in one blow... Even the president's palace was destroyed."

Ben watched in horror as photographs came on the screens.

"I see the satellite photos," Sammy said. "Unbelievable... You're right...not much is still standing."

"There are no services whatsoever—no banking, post, electricity, water, or government administration. The only entry point into Port-au-Prince is a single-lane airstrip, which means our options are limited."

Ben began mentally ticking off a list of response assets: food, staff, logistics, IT. The local airstrip wouldn't be able to accommodate cargo planes. They'd have to establish an air bridge from the regional supply hub in Panama City to the Dominican Republic.

"The aid community has been impacted by the loss of staff and assets, which will further compromise the relief effort. The UN building collapsed, and a hundred people died, including the UN representative and head of the Peacekeepers. We're meeting later today with the Haitian government, the UN, the U.S. military, and all the NGOs to coordinate our response."

"Do you have a response plan yet?"

"We have to reach three million people with enough high-energy biscuits for one week until cooking facilities can be established at the shelters, clinics, and schools."

Sammy nodded and looked around the room. "How much have we lost there?"

"We were able to salvage a few phones, our fleet of vehicles where we plan to sleep tonight, and our warehouse stocks. But our offices, our communications, and our homes are gone. We need everything from toilet paper to toothbrushes."

"We'll get you everything you need," he said, closing his eyes and pinching the bridge of his nose.

He spoke into the Spider to Washington, New York, Brussels, and Panama while looking around the table at his team in Rome. "The people of Haiti need us, and we're not going to let them down. Given the complexity of the relief effort," he glanced at Ben, "Ben Tano, our director of emergencies, will be deployed to Port-au-Prince immediately to coordinate all aspects of this operation."

Everyone turned to Ben, who was staring at Sammy. This would be his first operational assignment since Somalia. Sammy must think he could handle it, but his performance during the hostage transfer couldn't have inspired much confidence. And he was reeling from the shock of Melissa's death.

Sammy gave him a confident smile and said, "Okay, Ben, I'm turning the floor over to you."

Ben began tentatively, feeling his colleagues' sympathetic eyes. He had to sound in control. "The next seven- to ten-day period is the critical window. FFL must act now to deliver supplies. The threat of more lost lives and widespread disease is hanging over Haiti."

"Petra," Ben asked, leaning into the speaker phone, "what about the available stocks of food? The figures we have are 10,000 metric tons in the central warehouse and another 5,000 at the port."

"That's correct on paper, but we can't reach them. The police have cordoned off our warehouse until the structure can be certified by a city engineer, which is going to take time. They have other priorities—hospitals, banks, schools, military barracks."

"We could send an engineer. Would that speed up the process? What about the port?"

"The port was damaged, and all the agencies are fighting to get their stocks out. It's operated by a mafia of three families who serve the highest bidder."

"Petra, I can take care of that problem," Sammy interjected. "I'll speak to the American ambassador...the U.S. owes me a favor."

"Sammy, Ben," Petra said, "hang on. I'm getting some news... I've just heard that SOUTHCOM, the U.S. military base on the northern side of the island, is intact. The U.S. has agreed to allow the humanitarian organizations to use their airstrip and warehousing and will give us tents to serve as our offices until we regain our operational capacity."

"Excellent!" Ben turned to their aviation expert, a former military officer from France. "Nicolàs, identify all available aviation assets. We'll create an air bridge from our regional supply hub to SOUTHCOM. Samuel and I will negotiate the landing slots, which should streamline the supply chain and reduce the bottlenecks they would have faced flying into the Dominican Republic."

"Is Panama still on the line?" Ben asked, finding his stride.

"Affirmative, Ben," said Pablo Mendes, the FFL regional director.

"Pablo, airlift supplies from our contingency warehouse in Panama to Haiti: biscuits, prefabs, beds, blankets, tents, cooking utensils—whatever you can lay your hands on. I want that warehouse emptied and refilled within 48 hours. Do you copy?"

"Yes, Ben, we'll be ready with the first planeload within two hours. The question is whether or not we can secure a landing slot at SOUTHCOM. We may need headquarters to liaise with the U.S. military on this," responded Pablo.

Sammy nodded in agreement.

Ben turned to the shipping officer, Karl Dricker, a Brit with thirty years' experience. "Karl, track all the vessels on the high seas to identify which of them can be diverted to Haiti. And look into cruise ships that can be converted into a hotel for staff lodging. It can be anchored offshore. We need to give them a place to clean up and rest. There aren't enough tents, cots, portable toilets, and showers to accommodate the influx of the response teams.

"Fritz," Ben said to the director of procurement, "within two hours, I'll need a list of all the stocks in our warehouses in Latin America, as well as all ongoing food purchases." He turned to the tireless director of donor relations and said, "Claudia, liaise with the U.S. to see if they can donate those ready-to-eat meals the military uses. The Haitians will need food they can open and eat on the spot. We'll use the air bridge to fly it in. Activate our emergency supplier agreements to start delivering 100,000 tons of cereal. Once people start to cook again, the demand will go through the roof, and we need to be ready."

"Rose," he nodded to the director of personnel, "prepare to deploy a surge of staff capacity. Directors, I expect you to put forward your very best people. It's gonna be tough out there. We need experienced staff with proven track records who have cut their teeth on our complex emergencies: the tsunami, Pakistan, the Horn. I want this to be the strongest team we've ever put together. The list should be finalized by lunchtime today. Thank you, everyone. That's all for now. Sammy, over to you."

"Petra," Sammy said, "tell us about security."

"There's been extensive looting, a total breakdown of law and order. Four thousand prisoners are on the loose. We'll need to bolster the existing security arrangements…escorts during distributions, armored vehicles, and so on."

"Is New York on the line?" Sammy continued.

"Affirmative, sir."

"Mohamed, monitor how the Security Council is planning to respond."

"I've been told it plans to meet tomorrow, but the time is not confirmed."

"Washington, Brussels, are you there?"

"Affirmative."

"Find out what the U.S. and the European Commission are considering in terms of funding. I've instructed finance to advance one hundred million dollars in start-up costs, and I want assurances that this is in line with donor pledges."

He looked at Ben who nodded. "Start working the phones with our other donors—including the private sector—until we reach our target. For our next meeting, I want the list of donors and their pledges."

Sammy stood up and began collecting his notes. "We'll wrap this up for now. Thank you all for coming. We'll reconvene tomorrow at 15:00. Now, let's get cracking. We have three million hungry Haitians to feed." Then he turned on his heel, exited the door, and started down the hall.

Ben dashed after him. As the elevator doors were closing, he stuck his foot between them until they reopened to allow him inside. "Sammy, we need to talk."

"What is it, Ben?"

"Why am I the last to know what's going on, especially when it concerns me?"

"Do you mean my decision to send you to Haiti? FLITE is up and functioning now. There's no one better suited to handle this. All things considered, it might be best for you to get away from Rome and back to the field. Go do what you do best, Ben. You need that." Sammy locked eyes with Ben, and without having to say another word, Ben knew that he was right. But he would be on shaky ground, literally.

"I just wish you'd talked it over with me first." Ben still had a hard time making decisions, and Sammy was pushing him too fast. With the successful launch of FLITE, he had started feeling comfortable working at headquarters, but now, without Melissa, he felt rudderless again. He wasn't sure he could handle the stress of being thrown into a major humanitarian crisis.

"I didn't mean to spring it on you," Sammy said. "I looked around the room and didn't see anyone who could do the job better. You're the only chap I trust to be my operational arm on the ground. Now pull up your socks, and have a safe journey!"

Before Ben could argue, the elevator doors had opened and Sammy was gone.

Chapter 29

Ben took the first available flight from Rome to Madrid, then on to Santo Domingo, the closest airport to Haiti. He was traveling with just a knapsack and a gym bag loaded with FFL emergency cash so he could breeze through customs. He expected to be met by an FFL driver who would take him overland to Port-au-Prince, but a representative of United Parcel Service greeted him holding a cardboard sign with his name scrawled on it. This man knew the area better than even the FFL drivers, all of whom were busy assisting volunteers and families anyway.

He followed him to a cargo plane carrying food, tents, sleeping bags, and office equipment. It all felt so familiar, as though he had come home. Sammy had been right. He was energized by the challenge of providing life-saving food to three million Haitians—a greater purpose beyond wallowing in his own grief.

Thirty minutes later, they reached SOUTHCOM, a U.S. military base established to keep an eye on Cuba and monitor narcotics traffic. Before landing, the pilot conducted a flyover to study the strip. Ben peered through the window, surveying the damage. The landscape had been reduced to smoldering ruins. The magnitude of the devastation was staggering. He knew it would take billions of dollars to rebuild one of the world's poorest countries.

The plane circled the small base for ten minutes before it was given a slot, then landed fast and hard to make way for other planes still in a holding pattern. When the hatch at the back of the plane opened, the combined noise of arriving and departing aircraft and forklifts was deafening. People ran helter-skelter in all directions, while pallet after pallet of relief goods were stacked like towers along makeshift streets. The available warehousing was filling up so fast that all new cargo had to be stored outside, protected by tarps.

Food for Livelihood's NGO camp was somewhere inside the compound, but Ben needed directions to find it. When he tried to approach one of the people rushing by, he got a look that said, "Don't bother me. Can't you see I'm busy?" He spotted a U.S. Marine guard patrolling the gates and waved his Food for Livelihood ID card, shouting, "Where's…Food…for… Livelihood?"

"Straight ahead…half mile…left side… Look for the flag."

An overwhelming stench emanated from outside the compound where thousands of corpses were laid out on the streets waiting to be identified, and packs of starving dogs roamed among them, snarling and snapping their jaws in a frenzy as they tore into the rotting flesh. Ben stood there, immobilized, adrenalin pumping. He told himself that he wasn't in danger and tried to control his breathing.

The sight of the familiar Food for Livelihood flag fluttering in the light sea breeze focused him, and he began to methodically tick off the key information he'd received. A large, green military tent was serving as a makeshift office for thirty people while the additional tents Pablo had flown in from Panama were being erected by a team of logisticians. The IT staff had mounted two communication towers.

Inside the tent, he recognized a tall imposing woman wearing an FFL vest and cap. Petra had served in some of the most difficult conflict countries—Iraq, Burundi, and Sierra Leone—and had accepted an easier assignment in Haiti to catch her breath.

Ben approached her from behind and gently tapped her shoulder, but she was so absorbed in her briefing, she ignored it. When she finally looked up from her notes, her staff were smiling and pointing at him.

"Petra?"

"What?" she barked impatiently. Then she turned and saw him. "Ben Tano! You made it! Happy to see you."

"Well, you know Sammy. He makes it all happen. How are you holding up?" He hugged her.

She was pale and thin and looked as though she hadn't slept since the earthquake.

"Well, I was lucky. My house was destroyed, and I lost all my things, but I found my Dan," she said with a smile.

Ben whistled. "That was a close call."

"Still, the death toll keeps rising. Two nights ago, I had dinner with twelve of my closest friends, and now only seven of us are alive. My staff are suffering tremendous losses. My deputy, Lucien, lost most of his family. It's just him and his youngest son now." For a moment, she struggled to pull herself together then continued with forced cheeriness, "Jean-Bertrand is filling in for him… You'll meet him. Now, what about you? I heard through the FFL grapevine that you've been through a rough patch since Kabuk. I'm sorry about the team…I know you and Leo go way back, but I was surprised that you and Serena split up. I thought she was good for you."

"Maybe, but I couldn't keep it all together as you do."

"I'm lucky. Dan inhabits our world and can travel with me to dangerous places. He knows my career comes first, but he also knows I love him. We share those parts of ourselves that meet beyond the hustle and bustle of saving the world. I need that, and I'm sure you do too."

"Yeah, maybe… Anyway…tell me what you need."

"Frankly, we're struggling. As you see, our temporary quarters aren't fully set up yet, although we expect to be finished within a few hours. The only good news is that our cell phones are working again, but service is sporadic. We're lucky to have internet in the compound, but the system can't cope with so many users."

"What else have we got to work with?"

"Pablo's planes arrived this morning, which is a start, but it's not enough. We've got clothes, food, and supplies to last us one week at most."

"Before I left Rome, I approved twenty million dollars in biscuits, warehousing, portable offices, housing, and IT equipment for the Panama City office to replenish our humanitarian hub and set up an air bridge to Haiti. And this should help a little in the meantime," he smiled as he handed over the gym bag. Her eyes widened when she unzipped it. "Wow! How much is in here? We'll deposit it immediately."

"Five hundred thousand, but I thought the banks had collapsed. That's why we couldn't send anything to you directly."

She grabbed his arm and walked him around the corner of the tent where a white 2006 KIA Sportage was parked, covered in debris. "That's our FFL bank."

"You're fuckin' kidding me. How much do you plan to keep there?"

"With your deposit, we'll have about a million and a half, but we'll need double that to restart our operations. It's as safe there as anywhere else."

He laughed and said, "When you have time, you can count it and give me a receipt." How ironic that they were ready to roll out blockchain technology in the capital city of a country where the whole banking system, physical infrastructure, and IT connectivity networks had been swallowed by an earthquake. They wouldn't be able to tender, input contracts, or pay upon delivery online until the infrastructure was rebuilt. He was operating like a drug cartel mule, hand-carrying cash. While the chances of a major catastrophe of this magnitude reoccurring in a capital city were small, the FFL response teams would be better prepared next time.

As they strolled back to the tent, he asked, "What's the status of our operational response?"

"About an hour ago, we began the first distribution to twelve thousand victims living in shelters—biscuits, water, and purification tablets, which we borrowed from the UN peacekeepers."

"Well done. How the hell…?"

"They don't call me 'the bull' for nothing."

"Let's get down to business then, shall we?" As they sat at a small folding card table, the earth beneath them began to tremble, and the light bulbs hanging from the ceiling began to swing wildly. Yet another aftershock.

"Everyone, take cover!" Petra yelled, and they all dove to the ground, covering their heads and bracing themselves. Sirens screamed, and people staggered past them like drunkards leaving a bar.

When the aftershock finally passed, they got back up and checked for damages. Somehow, it all seemed normal. But they were not normal people, and this was not a normal life.

"Where were we before we were interrupted?"

"How is the situation evolving?" Ben asked. "I want to make sure your requirements are fast-tracked so we're able to respond to the changing scenarios."

"Food for Livelihood and the other humanitarian organizations are facing an impossible task. The needs are overwhelming, and even as we refine our assessments, they escalate. Plus, we're hampered by all these after-shocks. Food isn't the only problem right now."

"What is?"

"The biggest concern is an outbreak of disease. The city's water and sanitation systems are badly damaged, and people are living out in the open without potable water or toilet facilities, so the danger of cholera is very real. We're working closely with the UN to coordinate our sector priorities in food, logistics, shelter, water, sanitation, and health."

"The question is, how long will it take before we can go to scale?" Ben had to yell over the noise of airplanes taking off and landing.

"For homeless families moving to the camps, we plan to deliver hot meals from mobile kitchens, but our stocks will only last a few days." She yawned, unable to hide her exhaustion. "We'll need the equivalent of thirty thousand sacks of grain per day to start them up in the next ten to fourteen days. I've been told the U.S. military is ready to release five million of its ready-to-eat meals, but it's hardly enough when you're dealing with such a large caseload."

Ben listened carefully to every word and jotted notes so he could give Sammy a summary. "What about the staff?"

"What do you mean?"

He already knew how she would react. "Sammy thinks they should be evacuated to Santo Domingo for a few days of rest and recuperation once we have the new team in place. You can't keep working them for weeks on end in these conditions."

"You know as well as I do, they won't agree. We're a team. They know the country, the programs, and the people. They won't turn their backs on Haiti now when they're needed the most. Maybe they'll consider Sammy's offer when things stabilize."

"And what about you? You've lost your home, friends, staff. It takes time to recover from these things. When are you going to take a few days off?"

She understood where the discussion was leading and exploded, "What can you be thinking?! I've got millions of people who don't know where their next meal is coming from, and you're asking me to take a vacation? My place is right here. We'll worry about the Haitians now and about me later…case closed."

Chapter 30

The next morning, Ben woke up to the smell of coffee brewing on an open fire. It wasn't yet five, but the local team was already in full swing. Despite the physical discomfort, he'd slept peacefully for the first time since Melissa's death. Coming to Haiti had been the right decision. Surrounded by a team like old times, he felt comforted, renewed. He emerged from his sleeping bag, splashed some water from a jerry can on his face, and with a quick change of underwear, he quickly dressed and was ready for action. Water was restricted until portable showers and toilets could be set up. At the breakfast table, he found Petra and her staff, coffee, bread, jam, and canned juice.

Petra reviewed the day's plans with Ben and her team. The French military had just finished clearing away the rubble at the market square where they'd make their distribution. "You all know the drill," she said. "Register the beneficiaries and distribute the biscuits, water, and tablets. Okay, let's move out."

The two-mile drive to the distribution point took nearly an hour. The roads were filled with rubble and pitted with gaping holes. When they arrived, people were already milling around, anxiously waiting for their trucks. Community leaders were trying to organize them into lines. Petra requested a military escort in case things got out of control and their stocks were ransacked.

The minute they were spotted, crowds began pushing and shoving. The escort fired shots in the air to prevent children and the elderly from being trampled to death. Ben considered the size of the crowd and worried what would happen if they had to turn some people away empty-handed.

"This is not good," Petra said. "We didn't plan for this many people. Our estimates were around 12,000 from this neighborhood, but I'm guessing we're looking at 50,000 or more. We risk mass rioting."

"Call your deputy," he said. "Tell him to bring everything you've got in stock. We can't contain a crowd this big."

Petra picked up her satellite phone and called Jean-Bertrand. "Jean? Écoute, we need more food. Empty whatever you've got in the warehouse. Get it to Market Square. *Oui, oui…tout.* We need it now to avoid a stampede. *Dépêche-toi.*"

In the middle of all this, Ben's phone rang. "Hello, Sammy."

"I've got just a few minutes. How's it going?" asked Sammy.

"Honestly, it looks like Armageddon. All the organizations are struggling to provide the most basic form of aid without adequate staff, communications, or logistical support. I'm at a distribution point with Petra. She's clearing out all the stocks from the warehouses, but it won't be enough. The demand is too great. She and her staff are exhausted. We need to get reinforcements in here right away."

"Understood, Ben. We're working to gear up, but it will take time before we become fully operational. The mobile kitchens should be arriving tonight, and I've diverted a 60,000-ton liner. The one hundred emergency staff you requested should be arriving within twenty-four hours, followed by a floating hotel. But until we get up to speed, you're going to have to prioritize."

"Easy to say, but how do you prioritize hunger?" He remembered how this felt, the pressure to match Sammy's expectations and the demands of the donors and the press when operational realities were severely limited. Sammy was working to support them, but meanwhile, they were left on their own to optimize whatever food they had with on-the-spot decisions.

He heard Sammy's exasperated sigh. "Well, at least you can tell Petra I've solved her little problem at the port. You've got three days to get the food out. It should tide us over until shipments start flowing through the supply chain."

"Let me guess…Secretary Howard?"

"It was well worth the favor. Please keep me informed."

"Will do."

"Howard, who's Howard? Does he work for us?" Petra asked as she walked up behind him.

"Not exactly. Sammy called in a favor. He says you're free to pick up the cargo from the port. He's cleared it."

"Whew! That must have been some favor. The authorities here have expensive tastes. Now we can get the mobile kitchens started."

Ben was about to return to the supply chain crisis when, out of the corner of his eye, he saw a frail old woman being turned away from the distribution line. He rushed past Petra and dashed into the crowd.

"Ben, where are you going?" she called after him.

"Just a sec," he yelled over his shoulder.

He approached the field monitor who was doing the registration and asked him in rudimentary French, *"Excusez-moi, pourquoi avez-vous refusé cette femme?* Why have you turned that woman away?"

"She refused to be registered. She remembers the fingerprinting by Papa Doc's secret police," he answered in English.

"Take a look around you. Today we feed everyone and worry about the registration later, okay?"

"But Madame Petra…"

"I will speak with Madame Petra."

He put together a sack of biscuits, water, and purification tablets, ran after the old woman, and placed the sack of rations in her arms. *"C'est pour vous."* The sack was too heavy for her to carry, so he gently took it back and motioned for her to lead the way.

"Notre maison est là-bas…" She pointed sadly to the other side of the square. What remained of her home was nothing more than a mound of rubble covered in crucifixes. Ben followed her and paid his respects at the makeshift graveyard. In halting Creole-laced French, she told him that she had lost her husband, her son, and daughter-in-law, all of them buried

beneath the wreckage of their home. A small boy tugged on the old woman's apron. Her four grandchildren, who had been playing outside when the ground started to shake, had managed to survive.

When he got back to the distribution site, Ben found Petra supervising the off-loading of new deliveries from the warehouse. "What the hell was that all about…changing my instructions? Imagine if everyone started doing his own thing! This operation would spin out of control before it got started. I need to keep a tight grip."

"Petra," he smiled, hoping to calm her down, "today I'm reminded of what Sammy once told me: 'Managers do things right, but leaders do the right thing.' We've got to go with our instincts on this one. I learned that lesson in Somalia. We'll refine the process as we go, but let's feed everybody we can right now."

In the early afternoon, Petra took him to the airport where a Russian Ilyushin aircraft, chartered by Food for Livelihood, stood waiting. It had been quickly converted into a cargo plane to ferry passengers and equipment back and forth between Panama City and Haiti. She stood on the tarmac as he climbed up the rickety stairs to the cabin then turned around to wave goodbye.

"Thanks for stopping in, Ben," she called out over the roar of the engines.

He gave her a thumbs-up and yelled, "I'll be back soon. Keep up the good work!"

Chapter 31

Ben stepped into the Ilyushin and strapped himself to one of the makeshift fiberglass benches along the sides of the fuselage. Also on the plane were thirty exhausted humanitarian aid workers and several of the most critically injured victims of the quake. The air was filled with the heavy stench of dried blood and body waste emanating from two rows of stretchers in the middle section. Immobilized, with blood-stained bandages, temporary splints, and portable IVs, the wounded lay staring vacantly at the ceiling as the plane flew westward over the Caribbean Sea.

When they hit pockets of turbulence, children whimpered and clung tightly to their caretakers. Ben saw the fear and shock in their eyes. They had surely been traumatized by the devastation of the earthquake and, now, the terror of the flight. He smiled at them and whispered comforting words.

He passed the time reviewing all the measures that needed to be put in place to get the supply chain up and running to scale. It seemed effortless. He was back in his element. His encounters with the old woman and the dedicated staff had made him feel part of something good and pure, and he was proud of his work. In that moment, his life had a higher purpose than his own survival.

The landing was rough. The pilot had to brake hard to avoid over-shooting the runway at Tocumen International Airport. The stretchers came loose from their moorings, and an IV stand whizzed by Ben's head, hitting the aid worker strapped in beside him. Blood was running down the man's face, so Ben pressed his bandana against the gaping wound.

The medical personnel onboard sprang into action, comforting their patients as they untangled the pileup of stretchers and IV stands scattered about like a game of pick-up sticks.

A line of ambulances met them at the gate, sirens blaring and lights flashing. The back hatch was lowered, and one by one, the stretchers were rolled down and loaded into them for transfer to the Panama City hospital.

When the last stretcher was loaded, Ben disembarked with the other passengers, leaving the discomfort of the nearly three-hour journey behind him.

The terminal was crowded with passengers, many of whom were aid workers traveling back and forth to Haiti. The long hallway leading to the customs area was decorated with colorful posters showcasing upscale restaurants, sandy white beaches, five-star resorts, and casinos. Panama had become a staging area for aid to Haiti, so the lines at customs clearance were unusually long and slow-moving. Ben waited nearly an hour before he was called forward.

"What brings you to Panama?"

"I've come from Haiti where I've been helping with the relief efforts," he said. "I'm with the NGO Food for Livelihood. I plan to spend a few days at our regional office and then fly back."

The woman in the booth took his passport and ran it through a scanner. Then she repeated the process, scrutinizing the screen more closely. "Just a moment, please."

"Is everything okay?" he asked.

"Wait here, please," she said. "I'll be with you shortly." And she hurried away.

Ben's nerves were already on edge. He had experienced these delays many, many times, and they were never pleasant. He might fit the profile of a drug runner or be shaken down for a bribe to get his passport back. He stood there, shifting his weight from one foot to the other, staring aimlessly at the passengers moving through the lines on either side of him. A few booths over, he spotted a distinctive looking man, tall and silver-haired, with a deep red birthmark on his forehead. He couldn't remember where he'd seen him before.

When he heard someone return to the counter, he turned to face a different woman; this one was attractive, toned, her deep brown hair tucked into a chignon. She appeared no-nonsense, with an understated power. *I bet she wouldn't take shit from anyone.* The thought made Ben smile unexpectedly. She was wearing a military uniform with a badge that read Alejandra López. "Your passport, Mr. Tano. There was a problem in the system, so we had to issue your visa manually. Please excuse the delay." She spoke with an accent clearly not Panamanian, but her English was perfect.

Her smile reassured him. "Thank you," he replied, realizing he was disheveled, a man traveling alone. *I fit the perfect profile of a drug runner.* He took a good look at her uniform. The insignia on the sleeve bore the yellow, blue, and red of the Colombian flag. *What was she doing at the airport in Panama?*

"I see you work for Food for Livelihood!" she said.

"Yes."

"My brother and I were enrolled in your school feeding program as children. It got us out of the barrios and gave us a future. Thank you for your service."

"Thank you for telling me that. Stories like yours keep me going." He was surprised by her friendliness. He liked her but wasn't a hundred percent sure he could trust her. The less he said, the less trouble he'd have, and the line behind him was restless. So, he moved on, but as he turned to leave, he said, "It was a pleasure to meet you, Officer López."

She nodded back at him then turned and walked away with a gait that spoke to her military bearing.

Outside the airport, a car was waiting to take him to the FFL regional office in a suburb called the City of Knowledge, which had once been the property of the U.S. government. In 1977, Jimmy Carter negotiated the return of the Panama Canal and the adjacent military base with its American-style homes, manicured lawns, and swimming pools. Now it was the location of research centers and humanitarian organizations such as Food for Livelihood, which was housed in one of the former Marine barracks.

Staffers were working the phones, shouting instructions, placing orders, and waving letters and contracts at the boss for his signature. Tables and desks were littered with coffee cups and empty pizza boxes. Sleeping bags and pillows were stashed in a corner. They had been working twenty-four seven to mount the massive logistics operation, along with colleagues in Port-au-Prince and Rome.

He scanned the space for his friend and called out when he heard the familiar Chilean accent. Pablo's head emerged from one of the partitioned offices. "Ben! I'm glad you're back, my friend. You're a welcome sight."

Pablo was now in his sixties and close to retiring after thirty-five years with Food for Livelihood. As a parting gift, Sammy had made him the regional director for Panama City so he'd be closer to home.

"Come in. Come in, Ben. Put down your bag and take a seat," he said, throwing an arm around him. His office had been converted into a situation room, replicating the one in Rome. The walls were plastered with maps of Haiti and two flat screens were tuned to news stations. The desk was cluttered with briefing papers, newspaper clippings, and brochures from regional suppliers who wanted to get in on the business generated by the region's biggest emergency.

"It's been too long, *amigo*," Pablo said. "How's it going in Port-au-Prince?"

"Have a look for yourself." Ben pulled out his smartphone and scrolled through the snapshots. "They're working night and day, but they're running out of supplies. People are still dying."

Pablo scrolled through the photos, the smile fading from his lips. "I'm monitoring every ship sailing within the vicinity," he said. "If there's anything on board that might be useful for Haiti, I'll divert it." He stood and moved to the window where a telescope was positioned. "Come over here. I want to show you something. Look out there at the Miraflores locks. There should be a large cargo ship passing through now…there it is. See the containers stacked along the top row?"

"I'm looking at the *MSC Copenhagen*, right?"

"That's it. Do you see the containers?"

Ben adjusted the lens to zoom in. "I see them now... Food for Livelihood containers...four of them!"

"I've asked Rome to check the manifest, but I'm still waiting for a reply."

Ben rotated the telescope to scan the rest of the ship. The tall, silver-haired man with a mark on his forehead crossed the viewfinder. "I know that man. I thought I recognized him!"

"Who?" Pablo lifted his head from the papers he'd been perusing. "What are you talking about?"

"That's Melissa's father."

"Who?"

He must be imagining it. He'd only seen the man in photographs and now through a telescope. It was probably just someone who resembled him. Melissa's father lived in Italy. *What would he be doing on a cargo ship in Panama?*

"Never mind," Ben said. "I don't know anything about that cargo. It can't be mine. Mine was headed to Haiti. We need to check on those containers. Hopefully the manifest will tell you what's in those and where they're going. We need to divert everything we find of relevance on the high seas to Haiti. We have no margin of error on this."

"Not a problem. I'll get back to you the minute I get the manifest. Well, I've got donor meetings for the rest of the day," Pablo said, checking his watch. "The U.S., Canada, the EU all want to be briefed. How can I do my job if I have to spend all my time in meetings? It's crazy."

"That's exactly why I'm here...to help you," Ben said. "I'll take over the day-to-day coordination between Rome, Panama City, and Port-au-Prince. We should be able to get this operation up and running within a week."

"Thanks, Ben. That'd be great. Meanwhile, here are your briefing notes," he said, handing over a heavy three-ring binder. Go to your hotel, grab a shower and a little R and R while you get up to speed. We'll start early tomorrow morning."

"I'm fine!" Ben protested.

But Pablo wasn't having it. "Go! And don't show your face around here until *mañana*, understand?"

Ben dropped his bags in his hotel room, grabbed a beer from the minibar, and flopped on the bed. He lay there mulling over the events of the past twenty-four hours when his smartphone rang.

"Ben, it's Sammy. Am I disturbing you?"

"No…no. You're the one who's working late. Let me grab my notes."

"We can discuss Haiti another time. I'm calling to share some good news. Do you remember our conversation when I asked you to oversee the FLITE initiative?"

"Uh…yes?"

"I promised you then that there would be better things in store… for both of us. Well, it's happened. The Secretary General called. I've been appointed the UN Special Envoy to Somalia. Our negotiations with the YLF ministers got their attention. No one had been able to open a humanitarian corridor, and we did it."

"Wow! Congratulations, Sammy, you deserve it! But what does this mean for us?"

"Hold on, Ben. I'll still be based in Rome…at FFL, but I want you to accompany me as my adviser whenever I go to Somalia on mission. I'll need you to back me up. What do you think?"

He didn't know how to respond. He'd always loved his work in Somalia until the YLF attack, but despite the successful negotiations on the humanitarian corridor, the country still rattled him. He wasn't sure he could press his luck and go back there again. Besides, Melissa's death was weighing on his mind and heart. He wanted to run away from his memories of Somalia, of Rome, of love and loss. He wanted to leave it all behind and move forward, but he didn't know how.

"You don't need to decide yet," Sammy's voice came through the phone. "Take time to think it over, and we'll talk when you get back to Rome. I have some other ideas percolating as well."

"I bet you do, Sammy! Anyway, thanks for giving me a heads-up for once." Whenever he got his feet planted firmly on the ground, Sammy pulled the rug out from under him. He told himself to forget about it, to concentrate on Haiti.

Chapter 32

Rome, that same evening at the Italian Parliament

At a corner table in the dining room of the Italian Parliament, Filippo Manenti, minister of foreign affairs, was finishing his espresso when he heard his name called and looked up to see Ivano Sorgente, minister of internal affairs, rushing toward him.

"Ah, *buona sera*. I see we both are working late this evening."

Ivano was nervous and edgy.

"*Tutto è a posto?*" Manenti asked. *Is everything okay?*

"Filippo, may I have a word with you? In confidence?"

"Of course. Sit down."

"Interpol contacted my office. They've been monitoring two Serbian arms dealers and have managed to get their financials."

Manenti put down his coffee cup and leaned in. "Go on."

"Five days ago, the Interpol money laundering unit put out a suspicious transaction report. The price of bitcoin jumped and took all the cryptocurrencies on the market with it, so they began an investigation. This morning, I was advised that they believe it was spurred by a series of bitcoin purchases valued at millions of U.S. dollars through Mitchell Bank in London, and they've traced the transaction to an international NGO headquartered in Rome, Food for Livelihood."

"*Da vero?* Tell me…how much are we talking about?"

"Twenty million dollars."

"*Che cazzo dici?*" Manenti raised his voice.

"Filippo, lower your voice," he said softly, looking around. "*Ma mi hai sentito bene*. Twenty million. A significant amount for an aid agency.

A smaller purchase of three and a half million in bitcoin was made two days before this one, also by a man called Benjamin Tano." Sorgente quietly continued, "We believe *Signor* Tano is embezzling money from the NGO Food for Livelihood as part of a bigger scheme. You're a personal friend of the president of that organization, no?"

"Yes, but wait a minute, the first transaction was legitimate—at my request. Food for Livelihood paid the YLF in bitcoin to free the hostages from Somalia. I'm unaware of the rest, but even if it is true, I find it highly unlikely that Dr. Adjei and his organization are involved. He is a man of integrity and trusts the people around him."

Sorgente raised an eyebrow. "Nevertheless, the evidence is compelling. I signed a search warrant authorizing our external intelligence and security agents to conduct a complete search of Tano's apartment and office tomorrow. I'm informing you as a courtesy."

"Where's *Signor* Tano now?"

"Panama City. Our colleagues there are monitoring his movements."

Manenti seemed to sink into his chair. "Ivano," he said, "it's delicate. Our government supported Dr. Samuel Adjei when he was given the UN position. Dr. Adjei called yesterday to thank me—not that he needed our support. After the hostage rescue, the U.S. State Department loves him."

"*E allora?*"

"Ben Tano is Dr. Adjei's right-hand man. We need to be discreet until we have more information. I want to speak to Dr. Adjei tonight before you begin the search. Is there anyone else involved? His wife?"

"*Signora* Tano doesn't know anything. They've been living apart. He was working with another woman, in and out of the office...if you know what I mean."

"Who is she?"

"Miliitsa Trasjic, Serbian. Calls herself Melissa Trask. She was working as a consultant to Food for Livelihood on behalf of Albatross, the blockchain provider."

"Was?"

"Yes, she died in a car crash under mysterious circumstances… possibly linked to the embezzlement of funds. I've sent agents to Puglia to speak with the investigating officers."

"*Brutta faccenda…*" Manenti shook his head, pushed back his chair, stood up, and buttoned his suit jacket. "I'll call you immediately after I've spoken to Dr. Adjei. *Stai attento…ti raccomando.*"

"Fine, Filippo, but I trust you won't reveal anything that would compromise my investigation."

"*Stai tranquillo.*"

Samuel Adjei had been on the phone since dawn, coordinating the Haiti relief effort when Natasha buzzed him to say that two agents from AISE, the Italian External Intelligence and Security Agency, were waiting for him at reception. Moments later, she ushered an older man and a younger woman into his office. He motioned them to sit down, hoping the meeting would be brief. He was preoccupied with the earthquake in Haiti and the refugee crisis on the Kenyan border.

The man proffered an identification card. "Agent Giorgio Troianni with the money laundering unit," he said, "and this is my colleague, Agent Barbara Guerrini. Thank you for receiving us."

Sammy leaned back in his chair and folded his hands over his belly. "Of course. I imagine you might be here to discuss our confidential dealings with YLF in Somalia. Perhaps you're not aware that the matter was cleared by—"

"Excuse me, sir. We're here on a different matter."

"I see." Sammy sat up and raised his eyebrows. "Well then, what can I do for you?"

"We're curious to know why a humanitarian organization like FFL would need to buy a large sum of twenty million dollars in bitcoin through Mitchell Exchange Bank in London."

"This is a misunderstanding," Sammy said. "We had an emergency. FFL purchased, on an exceptional basis, three and a half million U.S. dollars in bitcoin to save lives. That is all."

"We are aware of the first purchase, but this is the second in a series of bitcoin purchases made within a two-day period." The agent turned to his colleague who handed him a file folder.

"This is a record of the transactions," he said, handing the document to Sammy.

His face changed. "I'll need to verify this with our treasury," he said. "Please allow me a moment?" He swiveled his chair to face away from the agents and pressed an extension. "Marianna? I need you to confirm something for me… How is that possible? Forty-eight hours…late at night… I see… No, no… I'll get back to you."

He swiveled back to the waiting agents. "The anomaly was discovered this morning. We've initiated an internal investigation. We lifted safety constraints on our treasury module for forty-eight hours in order to execute the first bitcoin purchase. Evidently, someone got into the account late at night, minutes before the controls would have been reinstated."

Troianni said, "As you can see, the transfer appears to have been executed by a *Signor* Benjamin Tano, whom we understand is in Panama."

"He's organizing our relief efforts for the earthquake in Haiti." Sammy shook his head. "Ben Tano has served this organization with great integrity and dedication for a number of years, often risking his life to provide humanitarian aid. I hope you're not inferring that he embezzled these funds?"

"Dr. Adjei, the evidence is there. The withdrawal was executed from a Food for Livelihood account with his profile."

Guerrini opened the file and handed Sammy a photograph of a silver-haired man with a dark mark on his forehead. "Do you recognize this person?" she asked.

"No."

"Rasko Trasjic, former chief of staff to Slobodan Milošević. He's wanted at the Hague for acts committed during the Serbian war."

"Trasjic?" Sammy asked.

Guerrini handed him a second photograph. "Do you recognize this woman?"

Sammy nodded. "Melissa Trask, a consultant with the London firm Albatross, who served as technical support to our blockchain initiative. She might have had access to our systems, but she recently died in a car crash."

"Yes, we're aware. Rasko Trasjic is her father. Her given name is Miliitsa Trasjic. The car crashed in Puglia, on the coast road heading north. If you will notice on the transfer report, the transaction originated from a computer located in Puglia."

She handed him a third photograph. "This is her brother, Michael Trask, an officer at Mitchell Bank. Were you aware of him?"

"I've never met him. I was aware that her brother was affiliated with that bank but had no reason to see it as a problem. Are they suspects?"

Agent Troianni leaned across the desk. "I'm sorry, Dr. Adjei, but an international arrest warrant has been issued for Benjamin Tano, and we are here with a warrant to search his office."

Sammy took a deep breath and let it out slowly. "I'll ask his assistant to escort you to the third floor. None of this alters my conviction that he is innocent. Any chance FFL will recover the funds?"

"We're working on it."

Chapter 33

Panama City

Ben couldn't sleep. He was surprised by Sammy's news, which affected him too. He decided to get out of his hotel room and headed down to the lobby bar where he collapsed onto the nearest stool.

"Shot of tequila…no lime." He knocked it back. Cigarettes and alcohol were still his default for coping with stress. Too much had happened all at once. First, Melissa's death, immediately followed by his assignment to coordinate the response to the biggest humanitarian crisis in living memory, and now, an invitation from the UN to return to Somalia. When would he get off the roller coaster? He couldn't slow down, but this coaster was at risk of derailing. So, the cigarettes helped mellow him out, and the alcohol numbed the pain.

He ordered another shot and looked around. It was like any other hotel bar, nothing festive about it, and at that hour, nearly empty. He pushed a lock of hair off his forehead and put his head in his hands, leaning on the counter. He wouldn't let Sammy rush him. He was flattered to have been asked, but it was his life, his choice.

His phone began to vibrate in his jacket pocket. Serena.

"Is that you, Ben?" she whispered.

He cupped his hand over the phone and swiveled away from the bartender. "Serena, are you alright? Where are you?"

"I'm in the apartment. I came over to pick up the rest of my stuff. Six agents from Italian security are here with a search warrant signed by the minister of the interior. They're confiscating everything with your name on it…sniffing around the bedroom. Are you in trouble?"

"I don't think so. Honestly, I have no idea what this is about."

"Ben," she whispered into the phone, "have you heard that twenty million dollars were embezzled from Food for Livelihood? It looks like they think you did this."

"What?! No! I spoke with Sammy in Rome a while ago. He would have said something."

"I believe you. I do," Serena whispered. "I'm going to hang up now. I'm in the bathroom because I don't want them to know I'm talking to you, and they'll be suspicious if I don't come out soon. Be careful, Ben."

Ben swiveled back to the bartender and signaled him for another shot. None of this made sense. Who would embezzle that much money from a charitable organization? And why would they think he had anything to do with it? No one who knew him would believe he was capable of stealing from FFL. There had to be some mistake.

His thoughts were interrupted by the invasion of a group of sailors who crowded around the bar laughing. Ben noticed the crest on the sleeve of the man beside him and grabbed his arm. "Were you working on the *MSC Copenhagen*?"

The sailor looked startled. "Yes. What's it to you?" He glanced at his crew.

"Where is it headed?"

He shrugged.

"Please? I need to know."

The sailor shook off Ben's grip and said, "Colombia...Buenaventura."

Ben began swiveling nervously back and forth on his stool, trying to work it all out. *How was it possible that twenty million dollars were embezzled from Food for Livelihood? Wouldn't Sammy know this, and why wouldn't he have said something on our call? What the hell is going on? What evidence could the Italian intelligence agents be looking for in my apartment?*

Suddenly, he thought of Melissa's father on the ship. His gut told him there was a connection…but what? He needed to find out what cargo was in the containers and why they were heading to Colombia. It was after three o'clock in the morning, which meant nine o'clock in Rome. He took out his smartphone and called the FFL shipping officer.

"Karl, it's Ben… I need your help."

"Ben, I can't talk now. We're under the gun. We're sitting on a hundred thousand tons of commodities that Sammy wanted delivered to Haiti yesterday."

"I know, I know, but please, this is important."

"Okay, what is it?

"Listen, I'm in Panama, and I saw the *MSC Copenhagen* passing through the canal with our containers," Ben said.

"And?"

"Why is it heading toward the Pacific? Last time I checked, Haiti was in the other direction."

"The *Copenhagen* isn't carrying anything we can deploy to the Haiti operation. You should know that."

"How should I know that?"

"Because it's carrying your cargo!" Karl said incredulously.

"My cargo? Please, refresh my memory if you can. I would appreciate it."

"Okay, hang on while I find the papers… Oh," he laughed, "they're right in front of me."

"So, what's in the containers?" Ben asked, feeling the suspense.

"It's listed as IT equipment…for Colombia. It's going to an FFL warehouse near the port at Buenaventura."

Ben froze. "I didn't approve any new IT equipment. I only signed off for supplies to be sent through Panama to Haiti."

"Well, according to this requisition order, you issued the payment of twenty million dollars yourself."

"That's nuts! There must be something wrong. I never issued that payment."

"Listen, Ben, I've got to deal with a shipment to Haiti right now. The broker is on hold. Call me later if you have to."

Ben stared at the phone, not knowing what to do next. How could he be on record approving a twenty-million-dollar expenditure? And why were the containers being sent to Buenaventura, Colombia? He'd call Dalia. Maybe she could explain what happened.

"Dalia, can you confirm something for me? Karl has a document authorizing payment of twenty million dollars for IT equipment. Do you have a copy of that? I don't remember it at all, so I thought you might have set up the transaction."

"Just a minute… Yes, I've pulled it up on my screen… You approved the transaction before you left. I thought it was strange you didn't alert me at the time, but I assumed it was urgent because it was executed just before midnight. What's going on? The building administrator opened your office for a couple of agents with AISE badges. They've confiscated your files."

"Dalia, I haven't done anything wrong. Please believe me."

"I believe you, but I overheard one of them speaking on his phone about Interpol putting surveillance on you. Then he said, 'We need to get to him first.' I'm scared, Ben. What's this all about? Are you there? Ben…Ben?"

But the line had dropped.

Chapter 34

Ben went back up to his room and spent the remainder of the night pacing back and forth like a caged animal, trying to connect the dots. His name on that document made him the mastermind. Who would have authorized the release of so much money in his name? No one else had that level of authority. Melissa had set up the bitcoin purchase when they'd ransomed the American hostages. She'd insisted that the financial controls had to be lifted for forty-eight hours to execute the ransom payment. *When was that?* He counted off the days, the hours.

Had Melissa deceived him? Had she seduced him, pretended to care for him so that she could pull off a fraud? Had it been her plan all along to embezzle money from Food for Livelihood? According to what he'd just heard from Karl and Dalia, the payment was issued after her death. So, even if she had set up the fraud, then someone else had carried it out. But who?

He couldn't, wouldn't believe that she'd deceived him. He reviewed every moment they'd spent together. The way they grew to know and trust each other, confided in one another. She said she loved him in her last voice message—her last words to him before she died. It sounded very real to him, heartbreakingly so. He didn't know what to think now. How could she have set him up this way?

Ben's thoughts turned back to her father in the photograph; he'd worn the uniform of a Serbian officer, which was suspicious in and of itself. Melissa had called him a bureaucrat and hadn't wanted to talk about him. But he was wearing a lot of medals in that photograph. If he had been a high-ranking Serbian war criminal, he would have been tried in the Hague by now.

Why was he here in Panama on a ship with FFL containers? And her brother...what was his name? He purchased the bitcoins for the hostage exchange. He could have found a way to transfer more funds through bitcoin using my temporary account. Why would Melissa and her family have wanted twenty million dollars' worth of IT equipment, and why was it going to Colombia?

He worried that if the Italian secret service tracked him to Panama City, they would be coming there to arrest him. Dalia had heard the agent say, "We have to get to him first." Was someone planning to kill him? Did someone murder Melissa? If so, why? Ben's head was spinning with all these questions, and he was beginning to think that if he didn't get some answers, his life might hang in the balance.

When his phone buzzed, he jumped then hung his head when he saw Sammy's name on the screen. It was morning in Rome. He must have been told about the embezzlement. He'd want an explanation, and Ben didn't have one. He couldn't clear his name without more information.

Once the press got a whiff of the scandal, the reputation of FFL would be ruined. Donors' trust would evaporate when they discovered that FFL had lost track of twenty million dollars. Sammy would go down with him. Ben let the phone ring. He couldn't answer. Five minutes later, he heard a beep. Sammy had sent a text: "Return to Rome immediately and be careful. You may be in danger."

He had a terrible feeling that he was being watched. Someone could be standing outside his door, lurking in the hallway, waiting for the right moment to take him out.

He stared out the window of his room. Dawn was breaking, and the first light cleared his mind. He had to get to Colombia and prepare for the arrival of the ship loaded with Food for Livelihood containers. He packed his things. He'd take the first flight to Bogotá.

At the hotel coffee shop, he gulped down a double espresso, scanning for anyone who might be carrying a gun. A well-dressed young man was seated alone at the other end of the counter. He might have been anyone having an early morning coffee, but when he placed a set of keys and a phone next to his plate, Ben imagined it was a surveillance device and rushed out of the hotel.

The doorman asked if he needed a taxi, but he ran past him toward the intersection, ditching his smart phone in a sewer along the way. Food for Livelihood had them all fitted with global tracking devices for safety reasons.

He waved down the first taxi, hopped in, and summoned his college Spanish. "*El aeropuerto, tan rápido como puedas.* As fast as you can." Curled up on the back seat, he finally began to doze off, but the driver wanted to talk. "*Señor*, I am Rigo, and you?"

"Rigo, *me gustaría dormir.*" *I'll just sleep, if you don't mind.*

"*Sí, sí...*"

Ben looked up and caught him turning off the main highway. Maybe the man was stalking him. Maybe he'd been planted at the intersection to kidnap him. "Shouldn't we stay on the main highway and go south rather than west?"

"No, *Señor*. The American Bridge is faster."

Ben was not reassured. He was severely sleep deprived and frightened, facing either arrest or death, and he was desperate to get out of that taxi. When he saw a gas station ahead, he tapped Rigo's shoulder.

"*Sí, Señor?*"

"*Necesito usar el baño.* Can we make a quick stop at that gas station?"

"*Claro, Señor.* I'll take you to my brother-in-law's café. He has a very clean bathroom there."

Ben tried to protest, but his Spanish failed him, and Rigo drove past the station and raced down the road to a deserted café.

Before the cab had come to a full stop, Ben jumped out. He looked around and saw the sign to the restrooms. Rigo was right behind him.

He smiled and tried to sound casual. "While I'm in the bathroom, could you order me a coffee, *por favor*?"

He watched Rigo go to the counter and begin chatting with the barista then ran into the restroom and locked the door. There was an open window big enough to crawl through. He wondered if he was being ridiculous. But what if he was really in danger? He didn't know Panama City well. Why hadn't the driver taken the highway that led to the airport? He jumped on the toilet seat, pushed his knapsack through the window, and hoisted himself up, grasping the ledge with both hands. His shoulders were too broad, so he repositioned them at an angle and shimmied out, scraping his elbows on the rough wooden frame. Halfway through, he could balance on his stomach. The distance to the ground looked to be less than ten feet. He arched his back and pushed up to drag the rest of his body through. With his feet still anchored on the window frame, he flopped down and dangled against the side of the building then hit the ground hard a few feet away, sprawled on his back.

Ben got up slowly and peered around the corner of the building. Another taxi was coming down the road. It slowed and turned off in front of the café. The place must be a cabbie hangout. He ran and jumped into the back seat just as it stopped.

"Where to *Señor*?"

"To the airport. *Rápido!*"

Chapter 35

At the departure terminal, security personnel were patrolling the premises for drugs, and maintenance workers coming off the night shift were packing up their floor-polishing equipment. The *MSC Copenhagen* would have passed through the Miraflores locks by now, so it would berth at the Colombian port of Buenaventura the next day. Ben waited at the Copa Airline counter until it opened then bought a ticket for the 6:00 a.m. flight to Buenaventura via Bogotá. On board the plane, he finally relaxed. At least he'd be safe during the ninety-minute flight. Once in Colombia, the connecting flight to Buenaventura would be riskier.

He eased into his seat and propped the pillow up against the window, hoping to fall asleep. From time to time, he watched the normal predeparture activities on the tarmac—fueling, loading luggage, and stocking food trays in the galley. The aisle was crowded with passengers carrying flat-screen television sets, computers, and other duty-free items. He had just closed his eyes when he felt a thump in the seat beside him and was shocked to discover the immigration agent who'd returned his passport when he'd arrived the day before. She was dressed differently now, in a flak jacket and cargo pants, her dark hair twisted in a tight bun at the nape of her neck.

"You remember me, don't you?" she asked.

He wasn't happy to see her. *Was she tracking him? Did she plan to impound his passport?*

"Officer López, right? This can't be a coincidence."

She smiled and whispered, "No, it is not. I know everything."

"You do?"

"Yes, and I'm not Panamanian."

"No kidding. I noticed the insignia on your uniform at the airport."

"I'm Colombian Secret Service. We're working closely with Interpol." She opened her jacket to flash her badge. "We know about the twenty million, Trasjic, and the containers. We're on the trail of something important, and you've been helpful in leading us in the right direction."

"How did you find me?"

"Do you remember when I processed your passport?"

"How could I forget? It took forever."

"When I took your passport to the back office, our surveillance experts slipped a tracking device between the pages. It's a tactic we often use to track suspected drug traffickers who enter the country."

"So, are you going to arrest me?"

Her eyes shifted. "We're going to need information."

"What information?"

"Who is receiving the shipment in Buenaventura?"

"And if I tell you, then what?" Ben didn't trust this woman.

She leaned in and whispered, "Listen to me. Two men sitting at the back of the plane are going to kill you the minute you set foot in Colombia. If you want to stay alive, you'll need me to get you off this plane, so I'm going to pretend to arrest you, and you're going to pretend to resist arrest, unsuccessfully."

"Really?" Ben pulled away to get a good look at her face. "Who are they, and why do they want to kill me?" He was terrified but relieved that he hadn't been completely paranoid.

She held his eyes. "We don't have all the answers yet, but with your cooperation, we hope to piece together the rest."

Ben considered that if she really was with the Secret Service, she might be an ally. She was a professional, she knew what she was doing, and he was just an aid worker, in way over his head.

"Now, can you tell me who is receiving the merchandise at Buenaventura?" she asked.

He was silent for a moment, weighing his options. He'd have to trust her. She already knew about the delivery, and if she was telling the truth about the assassins on the flight, he'd be killed if he didn't go along with her plan.

"Look, I have no idea who is receiving the shipment, although I could have sworn I saw Trasjic on the ship yesterday. Our shipping officer in Rome told me that the containers are supposedly carrying IT equipment purchased under my name. It will be delivered to a Food for Livelihood warehouse near the port. That's why I need to find out what's inside…to clear my name and restitute the stolen money to FFL. Does that help?"

"Yes. We have undercover agents monitoring the ship as it unloads its cargo, but this will save us time. I'll put out an investigation of the warehouses in the area. We'll look for one registered to Food for Livelihood and arrange backup to surveil the site."

———————————

For the remainder of the flight, neither Ben nor Officer López spoke. He was exhausted and tried to sleep, but his thoughts tormented him. This woman knew more than she was telling him. She might know what was really in those containers. The Colombian Secret Service wouldn't bother tracking down IT equipment. No, it was something bigger than that— a threat to national security, and to him. He suddenly felt that the end of his journey was near. He had always been in a dance with death, choosing Food for Livelihood over Serena, leading the wrong mission, falling for the wrong woman who betrayed him and set him up as a criminal. He had made some bad choices, and now he was alone, soon to be murdered or arrested. He'd impulsively decided to fly to Colombia, risking everything to prove his innocence. Right now, death was looking infinitely preferable to disgrace.

As the plane taxied slowly toward the gate at Bogotá's Aeropuerto El Dorado, Officer López turned to him. "Are you ready?"

"Ready." He forced a smile.

She pulled a set of handcuffs from her back pocket and announced in a loud voice, "Benjamin Tano, *está detenido por malversación y fraude.*" She was arresting him for embezzlement and fraud.

The passengers, who had been crowding the aisles, pulling their belongings from the overhead compartments, stopped and turned to stare.

"What?" Ben jumped up in protest as she snapped cuffs on him. "No! No, you've got the wrong man! I'm innocent, I swear…"

"*No hagamos una escena, Señor Tano. Vamos a desembarcar tranquilamente,*" she said. "Let's not make a scene. We're going to disembark quietly."

A female passenger sitting on the other side of the aisle screamed, "*Ayuda!* Help! Help! *Hay una terrorista!*" *There's a terrorist on board!* Dozens of terrified passengers began pushing and shoving each other toward the exits. Officer López waited until the flight attendants had succeeded in herding most of them back to their seats then held up her badge to clear a path down the aisle.

"This is a mistake!" shouted Ben.

"*No lo hagas difícil. Superar!*" *Don't make this difficult.* She gave him a push—harder than she needed to, perhaps to remind Ben that even though this was an act, she was still in charge.

At the rear of the aircraft, they passed two men sitting calmly in their seats. The younger one appeared to be sleeping, his arms folded over his chest, while the older bald man was grinning while reading his newspaper. Ben thought he'd seen the bald man before. But where? It might have been at an airport…maybe at Leonardo da Vinci, while he waited with Sammy in the café. They could have been tailing him since Rome.

At the bottom of the stairs, they were met by the Colombian Dirección Nacional de Inteligencia. A pair of heavily armed agents bundled Ben into the back of a waiting Jeep. Officer López turned to him from the front seat and smiled. "That was very good, Mr. Tano."

"Where are we going? We're losing precious time. We have to get to the drop site before they do."

"I'm sorry, but this is your one-way ticket back to Rome." She handed him a manilla envelope. "One of our agents will accompany you. The Italian authorities want you for questioning."

"Oh, no. I'm coming with you."

"That's out of the question. I'm obligated to arrest you and send you back to Interpol in Rome," she said firmly.

"No, please. I'm just asking for a few hours. I need to recover that money...to prove my innocence," pled Ben. "And I'm your only witness. I tracked the containers to Colombia and identified the Serbian general in Panama. This conspiracy revolves around me. You need me to finish it."

She looked at Ben as if trying to determine if he was worth the effort. "Give me a moment," she said. "I have to make a few calls." She got out of the Jeep and stepped away.

A few minutes later, she stuck her head into the back seat. "All right, Mr. Tano. You're cleared to accompany me, but you're under arrest. You're in my custody, and you will follow my orders to the letter. Any undermining of my authority, and I will put you on a plane back to Italy. Understood?"

Ben nodded, chastened, and watched her return to the front seat.

"*Vamos!*" she barked, and the driver headed to the adjoining military air base where a Cessna A-37 Dragonfly was fueled and ready for takeoff.

Chapter 36

Buenaventura, Colombia, the next day, 10:00 a.m.

They arrived at the warehouse, located in a remote section of the city. It was ideal for unloading twenty million dollars' worth of contraband. Faded green letters spelling out "Food for Livelihood" were still visible over the main doors, but the place looked as though it hadn't been in use for some time. All that remained were old sewing machines and burlap sacks. Broken furniture was piled up against a rusty Ford truck.

Six hours later, Ben was tired and restless, and his body ached from lying on the cement floor to nap. Officer López's encrypted micro-com device informed her that the ship had docked, but it would take time to unload the containers onto the trucks and drive them to the warehouse. He began to wonder if they were in the right place, if Trasjic and company would ever show up, and whether he'd make it out alive if they did.

Although the area surrounding the warehouse was deserted, they spoke in whispers. He asked her why the Colombians hadn't confiscated the containers in Panama and arrested the culprits there, which would have cleared him.

"Has it ever occurred to you that we're fishing for sharks?" she whispered. "Not small fry like yourself and those three stooges."

"Is the third one Trasjic?"

"Yes, he's an ex-Serbian general under indictment by the International Criminal Tribunal for war crimes."

"I see." That explained why Melissa hadn't wanted to talk about her father.

It was dusk when they finally heard the roar of a fleet of approaching trucks and took cover under the old Ford, where they would be well-hidden but could monitor everything that transpired. Minutes later, the heavy doors were rolled back.

"Follow my every move," she whispered, "and we'll leave here alive. Whatever you do, keep down. Okay?"

They watched four big-rig flatbed trucks roll into the center of the vast space, each loaded with a Food for Livelihood container. Headlights illuminated the warehouse, so Ben was able to get a good look at the three men who jumped down from the cab and stood in front of the first truck. "That's Trasjic," he whispered. "And I'm pretty sure I recognized the other two guys on the plane. They must have been tailing me."

"Mr. Neri and Mr. Bosco," she whispered back. "They're from the Camorra crime syndicate in Bari…specializing in extortion, money laundering, drugs, and bounty hunting. They work for someone higher up and much smarter than they are. Neri is a trusted lieutenant. He's been with them since he was a kid, but it's likely he is trying to get out after this big job. I think they're playing him. Nobody ever gets out really. Bosco is family but not much in the brains department. Neri is grooming him to be more useful. We're working on taking down the whole operation, top to bottom. These two are a good start."

"*Signori*," Trasjic said, gesturing to the trucks, "I have followed your instructions to the letter. I have escorted your cargo here. Now, if you hand over what's mine, I will be on my way."

"Not so fast," Neri smiled coldly as he shook his head. "A man with your experience could be valuable in our negotiations. You never know when things may get out of hand. So, what do you say?"

Neri pulled a Beretta from the inside pocket of his jacket and pointed it at the general, waited until he nodded his agreement, then lowered his weapon and handed it to him with a laugh. "Here, you may need this. It's better than that Russian job you've got tucked away in your vest. Just remember whose side you're on and who has your money and your new papers," he said, patting his breast pocket.

The general reached out and carefully inspected the gun to be sure it wasn't another trick. His hand tightened around the handle as his finger reached for the trigger.

"Now, now, General, don't do anything stupid. None of us will leave until we close this deal. Besides, what my people will do to you if you turn on them, well...you've already gotten a taste of what can happen. So, play nice, General, and we will all walk out of here a lot happier and richer than when we came in. You turn on me, you turn on them, *capisce*?"

The general clenched the gun so tightly his knuckles turned white. "How did you do it?" he seethed.

"Accidents happen. Don't take it so hard. This is business. You'll be a free man once the containers are handed over. Here," he patted the envelope again, "I have everything you need to join your wife and son in Brazil."

Ben and Officer López heard more vehicles approaching and watched two Dodge Ram double-cab pickups park outside the main doors.

"Who's that?" the general asked. Ben could see his body tense.

"It must be our buyers," Neri said and turned to welcome them.

Six heavily armed Colombians in army fatigues moved stealthily toward the three men. The leader wore his cap pulled down over his face so that all Ben could see was his grey-streaked beard. At his signal, two of his men closed the warehouse doors and bolted them shut from the inside.

"Who are they?" Ben whispered to Officer López.

"FARC, The Revolutionary Armed Forces of Colombia. The bearded man is their second in command, our shark. His name is Marridas, but he's known as 'El Santo.'"

El Santo, "the Saint," shook hands with Neri and Bosco. When he approached the general, he must have recognized the posture and demeanor of a military man like himself because he saluted him. "So, what do you have for me?"

The general thrust the documentation into El Santo's hand.

"Only the best…all Russian-made…the latest in military technology: AK-47s, RPG-7s, Kornet ATGM," Neri said. Marridas looked at the document in his hand. "We've held up our end. We will need you to do the same," Neri continued anxiously.

So, they were using FFL money to traffic arms. Now Ben understood why the Colombian Secret Services was involved and why Officer López insisted on following the containers to their destination. More was at stake than recovering the cargo and aid money. The Colombians were fighting terrorism. The danger was everywhere. The poverty, hunger, and hopelessness that fueled these movements were the enemies he'd been fighting against with food. His fear dissolved.

Marridas chewed off the end of a cigar, spit it out, and ordered his soldiers to bring three large suitcases, dropping them at the general's feet. Two other men began to open the containers. Marridas struck a match against the sole of his boot and smoked as he inspected the paperwork. His men removed crates of varying sizes from each container that were marked with labels indicating they held computers, wiring, phones, and other IT-related items. They pried loose the wooden lids and pulled out shiny AK-47 machine guns, rocket-propelled grenades, anti-tank guided missile launchers, and belts of ammunition.

"How much?" El Santo asked.

"Thirty million dollars, as agreed," Neri replied. "This is a straight cash-and-carry deal."

El Santo loaded an automatic rifle and shot a round into the air, sending bullets ricocheting off the metal walls and ceiling. Neri and Bosco dropped to the ground, and Officer López threw an arm over Ben to shield him. Only the general remained standing. He had seen these childish charades before.

When the shooting stopped, Ben propped himself up on his elbows to get a better view and bumped his head against the rusty muffler with a thud that reverberated throughout the enclosure.

"*Estúpido!*" Officer López hissed.

"*Qué mierda fue eso?*" El Santo barked. "Neri, I swear to God, if you're playing games with me, I will remove your *cojones* with a pair of pliers and send them to your wife in a box!"

"You're not the only one whose ass is on the line here," Neri replied nervously.

"Boss, the truck!" Bosco yelled.

Ben watched three sets of boots run toward the truck and held his breath as two of them passed within inches of his face. Then he felt something poking his backside.

"*Aquí! Aquí!* I've found them!"

El Santo's men dragged Ben and Officer López out from under the truck, ordered them to kneel with their hands over their heads, and frisked them for weapons. Ben was only carrying his wallet and passport, but Officer López was armed with a pistol, a set of handcuffs, the com device, and a spool of thin wire. The men threw her down and removed her boots where she had been hiding a two-shooter Colt and a switchblade.

"*Bueno, bueno.* What do we have here?" El Santo smirked.

"I underestimated you, Tano," Neri said. "You and your friend put on quite a show back there on the plane. I thought you would take the rap and spare us the trouble of killing you. You should have known better than to meddle. Now, we'll have to shoot you both."

El Santo was not pleased. "Neri, *quienes son estos hijos de puta?* Who are these sons of bitches? You know them?"

"Ben Tano is our phish. He was meant to take the rap for this. I presume the *signora* is with a government intelligence agency. We saw her haul him off the plane in Bogotá. I don't know how or why she got tangled up in this, but someone must have tipped off Interpol."

Ben stared at Officer López, whose face betrayed neither fear nor panic.

El Santos took a drag of his cigar. "Interpol! You think this is a game? You think we're fucking around?" He began pacing furiously.

"No, of course not." Neri's face darkened.

"I should waste you both now to teach you fucking amateurs a lesson!"

"That won't be necessary," Neri said. "Bosco, tie up these loose ends!"

"Is it prudent to kill them?" The general spoke calmly.

"If we don't," Neri said, "we'll be hunted for the rest of our lives."

"Not if you remain in Colombia," El Santo snorted.

Ben's life had been threatened before. He'd developed the ability to think brilliantly in circumstances that would paralyze most people. He knew he had to turn El Santo's attention back to his business deal.

"Hey, Neri!" he said. "Wasn't the twenty million you embezzled from Food for Livelihood enough for you? Why are you charging El Santo an extra ten million?"

El Santo coolly blew a cloud of his smoke in Neri's face. "What the hell is he talking about?"

"Shut your stupid mouth, Tano!" Neri began to sweat.

"Go on," El Santo turned to Ben.

"He's asking you for thirty million dollars when I can bet you there's only twenty million dollars' worth of weapons in those containers."

"*Stronzate!* How would he know? He works for a charity," Neri said. The noose was slowly tightening around his neck.

"You've got that wrong. I'm the phish, remember? My name is on the bank transaction."

"*El tiene razón,*" Officer López said. "We've verified it."

"Neri, what the fuck is going on here? You confirmed thirty million in merchandise. You're not trying to screw with me, are you?" He looked from Neri to Ben, waiting for a reply.

"Uh...the deal holds," Neri stalled. "The merchandise was paid for and delivered. If there's a problem, the general will have to explain. He was in charge of delivery."

The general shook his head in disgust.

Bosco was stealthily backing toward the doors, but one of El Santo's men saw him and fired off a round, nicking his leg. He brought him back limping with a rifle pressed to his back.

"You tried to screw me." El Santo's voice was calm. "We had a deal. You broke my trust. Do you know what happens to people who break my trust?"

Bosco's face was white, and he was grimacing in pain. "My uncle makes me work for Neri, so I do whatever he says. Nobody tells me nothing. I don't know nothing about...anything."

"Don't look at me. I just follow orders," Neri replied frantically. He shot a look at Bosco that said "keep your big mouth shut."

"It's not my mistake," Neri said. "I was told by this man," he said, pointing to the general, "that the deal you made was for thirty million, but if you say twenty, okay...twenty..."

El Santo's men reached for their machine guns.

"I swear I knew nothing," Bosco whimpered. "I was just following..."

Before he could finish his sentence, El Santo whipped a pistol from his side holster and shot him between the eyes. "That is for traitors!"

Neri tried to reach for his gun, but El Santo whirled around and shot him in the chest before he could even touch it.

"And that," El Santo said with a guffaw, "is for trying to screw me."

Ben closed his eyes, expecting the next bullet to kill him. He'd been here before and survived, but this time he wasn't running for his life. He surrendered, at peace with his conscience.

El Santo turned to the general, the only one of the three still standing. "And you? Where do you fit in?"

The general's eyes were fixed on the bodies lying in their own blood on the cement floor. "I'm just a retired Serbian general. Neri used my military record to blackmail me and my family. My children got him the money, some ex-military colleagues got him the guns, and these two got what they deserved. Like Mr. Tano here, I'm only a fall guy."

His suspicions were true. Melissa had betrayed him. Ben was overwhelmed with a grief so profound he could barely breathe. She had been involved from the beginning, and now her betrayal would end in his death. How fitting that he should die in an abandoned FFL warehouse.

With a quick wave of his hand, El Santo ordered his men to load the crates back into the container. "You," he said, looking down at Ben, "you just saved me ten million dollars... No," he paused to laugh loudly, "thirty million, and I thank you for that. But, *amigo mio*, I'm afraid you know too much. And you, my dear," he cooed to Officer López, fingering a strand of her hair, "you are much too beautiful to kill. You will come with me." She stared ahead defiantly.

Hostages taken by FARC could be held for years in the jungle without contact with the outside world. Ben glanced around and realized that Melissa's father had been trying to catch his attention, furtively darting his eyes in the direction of Neri's gun, which was lying forgotten on the ground where it had fallen. Ben was on his knees and couldn't risk standing up, but he had a chance.

"You should leave the woman," the general said.

"What was that, General?" El Santo confronted him.

"You have what you came for. Killing an aid worker might raise a few eyebrows, but if you take one of their agents, the Colombian authorities will hunt you down with the regional drug enforcement agencies. It may take a month, it may take a year, but they will find you. And they will kill you."

"General, I will give you a warning before we part ways. Keep your nose the fuck out of my business!"

He was purposely distracting El Santo while Ben inched toward the gun.

"I'm saying..." the general continued as though he had all the time in the world to chat, "there's no point in making life complicated. Unless, of course, you have difficulties finding a woman in Colombia?"

El Santo lunged for the general's throat, which gave Ben time to pounce on Neri's gun and toss it to Officer López. She fired off a shot, hitting El Santo in the chest. His cigar hit the ground, then he sank to the floor, screaming "*Chucha!*"

An explosion blew open the warehouse doors. Colombian soldiers burst into the warehouse, guns blasting. Officer López and Ben raced to take cover as El Santo's men returned fire. Ben saw the general snatch something from Neri's pocket and run the other way, dodging the gunfire.

Bullets ricocheted off the metal walls. Soldiers screamed as they were hit. Officer López fired another shot, hitting one of the FARC soldiers in the neck. They heard a wail of sirens, and Colombian police stormed the warehouse.

Then silence.

When the smoke cleared, the last of the FARC soldiers surrendered.

The captain of the Colombian Special Forces unit shook Officer López's hand. "*Felicitaciones por tu coraje.* Congratulations on your courage... and for netting us the FARC leadership. You killed Marridas?"

"Finally," Officer López replied. "I've been tracking him for years."

"Why didn't you signal us? We waited forty minutes after the trucks showed up on our surveillance cameras, then I decided it was too dangerous, and we rolled out."

"*Gracias a Dios!*" She crossed herself and pressed her palms together. "We were next in the line of fire. El Santo's guys confiscated my com device. I kept praying to Madre Maria that you'd show up, and she answered me, even knowing I haven't always been faithful."

Ambulances arrived. Paramedics tended those who had been hit but were still living, while Officer López spoke with the Colombian police.

Ben sat off to the side on a broken chair. He felt different after this traumatic event than he did after the massacre in the Somali village. He felt… calm and lucid. While he had just lived through more gunfire and death, this time, he wasn't shaken. Ben had seen the face of YLF in El Santo when he threatened Officer López, so he fought to protect her as he had failed to protect his friends. He had reenacted that horrifying scene of their deaths in Somalia, only this time with a different ending. He felt lighter—perhaps even freed from that moment of his past hidden in the recesses of his mind and body.

The warehouse was a bloody battlefield: the bodies of Marridas and his men and Neri and Bosco were still lying on the cement floor.

Officer López came over and asked Ben if he was ready to go.

"Go where?"

"You're still in my custody, remember? And we both need a drink."

Chapter 37

By the time Ben joined Officer López on a curved couch at the Marriott Airport hotel, night had fallen, and the lights of the city sparkled through the windowed wall. He had rested and showered, and she had shed her military attire for a flowered shirt and jeans.

"What are you drinking, Ben?" she asked, sipping aguardiente.

"*Una cerveza*, thanks. Time to kick the hard stuff."

She signaled the barman and said, "Dorado Pils." He hurried over with the cold beer and poured it into a tall glass, allowing the froth to peak.

"*Salud*, Ben," she said, as they clinked glasses and enjoyed the refreshing feeling in their throats. "Do you feel better now with this behind you?"

"Yes, Officer López, I am alive, and Food for Livelihood will get its money back."

"I'm off duty now. Please call me Alejandra…and you did save my life. I'm glad I made the decision to bring you along. The way you handled yourself was very professional. How did you manage to get hold of the gun and toss it to me? That was courage under fire."

"It was the general who saved us by signaling that the gun was there. I was already facing a lose-lose situation. If El Santo's men had caught me going for the gun, they'd have killed me instantly, and if I hadn't gone for the gun, they'd have killed me eventually. I got lucky. What happened to the general, by the way? I lost track of him in the shootout. Why do you think he wanted to keep us alive?"

Alejandra shook her head. "I don't know anything about his motives, but if I had to speculate, losing his daughter might have brought out the humanity in him. Maybe he's seen enough death in his lifetime and didn't want ours on his conscience. The police believe he slipped out in the crossfire.

He must be on his way to Brazil where there's no extradition treaty. They'll catch up with him before he crosses the border."

"What was he even doing here?"

"Most of the money was wired to two Serbian arms dealers. The Italians tracked it down and put the dealers under surveillance. The rest went to an account linked to Neri but was tied to the bigger operation he worked for. They've had an eye on him for years because of his connection with the mob. They put the dealers under surveillance and discovered that they were delivering a shipment of arms to Cuba, but they were too late to intercept it before it made it onto the ship. The surveillance netted us Trasjic there when he was meeting the arms shipment. Interpol spotted him again at the airport in Panama. After the death of his daughter, he might have cooperated with us, but they had a shadow on his wife and threatened to kill her. So, the decision was made to follow the shipment to the final destination and net the entire operation, including the buyers."

"And the son? I think his name is Mihailo."

"*Ay, el hijo*. Italian authorities intercepted him at the airport in Naples where he was about to board an Air France flight to Rio. He despises Neri and was ready to cooperate with the authorities in exchange for a reduced charge. Still, that might not help him much; there is no sympathy for a man who steals from hungry children. I remember a case in the U.S. where the president of an NGO was sent to jail in Rikers Island for that crime."

Ben turned to stare through the windows at the dark sky. The pieces were starting to fit together. When he was assigned to head up the Albatross transition, Melissa charmed him into trusting her so she could feed her brother information. Mihailo would have known exactly how to hack into the FFL network.

"Alejandra, do you know what happens to the money? Does Food for Livelihood get it back now?"

"I'm sure we'll find more than enough in those suitcases to cover your losses, but we'll have to follow procedures, of course. We'll also embargo the arms and freeze the dealers' accounts. The money was divided into smaller amounts to buy bitcoin, so it may take a while to trace the rest of it, but they'll get it back. We'll also dismantle their network of forgers and corrupt officials to protect the integrity of legitimate businesses and organizations like yours."

They sipped their drinks in silence for a moment, then she put a hand on his arm. "Aren't you going to ask me about Melissa Trasjic?"

"Why? Didn't she set me up?"

"We won't know everything until Mihailo has been questioned further, but he told the authorities that Melissa was used as bait to get to you. When she tried to back out and warn you, she disappeared."

"She tried to back out?"

"According to her brother, she refused to go through with it at the last minute."

"And that's when she disappeared? She died in a car crash...or did someone kill her?"

"We don't know for sure, Ben. We don't know why she drove off the road. It was assumed to be an accident, but there was no reason for her to lose control of the car."

"Oh, God," Ben said softly. "I was involved with her. Did you know that? I was starting a serious relationship with her."

"I'm sorry, Ben, but even if she couldn't stop it, she died trying and that means something. Now, what about you? What do you want in your life now? You're still married to your wife, Serena, no?"

"You know everything! Yeah, Serena...married, yes, but we're separated now. She's been my rock since we first met in Rome. I loved her. I mean...I think I'll always love her. I've been gallivanting all over the globe on a noble crusade to save lives, rebuild livelihoods, get kids into school. Meanwhile, the world became more dangerous, the conflicts and disasters more frequent, the aid workers targeted by terrorist groups. I was sent out more on missions to the most dangerous and remote places. She was home alone, waiting for me to come back alive. But after I nearly died in Somalia, she drew a line in the sand, saying no more. She expected me to give it all up, which I wasn't ready to do. So, we agreed to separate. I've been hooked on saving the world, but I couldn't save my own marriage. And then, Melissa came along...and I fell too fast and, with everything that happened, figured I'd been played. Now, I learn she refused to betray me...so maybe..."

"*Ella te amó estoy segura.* I'm sure she loved you, Ben. But she's gone now, and it's not your fault."

Ben ran a hand over his face. "Can I smoke here?"

"No, but we'd better get you more beer."

"What about you? Do you have a family?"

"*Sí.* Jorge is in Medellín with our seven-year-old son. I try to be with them whenever I can. Jorge is a special Latino man. He accepts that my job is dangerous, but I do it because I believe fighting FARC, the drug lords, and other bad actors to protect my country is a cause worth dying for. Like you, my work is my primary focus now. I have to stay mentally and physically sharp at all times, always ready to respond to the next crisis. But I won't do this job forever. I promised Jorge that I would eventually choose more predictable assignments, using my skills to train new recruits or analyze intelligence. I love my work, but I also love my family. You might consider what that means for you, Ben."

Ben nodded. "I understand. I've dedicated my life to being a humanitarian but...I took Serena for granted, putting my career first, unable to find a middle way to be happy together. When I found out that Melissa was dead, I went straight back to her. What does that make me?"

"It makes you human, Ben, and it tells me that you still care for each other. Here's the waiter with your drink."

He took a long sip. "My boss, Sammy, is also bugging me to take an advisory position that would require more missions to Somalia. That's another decision to add to the mix."

Alejandra smiled and said, "You do have choices, Ben. What do you want? Your work does not define who you are. If you make it to retirement, do you really want to be alone, with only your memories to keep you company? It seems now is a good time to figure it out. You've already lived your nine lives."

"Okay, maybe it's not too late. Maybe I can still find a way to repair things with Serena and somehow factor in Food for Livelihood. I owe that much to her."

She signaled for the check. "You owe that to yourself. It seems she's always been your safe haven. Order what you'd like if you want to eat something, compliments of the Colombian government. You can sign for it. I'm going up. I'm exhausted. While you were napping, I was being debriefed. Your flight leaves at ten in the morning. I'll meet you in the lobby at eight and escort you onto the plane." She stood up and put a hand on his shoulder.

"Do you think I'll be arrested when I land in Rome?"

"No, Dr. Adjei has declined to press charges against you."

"He probably thinks I'm a fool."

"I don't know. I'd be willing to bet that he sees you as a hero...someone willing to risk his life for any humanitarian cause. Don't sell yourself short. I don't think Dr. Adjei will."

Epilogue

When Ben returned to Rome, he summoned the courage to talk to Serena. The episode at the Colombian warehouse had helped him to rewrite his story. He was no longer frozen in the trauma of his helplessness in Somalia, but it had also been a brutal reminder that life was short. At this point, he had nothing left to prove. He opened up to his wife for the first time about what he had been going through since Somalia, breaking down at times when words were inadequate. He apologized for being absent from their marriage.

Serena listened to him, comforted him, and ultimately forgave him. Ben already knew the changes that he would have to make, and he was ready to recommit, knowing that their happiness together was what mattered to him now. He still struggled to rein in his drinking and smoking, but he spent a year in therapy, never once regretting it, particularly with all the new modalities available to war veterans and others suffering from PTSD. He would always have triggers to manage, but he suffered less from anxiety and panic attacks, and the nightmares of the past were receding.

South Somalia, two years after the attack on the FFL mission

When the rains finally returned, the villagers came out of their huts, heads raised to the sky, open-mouthed, drinking it in. They stomped and danced on the wet ground and let the rain wash the dust from their bodies. They lifted their arms to the heavens and praised Allah.

The once desolate land was blooming yellow and orange with wild-flowers, and an FFL Land Cruiser navigated the vast green landscape under a blazing sun. Ben Tano was returning to the village of Kabuk, on a pilgrimage to silence the voices that had pursued him since the massacre and to honor the colleagues who had died that day. He wanted to see for himself that the ground was no longer soaked with their blood, that their spirits were no longer restless. And he wanted Serena to see Somalia, to see where he'd been, to understand why he'd come back to Rome a changed man.

Samuel Adjei sat beside him dressed in a smart safari suit. "How are you holding up?" he asked.

The African Union and Somali soldiers had pushed back YLF to the peripheries of Somalia, their leadership in disarray, but the militants were far from subdued. They'd continued their kidnapping and terrorist attacks, focusing on targets in Kenya.

But there was no sign of them under the blazing sun as the Cruiser approached Kabuk. "How am I holding up? More like *if* I'm holding up," said Ben, a strangled sound escaping his mouth, his best effort at a laugh. "Thanks for coming along today, brother."

Serena studied Ben's face, squeezing his hand. When they'd left Mogadishu that morning, he'd seemed excited, talkative, joking with the driver, pointing things out to her, chatting with Sammy about his work, what he hoped to accomplish in Somalia, what it might be possible to accomplish. Sammy had taken up his assignment as Special Envoy of the UN Secretary General to foster the democratization process in Somalia. He'd spend a year commuting between Rome and Mogadishu, coordinating donor round-tables to promote poverty reduction, economic development, and food security programs.

After careful deliberation, Ben had decided not to accept Sammy's offer to serve as his adviser in Somalia. He realized that he'd do more good at FFL headquarters in Rome, working full-time as FFL's director of inno-vations, finding ways to use new technologies to empower people to feed themselves. And he knew his marriage wouldn't survive another separa-tion. For the first time in his life, he was close to settled, but he was still not entirely at peace with himself, as if he were trying on a new pair of shoes that needed breaking in to feel comfortable.

The YLF leader, whose rabid militants had nearly killed him, was running for office in the elections Sammy was there to oversee. Finally, the hope of peace glimmered in the war-torn country. The time was right for

Ben to return to the village that still haunted him, but he knew he couldn't stay in Somalia for long.

The closer they got to the village, the less he had to say, and he gazed over the flat, rocky terrain, saying almost nothing at all.

When the Cruiser pulled up at the village, Ben was amazed at how much—and how little—had changed. The villagers were no longer living on the brink of starvation. The rains had restored the fields so that the goats and camels could graze again. Those who had survived the refugee camps, the fighting, and the drought had returned to their ancestral homes, repaired their huts, planted crops. Babies had been born and flourished on their mother's plentiful milk. And the aid agencies were able to resume their development programs, maternal-child health, agricultural production, and school meals without the threat of being ambushed by YLF.

Women sat on their doorsteps weaving grass baskets so finely made they held milk or water without leaking. Old men were drinking tea, smoking. Little boys chased each other, shrieking.

But the poverty of the huts had not changed at all. Running water, toilets, electricity were still unimaginable, and food security remained unpredictable, dependent on the next rainy season. And when Hakim, the village elder, emerged with his council to greet them, he looked even frailer than Ben had remembered him.

He bowed his head at the village elder. "*Yaabaa*," he said. "I am Ben Tano. You saved my life." Before Bashir translated his greeting, Hakim took both his hands. "*Mahad Ilaah!* Thank God," he said. And the deep lines in his face folded into a joyous grin that lifted his cheeks and closed his eyes. He leaned on his walking stick with both hands, nodding, smiling, displaying his remaining teeth, as Ben and their driver, Bashir, introduced Sammy and Serena.

"We have brought gifts," Serena said. The driver unloaded baskets of sweet plump tomatoes, ripe yellow bananas, green papayas, dates, and tea, and boxes of pencils and notebooks for the children.

The elders bowed their heads in thanks. "Come," Hakim said. "You must drink tea at my home. We will distribute your gifts to those who need them." The old men and young women, who had been watching in amazement, timidly approached. The children stopped their play and gazed wide-eyed at the baskets of food. As Hakim led them through the narrow alleys, they were followed by a crowd of villagers, two or three small goats, and one little boy, who wrapped his thin arms around Ben's leg. Serena knelt beside the boy. "Who is this beautiful child?" she asked, touching the boy's cheek. His eyes were a startling blue, and in an instant, Ben remembered.

"I met a woman here with eyes like this. Where is she?" And he waited for Bashir to translate.

Hakim stopped walking and stood leaning on his stick. "I said goodbye to Suhila when she boarded a truck bound for Kenya. She was a blameless woman who cared only for her children. I am sure she has reached *Jannah.*"

"He says she is in Paradise," Bashir translated.

"She also had a baby girl?" Ben asked.

Hakim shook his head. "How could a child so new to this world survive so much misery? Only the boy returned. The driver of the truck brought him to us. A couple who lost all their children in the famine are caring for him. Geedi has not said a word since the driver found him. I fear he is annoying you and your wife."

"Geedi?" Serena said, reaching for his hand. "Geedi." The boy looked up at her. "Bashir, please tell the man that the boy is not bothering me at all."

"*Nac*," Geedi said.

Hakim looked at Ben in amazement. "The boy has not uttered a sound since he was brought back here."

"*Nac*," the boy said again.

Serena turned to Bashir, who explained, "*Nac* is the Somali word for candy."

Ben put a hand over his mouth. His brow wrinkled and his eyes filled. "How can he remember that?" he wondered. "I gave him a piece of candy that day when he was running from YLF with his mother and baby sister. Oh, God. Do we have any candy?"

Serena reached into her bag and produced a caramel wrapped in cellophane. She handed it to Ben, who knelt before the boy. "*Nac*, Geedi," he said.

"*Nac, nac!*" Geedi squealed, jumping up and down.

Ben cupped the boy's head in his hand and brought it close to his chest. "*Nac*," he whispered.

Hakim waited silently for a while before breaking the moment. He said something to one of the elders, and the man disappeared in search of the couple who had adopted Geedi.

Then he spoke to Ben. "You have brought flowers…"

"I came to honor my colleagues who died here. I wish to ask for their forgiveness because I still live and they do not."

Hakim shook his head. "But they are at peace, and you are not. We will go first to the school. Every day, the women organize the cooking. The children are eating together now."

The makeshift school building was still standing at the far end of the village. As they walked among the huts, Ben saw few young men. "We are a community of widows here," Hakim said. "Many men fled the drought, and few returned. But this boy will grow to be a man. And many more will become men as well."

They reached the edge of the village, the open plain where the FFL trucks parked that day, where YLF arrived with their weapons, eager to kidnap the aid workers. Ransom gained by machine guns was a vital source of revenue. The military had arrived in the nick of time to save them and sent the YLF running for their lives. But a teenager with a nervous trigger finger, and a thirst for blood, had decided to get revenge, taking aim at the hostages, the lost prize. The skinny lieutenant who had shot them all hadn't been more than fifteen years old.

Two of Ben's colleagues had fallen against the metal wall of the school, now painted in bright colors with images of plants and flowers created by the children. The sound of childish laughter drifted through a window, carrying the aroma of beans, rice, and onions.

Ben put an arm around Serena. "I feel as though I'm in a very strange dream," he said. "I wanted to leave flowers where Leo and Hassan, Khaled and Jhamal died. It seems so unreal now. This is not a place of death and terror, but of life—joy even."

He walked around to the back of the school, half expecting to find the ground soaked in blood, but it was green now, the wild grasses chewed low by goats. He placed the flowers there, among the flat leaves of a yeheb bush, whispering the names of the fallen.

"*Kalaay.*" Hakim had followed him. "Come along. We will have tea."

As they set off for Hakim's hut, Serena grabbed Ben's arm and stopped. The blue-eyed boy was running behind them. He bumped into Ben's leg and held on with all his might. Ben looked at Sammy then at Hakim. "Allah has spared this child," Hakim said, "and Allah has spared you. You have found each other here in our village. You are truly blessed."

Ben reached down to put a hand on the boy's head. *These strange blue eyes watched his baby sister die of hunger,* he thought. *He has felt his mother's grief. Then, with a stomach that had been empty for days, he watched her die, and he was alone in a strange place surrounded by starving strangers. If the driver who brought him there hadn't discovered him and brought him back to his village, he, too, would have died.*

Hakim said, "The *djins*, the local spirits, still attack him, but he has new parents who love him as their own. He is the only child they have left. They will be so happy that he has begun to speak again, even if he says only '*nac.*'"

Ben bent down and lifted the boy, who rested his head in Ben's neck and sighed. Ben looked at Serena. "He is suffering from his wounds, which are so much deeper than mine," he said. "I thought I was scarred by the YLF massacre, but I had no idea what it was to be truly scarred. This boy knows."

Serena had been staring at the boy in Ben's arms. "Can we do something for him?"

Ben stopped stroking the boy's head for a moment. "We can be sure that the village school is always stocked with supplies. We'll keep track of Geedi. If he wants to study, we'll find a way to sponsor his education."

They sat in the cool shade of a tugaar tree near Hakim's hut, as its feathery leaves made dancing shadows in the breeze. Ben looked at the faces of the villagers and the elders while Geedi snuggled contentedly on the lap of the village woman who had adopted him. He looked at Sammy, his trusted friend. "Thank you for not giving up on me," he said.

Sammy nodded. "A little hope each day can fill the rivers to overflowing. I have more than a little hope…for you, for the future of this boy, and for his country."

Ben felt Serena's warm body brush against his. He listened to her calm breathing. Everyone around him was smiling. And he was at peace at last.

Afterword

"We know only too well that what we are doing is nothing
more than a drop in the ocean. But if the drop were not there,
the ocean would be missing something."

~ Mother Teresa

The Hunger Crime highlights the value of school meal programs, that incentivize the poorest parents to send their children, and girls in particular, to school. Girls who stay in school get married later, give birth to healthier and better educated children, and earn higher incomes, which benefit their families and communities. A nutritional meal costs fifty cents to feed a hungry child at school, which is an investment in health, education, and each child's future potential.

If you would like to give or learn more about the global food crisis, humanitarian operations or school meal programs you may visit the following websites:

UN World Food Programme (WFP)
https://www.wfp.org/

World Food Program USA
https://www.wfpusa.org/

The Hunger Crime
www.thehungercrime.com

Thank you.
John and Trudy

About the Authors

John B. Crisci recently served as the acting director of a UN World Food Programme's Supply Chain Division, keeping operations running smoothly in the face of the multiple global challenges posed by COVID-19, thereby enabling the UN to assist more than a 100 million people with food. He also ensured that the division used its global supply chain infrastructure, expertise, and experience to support the humanitarian community's efforts to deal with the pandemic.

John was instrumental in making sure all divisions worked closely together to assist close to a 100 million people, often in the most challenging emergency situations possible—conflict, natural disaster, climate change, economic collapse, or a combination of these. He has also served as deputy director of emergency response and director of the budget division. He has served in several field positions around the world, including the Sudan, the Republic of the Congo, and Sierra Leone, where he served as emergency coordinator for the Ebola outbreak in 2014.

John has over twenty-seven years of experience in general management, business development, and risk management. This is his first work of fiction.

A native of Princeton, N.J., Trudy E. Bower studied French literature at Smith College and international affairs at Columbia University. Inspired by the writings of Victor Hugo and an internship at the United Nations in New York, she embarked on an overseas career with CARE (Cooperative for Assistance and Relief Everywhere) and the UN World Food Programme spanning thirty years where her interests in social justice, languages, and travel intersected.  She managed food assistance programs in India, Bangladesh, Mozambique, Burundi, Madagascar, Cote d'Ivoire, and Ghana—the latter two as country director.

Her most challenging assignments were working in countries where political instability and violence coexisted with managing food emergencies and raising her two daughters.

In 2011, Trudy began co-authoring this book. In 2015, she joined a writing group in Rome, Italy, and started her memoirs. She has contributed articles to two published works of nonfiction. This is her first work of fiction.

Trudy currently resides in Florida.

Acknowledgments

We would like to honor our humanitarian colleagues for their courage and dedication.

We would particularly like to thank those who assisted us by reading the drafts and providing critical inputs to the story: Liliana D'Aniello, Paul Ares, Gawaher Atif, Anne Callanan, Judith Douglass, George Gegelia, Rebecca Hansen, Lourdes Ibarra, Michael Jensen, Allan Jury, Etienne Labande, Thomas Lecato, John Otieno, Georgia Shaver, Claudia Von Roehl, and Angela Van Rynbach. Other readers gave their valuable time and feedback: Ilaria Campone, Dr. Margaret O'Neill, Brenda Dean Lucero, Dr. Richard Bower and Savannah Pearson.

Alberto Cozzolino, Michael Gannon, and Rienzo Monferdini were invaluable for their research.

We are honored by Catherine Bertini, who agreed to write the foreword.

Over a decade, this story has been hewn to its essence with the assistance of talented writers and editors: Joie Davidow, Karen L. Tucker, Alexandra Pirinis, Lil Barcaski, and Anya Overmann.

We are grateful to Cathy Davis at Creative Publishing Partners for shepherding this book to publication.

We owe a great debt to Peter Levine and his seminal work, *Waking the Tiger*, which articulates the causes and manifestations of trauma experienced by many humanitarians.

Printed by Amazon Italia Logistica S.r.l.
Torrazza Piemonte (TO), Italy